Historical Mysteries

Andrew Lang

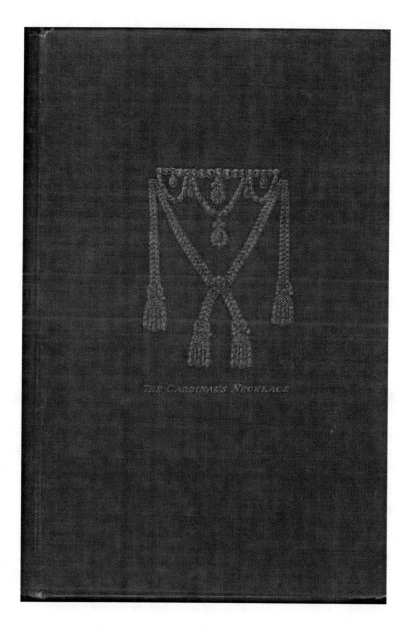

HISTORICAL MYSTERIES

BY

ANDREW LANG

WITH A FRONTISPIECE

SECOND EDITION

LONDON
SMITH, ELDER, & CO., 15 WATERLOO PLACE

1905

Elizabeth Canning.

PREFACE

THESE Essays, which appeared, with two exceptions, in *The Cornhill Magazine*, 1904, have been revised, and some alterations, corrections, and additions have been made in them. 'Queen Oglethorpe, ' in which Miss Alice Shield collaborated, doing most of the research, is reprinted by the courteous permission of the editor, from *Blackwood 's Magazine*. A note on 'The End of Jeanne de la Motte, ' has been added as a sequel to 'The Cardinal 's Necklace: ' it appeared in *The Morning Post*, the Editor kindly granting leave to republish.

The author wishes to acknowledge the able assistance of Miss E.M. Thompson, who made researches for him in the British Museum and at the Record Office.

CONTENTS

I. THE CASE OF ELIZABETH CANNING
II. THE MURDER OF ESCOVEDO
III. THE CAMPDEN MYSTERY
IV. THE CASE OF ALLAN BRECK
V. THE CARDINAL'S NECKLACE
VI. THE MYSTERY OF KASPAR HAUSER: THE CHILD OF EUROPE
VII. THE GOWRIE CONSPIRACY
VIII. THE STRANGE CASE OF DANIEL DUNGLAS HOME
IX. THE CASE OF CAPTAIN GREEN
X. QUEEN OGLETHORPE (*in collaboration with Miss Alice Shield*)
XI. THE CHEVALIER D'ÉON
XII. SAINT-GERMAIN THE DEATHLESS
XIII. THE MYSTERY OF THE KIRKS
XIV. THE END OF JEANNE DE LA MOTTE

PORTRAIT OF ELIZABETH CANNING. *Frontispiece.*

Footnotes

I

THE CASE OF ELIZABETH CANNING

> Don't let your poor little
> Lizzie be blamed!
>
> THACKERAY.

'EVERYONE has heard of the case of Elizabeth Canning,' writes Mr. John Paget; and till recently I agreed with him. But five or six years ago the case of Elizabeth Canning repeated itself in a marvellous way, and then but few persons of my acquaintance had ever heard of that mysterious girl.

The recent case, so strange a parallel to that of 1753, was this: In Cheshire lived a young woman whose business in life was that of a daily governess. One Sunday her family went to church in the morning, but she set off to skate, by herself, on a lonely pond. She was never seen of or heard of again till, in the dusk of the following Thursday, her hat was found outside of the door of her father's farmyard. Her friend discovered her further off in a most miserable condition, weak, emaciated, and with her skull fractured. Her explanation was that a man had seized her on the ice, or as she left it, had dragged her across the fields, and had shut her up in a house, from which she escaped, crawled to her father's home, and, when she found herself unable to go further, tossed her hat towards the farm door. Neither such a man as she described, nor the house in which she had been imprisoned, was ever found. The girl's character was excellent, nothing pointed to her condition being the result d'*une orgie échevelée*; but the neighbours, of course, made insinuations, and a lady of my acquaintance, who visited the girl's mother, found herself almost alone in placing a charitable construction on the adventure.

My theory was that the girl had fractured her skull by a fall on the ice, had crawled to and lain in an unvisited outhouse of the farm, and on that Thursday night was wandering out, in a distraught state, not wandering in. Her story would be the result of her cerebral condition—concussion of the brain.

It was while people were discussing this affair, a second edition of Elizabeth Canning's, that one found out how forgotten was Elizabeth.

On January 1, 1753, Elizabeth was in her eighteenth year. She was the daughter of a carpenter in Aldermanbury; her mother, who had four younger children, was a widow, very poor, and of the best character. Elizabeth was short of stature, ruddy of complexion, and, owing to an accident in childhood—the falling of a garret ceiling on her head—was subject to fits of unconsciousness on any alarm. On learning this, the mind flies to hysteria, with its accompaniment of diabolical falseness, for an explanation of her adventure. But hysteria does not serve the turn. The girl had been for years in service with a Mr. Wintlebury, a publican. He gave her the highest character for honesty and reserve; she did not attend to the customers at the bar, she kept to herself, she had no young man, and she only left Wintlebury's for a better place—at a Mr. Lyon's, a near neighbour of her mother. Lyon, a carpenter, corroborated, as did all the neighbours, on the points of modesty and honesty.

On New Year's Day, 1753, Elizabeth wore her holiday best— 'a purple masquerade stuff gown, a white handkerchief and apron, a black quilted petticoat, a green undercoat, black shoes, blue stockings, a white shaving hat with green ribbons, ' and 'a very ruddy colour. ' She had her wages, or Christmas-box, in her pocket— a golden half guinea in a little box, with three shillings and a few coppers, including a farthing. The pence she gave to three of her little brothers and sisters. One boy, however, 'had huffed her, ' and got no penny. But she relented, and, when she went out, bought for him a mince-pie. Her visit of New Year's Day was to her maternal aunt, Mrs. Colley, living at Saltpetre Bank (Dock Street, behind the London Dock). She meant to return in time to buy, with her mother, a cloak, but the Colleys had a cold early dinner, and kept her till about 9 P.M. for a hot supper.

Already, at 9 P.M., Mr. Lyon had sent to Mrs. Canning's to make inquiries; the girl was not wont to stay out so late on a holiday. About 9 P.M., in fact, the two Colleys were escorting Elizabeth as far as Houndsditch.

The rest is mystery!

On Elizabeth's non-arrival Mrs. Canning sent her lad, a little after ten, to the Colleys, who were in bed. The night was passed in anxious search, to no avail; by six in the morning inquiries were vainly renewed. Weeks went by. Mrs. Canning, aided by the neighbours, advertised in the papers, mentioning a report of shrieks heard from a coach in Bishopsgate Street in the small morning hours of January 2. The mother, a Churchwoman, had prayers put up at several churches, and at Mr. Wesley's chapel. She also consulted a cheap 'wise man,' whose aspect alarmed her, but whose wisdom took the form of advising her to go on advertising. It was later rumoured that he said the girl was in the hands of 'an old black woman,' and would return; but Mrs. Canning admitted nothing of all this. Sceptics, with their usual acuteness, maintained that the disappearance was meant to stimulate charity, and that the mother knew where the daughter was; or, on the other hand, the daughter had fled to give birth to a child in secret, or for another reason incident to 'the young and gay,' as one of the counsel employed euphemistically put the case. The medical evidence did not confirm these suggestions. Details are needless, but these theories were certainly improbable. The character of La Pucelle was not more stainless than Elizabeth's.

About 10.15 P.M. on January 29, on the Eve of the Martyrdom of King Charles—as the poor women dated it—Mrs. Canning was on her knees, praying—so said her apprentice—that she might behold even if it were but an apparition of her daughter; such was her daily prayer. It was as in Wordsworth's *Affliction of Margaret*:

> I look for ghosts, but none will force
> Their way to me; 'tis falsely said

> That ever there was intercourse
> Between the living and the dead!

At that moment there was a sound at the door. The 'prentice opened it, and was aghast; the mother's prayer seemed to be answered, for there, bleeding, bowed double, livid, ragged, with a cloth about her head, and clad in a dirty dressing-jacket and a filthy draggled petticoat, was Elizabeth Canning. She had neglected her little brother that 'huffed her' on New Year's Day, but she had been thinking of him, and now she gave her mother for him all that she had—the farthing!

You see that I am on Elizabeth's side: that farthing touch, and another, with the piety, honesty, loyalty, and even the superstition of her people, have made me her partisan, as was Mr. Henry Fielding, the well-known magistrate.

Some friends were sent for, Mrs. Myers, Miss Polly Lyon, daughter of her master, and others; while busybodies flocked in, among them one Robert Scarrat, a toiler, who had no personal knowledge of Elizabeth. A little wine was mulled; the girl could not swallow it, emaciated as she was. Her condition need not be described in detail, but she was very near her death, as the medical evidence, and that of a midwife (who consoled Mrs. Canning on one point), proves beyond possibility of cavil.

The girl told her story; but what did she tell? Mr. Austin Dobson, in *The Dictionary of National Biography*, says that her tale 'gradually took shape under the questions of sympathising neighbours, ' and certainly, on some points, she gave affirmative answers to leading questions asked by Robert Scarrat. The difficulty is that the neighbours' accounts of what Elizabeth said in her woful condition were given when the girl was tried for perjury in April-May 1754. We must therefore make allowance for friendly bias and mythopœic memory. On January 31, 1753, Elizabeth made her statement before Alderman Chitty, and the chief count against her is that what she told Chitty did not tally with what the neighbours, in May 1754, swore that she told them when she came home on January 29, 1753. This point is overlooked by Mr. Paget in his essay on the subject.[1]

On the other hand, by 1754 the town was divided into two factions, believers and disbelievers in Elizabeth; and Chitty was then a disbeliever. Chitty took but a few notes on January 31, 1753. 'I did not make it so distinct as I could wish, not thinking it could be the subject of so much inquiry, ' he admitted in 1754. Moreover, the notes which he then produced were *not* the notes which he made at the time, 'but what I took since from that paper I took then ' (January 31, 1753) 'of hers and other persons that were brought before me. ' This is not intelligible, and is not satisfactory. If Elizabeth handed in a paper, Chitty should have produced it in 1754. If he took notes of the evidence, why did he not produce the original notes?

These notes, made when, and from what source, is vague, bear that Elizabeth 's tale was this: At a dead wall by Bedlam, in Moorfields, about ten P.M., on January 1, 1753, two men stripped her of gown, apron, and hat, robbed her of thirteen shillings and sixpence, 'struck her, stunned her, and pushed her along Bishopsgate Street. ' She lost consciousness—one of her 'fits '—and recovered herself (near Enfield Wash). Here she was taken to a house, later said to be 'Mother Wells 's, ' where 'several persons ' were. Chitty, unluckily, does not say what sort of persons, and on that point all turns. She was asked 'to do as they did, ' 'a woman forced her upstairs into a room, and cut the lace of her stays, ' told her there were bread and water in the room, and that her throat would be cut if she came out. The door was locked on her. (There was no lock; the door was merely bolted.) She lived on fragments of a quartern loaf and water *'in a pitcher,* ' with the mince-pie bought for her naughty little brother. She escaped about four in the afternoon of January 29. In the room were 'an old stool or two, *an old picture* over the chimney, ' two windows, an old table, and so on. She forced a pane in a window, 'and got out on a small shed of boards or penthouse, ' and so slid to the ground. She did not say, the alderman added, that there was any hay in the room. Of bread there were 'four or five ' or 'five or six pieces. ' *'She never mentioned the name of Wells.* ' Some one else did that at a venture. 'She said she could tell nothing of the woman 's name. ' The alderman issued a warrant against this Mrs. Wells, apparently on newspaper suggestion.

The chief points against Elizabeth were that, when Wells's place was examined, there was no penthouse to aid an escape, and no old picture. But, under a wretched kind of bed, supporting the thing, was a picture, on wood, of a Crown. Madam Wells had at one time used this loyal emblem as a sign, she keeping a very ill-famed house of call. But, in December 1745, when certain Highland and Lowland gentlemen were accompanying bonny Prince Charlie towards the metropolis, Mrs. Wells removed into a room the picture of the Crown, as being apt to cause political emotions. This sign may have been 'the old picture.' As to hay, there *was* hay in the room later searched; but penthouse there was none.

That is the worst point in the alderman's notes, of whatever value these enigmatic documents may be held.

One Nash, butler to the Goldsmiths' Company, was present at the examination before Chitty on January 31, 1753. He averred, in May 1754, what Chitty did not, that Elizabeth spoke of the place of her imprisonment as 'a little, square, darkish room,' with 'a few old pictures.' Here the *one* old picture of the notes is better evidence, if the notes are evidence, than Nash's memory. But I find that he was harping on 'a few old pictures' as early as March 1753. Elizabeth said she hurt her ear in getting out of the window, and, in fact, it was freshly cut and bleeding when she arrived at home.

All this of Nash is, so far, the better evidence, as next day, February 1, 1753, when a most tumultuous popular investigation of the supposed house of captivity was made, he says that he and others, finding the dungeon not to be square, small, and darkish, but a long, narrow slit of a loft, half full of hay, expressed disbelief. Yet it was proved that he went on suggesting to Lyon, Elizabeth's master, that people should give money to Elizabeth, and 'wished him success.' The proof was a letter of his, dated February 10, 1753. Also, Nash, and two like-minded friends, hearing Elizabeth perjure herself, as they thought, at the trial of Mrs. Wells (whom Elizabeth never mentioned to Chitty), did not give evidence against her—on the most absurdly flimsy excuses. One man was so horrified that, in place of denouncing the perjury, he fled incontinent! Another went to a dinner, and Nash to Goldsmiths' Hall, to his duties as butler. Such was then the vigour of their scepticism.

On the other hand, at the trial in 1754 the neighbours reported Elizabeth's tale as told on the night when she came home, more dead than alive. Mrs. Myers had known Elizabeth for eleven years, 'a very sober, honest girl as any in England.' Mrs. Myers found her livid, her fingers 'stood crooked;' Mrs. Canning, Mrs. Woodward, and Polly Lyon were then present, and Mrs. Myers knelt beside Elizabeth to hear her story. It was as Chitty gave it, till the point where she was carried into a house. The 'several persons' there, she said, were 'an elderly woman and two young ones.' Her stays were cut by the old woman. She was then thrust upstairs into a room, wherein was *hay, a pitcher of water,* and bread in pieces. Bread may have been brought in, water too, while she slept, a point never noted in the trials. She 'heard the name of Mother Wills, or Wells, mentioned.'

Now Scarrat, in 1754, said that he, being present on January 29, 1753, and hearing of the house, 'offered to bet a guinea to a farthing that it was Mother Wells's.' But Mrs. Myers believed that Elizabeth had mentioned hearing that name earlier; and Mrs. Myers must have heard Scarrat, if he suggested it, before Elizabeth named it. The point is uncertain.

Mrs. Woodward was in Mrs. Canning's room a quarter of an hour after Elizabeth's arrival. The girl said she was almost starved to death in a house on the Hertfordshire road, which she knew by seeing the Hertford coach, with which she was familiar, go by. The woman who cut her stays was 'a tall, black, swarthy woman.' Scarrat said 'that was not Mrs. Wells,' which was fair on Scarrat's part. Elizabeth described the two young women as being one fair, the other dark; so Scarrat swore. Wintlebury, her old master, and several others corroborated.

If these accounts by Mrs. Myers, Mrs. Woodward, Scarrat, Wintlebury, and others are trustworthy, then Elizabeth Canning's narrative is true, for she found the two girls, the tall, swarthy woman, the hay, and the broken water-pitcher, and almost everything else that she had mentioned on January 29, at Mother

Wells 's house when it was visited on February 1. But we must remember that most accounts of what Elizabeth said on January 29 and on January 31 are fifteen months after date, and are biassed on both sides.

To Mother Wells 's the girl was taken on February 1, in what a company! The coach, or cab, was crammed full, some friends walked, several curious citizens rode, and, when Elizabeth arrived at the house, Nash, the butler, and other busybodies had made a descent on it. The officer with the warrant was already there. Lyon, Aldridge, and Hague were with Nash in a cab, and were met by others 'riding hard, ' who had seized the people found at Mrs. Wells 's. There was a rabble of persons on foot and on horse about the door.

On entering the doorway the parlour was to your left, the house staircase in front of you, on your right the kitchen, at the further end thereof was a door, and, when that was opened, a flight of stairs led to a long slit of a loft which, Nash later declared, did not answer to Elizabeth 's description, especially as there was hay, and, before Chitty, Elizabeth had mentioned none. There was a filthy kind of bed, on which now slept a labourer and his wife, Fortune and Judith Natus. Nash kept talking about the hay, and one Adamson rode to meet Elizabeth, and came back saying that she said there *was* hay. By Adamson 's account he only asked her, 'What kind of place was it? ' and she said, 'A wild kind of place with hay in it, ' as in the neighbours ' version of her first narrative. Mrs. Myers, who was in the coach, corroborated Adamson.

The point of the sceptics was that till Adamson rode back to her on her way to Wells 's house she had never mentioned hay. They argued that Adamson had asked her, 'Was there hay in the room? ' and that she, taking the hint, had said 'Yes! ' By May 1754 Adamson and Mrs. Myers, who was in the cab with Elizabeth, would believe that Adamson had asked 'What kind of place is it? ' and that Elizabeth then spoke, without suggestion, of the hay. The point would be crucial, but nobody in 1754 appears to have remembered that on February 21, three weeks after the event, at the trial of Mother Wells, Adamson had given exactly the same evidence as in

May 1754. 'I returned to meet her, and asked her about the room. She described the room with some hay in it ... an odd sort of an empty room.'

Arriving at Mother Wells's, Elizabeth, very faint, was borne in and set on a dresser in the kitchen. Why did she not at once say, 'My room was up the stairs, beyond the door at the further end of the room'? I know not, unless she was dazed, as she well might be. Next she, with a mob of the curious, was carried into the parlour, where were all the inmates of the house. She paid no attention to Mrs. Wells, but at once picked out a tall old woman huddled over the fire smoking a pipe. She did this, by the sceptical Nash's evidence, instantly and without hesitation. The old woman rose. She was 'tall and swarthy,' a gipsy, and according to all witnesses inconceivably hideous, her underlip was 'the size of a small child's arm,' and she was marked with some disease. 'Pray look at this face,' she said; 'I think God never made such another.' She was named Mary Squires. She added that on January 1 she was in Dorset— 'at Abbotsbury,' said her son George, who was present.

In 1754 thirty-six people testified to Mary Squires's presence in Dorset, or to meeting her on her way to London, while twenty-seven, at Enfield alone, swore as positively that they had seen her and her daughter at or near Mrs. Wells's, and had conversed with her, between December 18, 1752, and the middle of January. Some of the Enfield witnesses were of a more prosperous and educated class than the witnesses for the gipsy. Many, on both sides, had been eager to swear, indeed, many had made affidavits as early as March 1753.

This business of the cross-swearing is absolutely inexplicable; on both sides the same entire certainty was exhibited, as a rule, yet the woman was unmistakable, as she justly remarked. The gipsy, at all events, had her *alibi* ready at once; her denial was as prompt and unhesitating as Elizabeth's accusation. But, if guilty, she had enjoyed plenty of time since the girl's escape to think out her line of defence. If guilty, it was wiser to allege an *alibi* than to decamp when Elizabeth made off, for she could not hope to escape pursuit. George Squires, her son, so prompt with his 'at Abbotsbury on January 1,' could not tell, in May 1754, where he had passed the Christmas Day before that New Year's Day, and Christmas is a notable day. Elizabeth also recognised in Lucy Squires, the gipsy's daughter, and in Virtue Hall, the two girls, dark and fair, who were present when her stays were cut.

After the recognition, Elizabeth was carried through the house, and, according to Nash, in the loft up the stairs from the kitchen she said, in answer to his question, 'This is the room, for here is the hay I lay upon, but I think there is more of it.' She also identified the pitcher with the broken mouth, which she certainly mentioned to Chitty, as that which held her allowance of water. A chest, or nest, of drawers she declared that she did not remember. An attempt was made to suggest that one of her party brought the pitcher in with him to confirm her account. This attempt failed; but that she had mentioned the pitcher was admitted. Mrs. Myers, in May 1754, quoted Elizabeth's words as to there being more hay exactly in the terms of Nash. Mrs. Myers was present in the loft, and added that Elizabeth 'took her foot, and put the hay away, and showed the gentlemen two holes, and said they were in the room when she was in it before.'

On February 7, Elizabeth swore to her narrative, formally made out by her solicitor, before the author of *Tom Jones*, and Mr. Fielding, by threats of prosecution if she kept on shuffling, induced Virtue Hall to corroborate, after she had vexed his kind heart by endless prevarications. But as Virtue Hall was later 'got at' by the other side and recanted, we leave her evidence on one side.

On February 21-26 Mary Squires was tried at the Old Bailey and condemned to death, Virtue Hall corroborating Elizabeth. Mrs. Wells was branded on the hand. Three Dorset witnesses to the gipsy's *alibi* were not credited, and Fortune and Judith Natus did not appear in court, though subpœnaed. In 1754 they accounted for this by their fear of the mob. The three sceptics, Nash, Hague, and Aldridge, held their peace. The Lord Mayor, Sir Crispin Gascoyne, who was on the bench at the trial of Squires and Wells, was dissatisfied. He secured many affidavits which seem unimpeachable, for the gipsy's *alibi*, and so did the other side for her presence at Enfield. He also got at Virtue Hall, or rather a sceptical Dr. Hill got at her and handed her over to Gascoyne. She, as we saw, recanted. George Squires, the gipsy's son, with an attorney, worked up the evidence for the gipsy's *alibi*; she received a free pardon, and on April 29, 1754, there began the trial of Elizabeth Canning for 'wilful and corrupt perjury.'

Mr. Davy, opening for the Crown, charitably suggested that Elizabeth had absconded 'to preserve her character,' and had told a romantic story to raise money! 'And, having by this time subdued all remains of virtue, she preferred the offer of money, though she must wade through innocent blood '—that of the gipsy— 'to attain it.'

These hypotheses are absurd; her character certainly needed no saving.

Mr. Davy then remarked on the gross improbabilities of the story of Elizabeth. They are glaring, but, as Fielding said, so are the improbabilities of the facts. Somebody had stripped and starved and imprisoned the girl; that is absolutely certain. She was brought 'within an inch of her life.' She did not suffer all these things to excite compassion; that is out of the question. Had she plunged into 'gaiety' on New Year's night, the consequences would be other than instant starvation. They might have been 'guilty splendour.' She had been most abominably misused, and it was to the last degree improbable that any mortal should so misuse an honest quiet lass. But the grossly improbable had certainly occurred. It was next to impossible that, in 1856, a respectable-looking man should offer to take a little boy for a drive, and that, six weeks later, the naked body of the boy, who had been starved to death, should be found in a ditch near Acton. But the facts occurred.[2] To Squires and Wells a rosy girl might prove more valuable than a little boy to anybody.

That Elizabeth could live for a month on a loaf did not surprise Mrs. Canning. 'When things were very hard with her,' said Mrs. Canning, 'the child had lived on half a roll a day.' This is that other touch which, with the story of the farthing, helps to make me a partisan of Elizabeth.

Mr. Davy said that on January 31, before Chitty, Elizabeth 'did not pretend to certainty' about Mrs. Wells. She never did at any time;

she neither knew, nor affected to know, anything about Mrs. Wells. She had only seen a tall, swarthy woman, a dark girl, and a fair girl, whom she recognised in the gipsy, her daughter, and Virtue Hall. Mr. Davy preferred Nash 's evidence to that of all the neighbours, and even to Chitty 's notes, when Nash and Chitty varied. Mr. Davy said that Nash 'withdrew his assistance ' after the visit to the house. It was proved, we saw, by his letter of February 10, that he did not withdraw his assistance, which, like that of Mr. Tracy Tupman, took the form of hoping that other people would subscribe money.

Certain varieties of statement as to the time when Elizabeth finished the water proved fatal, and the penthouse of Chitty 's notes was played for all that it was worth. It was alleged, as matter of fact, that Adamson brought the broken pitcher into the house—this by Mr. Willes, later Solicitor-General. Now, for three months before February 1, Adamson had not seen Elizabeth Canning, nor had he heard her description of the room. He was riding, and could not carry a gallon pitcher in his coat pocket. He could not carry it in John Gilpin 's fashion; and, whatever else was denied, it was admitted that from the first Elizabeth mentioned the pitcher. The statement of Mr. Willes, that Adamson brought in the pitcher, was one that no barrister should have made.

The Natus pair were now brought in to say that they slept in the loft during the time that Elizabeth said she was there. As a reason for not giving evidence at the gipsy 's trial, they alleged fear of the mob, as we saw.

The witnesses for the gipsy 's *alibi* were called. Mrs. Hopkins, of South Parrot, Dorset, was not very confident that she had seen the gipsy at her inn on December 29, 1752. She, if Mary Squires she was, told Mrs. Hopkins that they 'sold hardware '; in fact they sold soft ware, smuggled nankin and other stuffs. Alice Farnham recognised the gipsies, whom she had seen after New Christmas (new style). 'They said they would come to see me after the Old Christmas holidays '—which is unlikely!

Lucy Squires, the daughter, was clean, well dressed, and, *teste* Mr. Davy, she was pretty. She was not called.

Historical Mysteries

George Squires was next examined. He had been well tutored as to what he did *after* December 29, but could not tell where he was on Christmas Day, four days earlier! His memory only existed from the hour when he arrived at Mrs. Hopkins's inn, at South Parrot (December 29, 1752). His own counsel must have been amazed; but in cross-examination Mr. Morton showed that, for all time up to December 29, 1752, George's memory was an utter blank. On January 1, George dined, he said, at Abbotsbury, with one Clarke, a sweetheart of his sister. They had two boiled fowls. But Clarke said they had only 'a part of a fowl between them.' There was such a discrepancy of evidence here as to time on the part of one of the gipsy's witnesses that Mr. Davy told him he was drunk. Yet he persisted that he kissed Lucy Squires, at an hour when Lucy, to suit the case, could not have been present.

There was documentary evidence—a letter of Lucy to Clarke, from Basingstoke. It was dated January 18, 1753, but the figure after 175 was torn off the postmark; that was the only injury to the letter. Had there not been a battalion of as hard swearers to the presence of the gipsies at Enfield in December-January 1752-1753 as there was to their absence from Enfield and to their presence in Dorset, the gipsy party would have proved their case. As matters stand, we must remember that the Dorset evidence had been organised by a solicitor, that the route was one which the Squires party habitually used; that by the confession of Mr. Davy, the prosecuting counsel, the Squires family 'stood in' with the smuggling interest, compact and unscrupulous. They were 'gipsies dealing in smuggled goods,' said Mr. Davy. Again, while George Squires had been taught his lesson like a parrot, the prosecution dared not call his sister, pretty Lucy, as a witness. They said that George was 'stupid,' but that Lucy was much more dull. The more stupid was George, the less unlikely was he to kidnap Elizabeth Canning as prize of war after robbing her. But she did not swear to him.

As to the presence of the gipsies at Mrs. Wells's, at Enfield, as early as January 19, Mrs. Howard swore. Her husband lived on his own property, and her house, with a well, which she allowed the villagers to use, was opposite Mrs. Wells's. Mrs. Howard had seen the gipsy girl at the well, and been curtsied to by her, at a distance of three or four yards. She had heard earlier from her servants of the arrival of the gipsies, and had 'looked wishfully,' or earnestly, at them. She was not so positive as to Mary Squires, whom she had seen at a greater distance.

William Headland swore to seeing Mary Squires on January 9; he fixed the date by a market-day. Also, on the 12th, he saw her in Mrs. Wells's house. He picked up a blood-stained piece of thin lead under the window from which Elizabeth escaped, and took it to his mother, who corroborated. Samuel Story, who knew Mary Squires from of old, saw her on December 22 in White Webs Lane, so called from the old house noted as a meeting-place of the Gunpowder Plot conspirators. Story was a retired clockmaker. Mr. Smith, a tenant of the Duke of Portland, saw Mary Squires in his cowhouse on December 15, 1752. She wanted leave to camp there, as she had done in other years. The gipsies then lost a pony. Several witnesses swore to this, and one swore to conversations with Mary Squires about the pony. She gave her name, and said that it was on the clog by which the beast was tethered.

Loomworth Dane swore to Mary Squires, whom he had observed so closely as to note a great hole in the heel of her stocking. The date was Old Christmas Day, 1752. Dane was landlord of the Bell, at Enfield, and a maker of horse-collars. Sarah Star, whose house was next to Mrs. Wells's, saw Mary Squires in her own house on January 18 or 19; Mary wanted to buy pork, and hung about for three-quarters of an hour, offering to tell fortunes. Mrs. Star got rid of her by a present of some pig's flesh. She fixed the date by a document which she had given to Miles, a solicitor; it was not in court. James Pratt swore to talk with Mary Squires before Christmas as to her lost pony; she had then a man with her. He was asked to look round the court to see if the man was present, whereon George Squires ducked his head, and was rebuked by the prosecuting counsel, Mr. Davy, who said 'It does not look well.' It was hardly the demeanour of conscious innocence. But Pratt would not swear to him. Mary Squires told Pratt that she would consult 'a cunning-man about the lost pony,' and Mr. Nares foolishly asked why a cunning woman should consult a cunning man? 'One black fellow will often tell you that he can and does something magical, whilst all the time he is perfectly aware that he cannot, and yet firmly believes that some other man can really do it. ' So write Messrs. Spencer and Gillen in their excellent book on *The Native Tribes of Central Australia* (p. 130); and so it was with the gipsy, who, though a 'wise woman, ' believed in a 'wise man. '

This witness (Pratt) said, with great emphasis: 'Upon my oath, that is the woman.... I am positive in my conscience, and I am sure that it was no other woman; this is the woman I saw at that blessed time. ' Moreover, she gave him her name as the name on the clog of the lost pony. The affair of the pony was just what would impress a man like Pratt, and, on the gipsies ' own version, they had no pony with them in their march from Dorset.

All this occurred *before* Pratt left his house, which was on December 22, 'three days before New Christmas. ' He then left Enfield for Cheshunt, and his evidence carries conviction.

In some other cases witnesses were very stupid—could not tell in what month Christmas fell. One witness, an old woman, made an error, confusing January 16 with January 23. A document on which she relied gave the later date.

If witnesses on either side were a year out in their reckoning, the discrepancies would be accountable; but Pratt, for example, could not forget when he left Enfield for Cheshunt, and Farmer Smith and Mrs. Howard could be under no such confusion of memory. It may be prejudice, but I rather prefer the Enfield evidence in some ways, as did Mr. Paget. In others, the Dorset evidence seems better.

Elizabeth had sworn to having asked a man to point out the way to London after she escaped into the lane beside Mrs. Wells 's house. A man, Thomas Bennet, swore that on January 29, 1753, he met 'a miserable, poor wretch, about half-past four, ' 'near the ten-mile stone, ' in a lane. She asked her way to London; 'she said she was affrighted by the tanner 's dog. ' The tanner 's house was about two hundred yards nearer London, and the prosecution made much of this, as if a dog, with plenty of leisure and a feud against tramps, could not move two hundred yards, or much more, if he were taking a walk abroad, to combat the object of his dislike. Bennet knew that the dog was the tanner's; probably he saw the dog when he met the wayfarer, and it does not follow that the wayfarer herself called it 'the tanner's dog.' Bennet fixed the date with precision. Four days later, hearing of the trouble at Mrs. Wells's, Bennet said, 'I will be hanged if I did not meet the young woman near this place and told her the way to London.' Mr. Davy could only combat Bennet by laying stress on the wayfarer's talking of 'the tanner's dog.' But the dog, at the moment of the meeting, was probably well in view. Bennet knew him, and Bennet was not asked, 'Did the woman call the dog "the tanner's dog," or do you say this of your own knowledge?' Moreover, the tannery was well in view, and the hound may have conspicuously started from that base of operations. Mr. Davy's reply was a quibble.

His closing speech merely took up the old line: Elizabeth was absent to conceal 'a misfortune'; her cunning mother was her accomplice. There was no proof of Elizabeth's unchastity; nay, she had an excellent character, 'but there is a time, gentlemen, when people begin to be wicked.' If engaged for the other side Mr. Davy would have placed his *'Nemo repente fuit turpissimus '*—no person of unblemished character wades straight into 'innocent blood,' to use his own phrase.

The Recorder summed up against Elizabeth. He steadily assumed that Nash was always right, and the neighbours always wrong, as to the girl's original story. He said nothing of Bennet; the tanner's dog had done for Bennet. He said that, if the Enfield witnesses were right, the Dorset witnesses were wilfully perjured. He did not add that, if the Dorset witnesses were right, the Enfield testifiers were perjured.

The jury brought in a verdict of 'Guilty of perjury, but not wilful and corrupt.' This was an acquittal, but, the Recorder refusing the verdict, they did what they were desired to do, and sentence was passed. Two jurors made affidavit that they never intended a conviction. The whole point had turned, in the minds of the jury, on a discrepancy as to when Elizabeth finished the water in the broken pitcher—on Wednesday, January 27, or on Friday, January 29. Both accounts could not be true. Here, then, was 'perjury,' thought the jury, but not 'wilful and corrupt,' not purposeful. But the jury had learned that 'the court was impatient;' they had already brought Elizabeth in guilty of perjury, by which they meant guilty of a casual discrepancy not unnatural in a person hovering between life and death. They thought that they could not go back on their 'Guilty,' and so they went all the way to 'corrupt and wilful perjury'— murder by false oath—and consistently added 'an earnest recommendation to mercy'!

By a majority of one out of seventeen judges, Elizabeth was banished for seven years to New England. She was accused in the Press of being an 'enthusiast,' but the Rev. William Reyner, who attended her in prison, publicly proclaimed her a good Churchwoman and a good girl (June 7, 1754). Elizabeth (June 24) stuck to her guns in a manifesto—she had not once 'knowingly deviated from the truth.'

Mr. Davy had promised the jury that when Elizabeth was once condemned all would come out—the whole secret. But though the most careful attempts were made to discover her whereabouts from January 1 to January 29, 1753, nothing was ever found out—a fact most easily explained by the hypothesis that she was where she said she was, at Mother Wells's.

As to Elizabeth's later fortunes, accounts differ, but she quite certainly married, in Connecticut, a Mr. Treat, a respectable yeoman, said to have been opulent. She died in Connecticut in June 1773, leaving a family.

In my opinion Elizabeth Canning was a victim of the common sense of the eighteenth century. She told a very strange tale, and common-sense holds that what is strange cannot be true. Yet something strange had undeniably occurred. It was very strange if Elizabeth on the night of January 1, retired to become a mother, of which there was no appearance, while of an amour even gossip could not furnish a hint. It was very strange if, having thus retired, she was robbed, starved, stripped and brought to death's door, bleeding and broken down. It was very strange that no vestige of evidence as to her real place of concealment could ever be discovered. It was amazingly strange that a girl, previously and afterwards of golden character, should in a moment aim by perjury at 'innocent blood.' But the eighteenth century, as represented by Mr. Davy, Mr. Willes, the barrister who fabled in court, and the Recorder, found none of these things one half so strange as Elizabeth Canning's story. Mr. Henry Fielding, who had some knowledge of human nature, was of the same opinion as the present candid inquirer. 'In this case,' writes the author of *Tom Jones*, 'one of the most simple girls I ever saw, if she be a wicked one, hath been too hard for me. I am firmly persuaded that Elizabeth Canning is a poor, honest, simple, innocent girl.'

Moi aussi, but—I would not have condemned the gipsy!

In this case the most perplexing thing of all is to be found in the conflicting unpublished affidavits sworn in March 1753, when memories as to the whereabouts of the gipsies were fresh. They form a great mass of papers in State Papers Domestic, at the Record Office. I owe to Mr. Courtney Kenny my knowledge of the two unpublished letters of Fielding to the Duke of Newcastle which follow:

'My Lord Duke,—I received an order from my Lord Chancellor immediately after the breaking up of the Council to lay before your Grace all the Affidavits I had taken since the Gipsy Trial which related to that Affair. I then told the Messenger that I had taken none, as indeed the fact is the Affidavits of which I gave my Lord Chancellor an Abstract having been all sworn before Justices of the Peace in the Neighbourhood of Endfield, and remain I believe in the Possession of an Attorney in the City.

'However in Consequence of the Commands with which your Grace was pleased to honour me yesterday, I sent my Clerk immediately to the Attorney to acquaint him with the Commands, which I doubt not he will instantly obey. This I did from my great Duty to your Grace, for I have long had no Concern in this Affair, nor have I seen any of the Parties lately unless once when I was desired to send for the Girl (Canning) to my House that a great number of Noblemen and

Gentlemen might see her and ask her what Questions they pleased. I am, with the highest Duty,

> 'My Lord,
>
> > 'Your Grace's most obedient
> > and most humble Servant,
>
> > > 'HENRY FIELDING.

'Ealing; April 14, 1753.
   'His Grace the Duke of Newcastle.'

'*Endorsed*: Ealing, April 14th, 1753
   Mr. Fielding.
   R. 16th.'

'My Lord Duke,—I am extremely concerned to see by a Letter which I have just received from Mr. Jones by Command of your Grace that the Persons concerned for the Prosecution have not yet attended your Grace with the Affidavits in Canning's Affair. I do assure you upon my Honour that I sent to them the moment I first received your Grace's Commands, and having after three Messages prevailed with them to come to me I desired them to fetch the Affidavits that I might send them to your Grace, being not able to wait on you in Person. This they said they could not do, but would go to Mr. Hume Campbell their Council, and prevail with him to attend your Grace with all their Affidavits, many of which I found were sworn after the Day mentioned in the Order of Council. I told them I apprehended the latter could not be admitted but insisted in the strongest Terms on their laying the others immediately before your Grace, and they at last promised me they would, nor have I ever seen them since.

'I have now again ordered my Clerk to go to them to inform them of the last Commands I have received, but as I have no Compulsory Power over them I cannot answer for their Behaviour, which *indeed I have long disliked,* and have therefore long ago declined giving them any advice, nor would I *unless in Obedience to your Grace have anything to say to a set of the most obstinate fools I ever saw, and who seem to me rather to act from a Spleen against my Lord Mayor, than from any motive of Protecting Innocence, tho ' that was certainly their motive at first.*[3] In Truth, if I am not deceived, I suspect that they desire that the Gipsey should be pardoned, and then to convince the World that she was guilty in order to cast the greater Reflection on him who was principally instrumental in obtaining such Pardon. I conclude with assuring your Grace that I have acted in this Affair, as I shall on all Occasions, with the most dutiful Regard to your Commands, and that if my Life had been at Stake, as many know, I could have done no more. I am, with the highest Respect,

'My Lord Duke,

'Yr. Grace 's most obedient and most humble Servant,

'HENRY FIELDING.

'Ealing; April 27, 1753.
   'His Grace the Duke of Newcastle. '

Endorsed: 'Ealing: April 27th, 1753.
   Mr. Fielding. '

II

THE MURDER OF ESCOVEDO

'MANY a man,' says De Quincey, 'can trace his ruin to a murder, of which, perhaps, he thought little enough at the time.' This remark applies with peculiar force to Philip II. of Spain, to his secretary, Antonio Perez, to the steward of Perez, to his page, and to a number of professional ruffians. All of these, from the King to his own scullion, were concerned in the slaying of Juan de Escovedo, secretary of Philip's famous natural brother, Don John of Austria. All of them, in different degrees, had bitter reason to regret a deed which, at the moment, seemed a commonplace political incident.

The puzzle in the case of Escovedo does not concern the manner of his taking off, or the identity of his murderers. These things are perfectly well known; the names of the guilty, from the King to the bravo, are ascertained. The mystery clouds the motives for the deed. *Why* was Escovedo done to death? Did the King have him assassinated for purely political reasons, really inadequate, but magnified by the suspicious royal fancy? Or were the secretary of Philip II. and the monarch of Spain rivals in the affections of a one-eyed widow of rank? and did the secretary, Perez, induce Philip to give orders for Escovedo's death, because Escovedo threatened to reveal to the King their guilty intrigue? Sir William Stirling-Maxwell and Monsieur Mignet accepted, with shades of difference, this explanation. Mr. Froude, on the other hand, held that Philip acted for political reasons, and with the full approval of his very ill-informed conscience. There was no lady as a motive in the case, in Mr. Froude's opinion. A third solution is possible: Philip, perhaps, wished to murder Escovedo for political reasons, and without reference to the tender passion; but Philip was slow and irresolute, while Perez, who dreaded Escovedo's interference with his love affair, urged his royal master on to the crime which he was shirking. We may never know the exact truth, but at least we can study a state of morals and manners at Madrid, compared with which the blundering tragedies of Holyrood, in Queen Mary's time, seem mere child's play. The 'lambs' of Bothwell are lambs playful and gentle when set beside the instruments of Philip II.

The murdered man, Escovedo, and the 'first murderer,' as Shakespeare says, Antonio Perez, had both been trained in the service of Ruy Gomez, Philip's famous minister. Gomez had a wife, Aña de Mendoza, who, being born in 1546, was aged thirty-two, not thirty-eight (as M. Mignet says), in 1578, when Escovedo was killed. But 1546 may be a misprint for 1540. She was blind in one eye in 1578, but probably both her eyes were brilliant in 1567, when she really seems to have been Philip's mistress, or was generally believed so to be. Eleven years later, at the date of the murder, there is no obvious reason to suppose that Philip was constant to her charms. Her husband, created Prince d'Eboli, had died in 1573 (or as Mr. Froude says in 1567); the Princess was now a widow, and really, if she chose to distinguish her husband's old secretary, at this date the King's secretary, Antonio Perez, there seems no reason to suppose that Philip would have troubled himself about the matter. That he still loved Aña with a constancy far from royal, that she loved Perez, that Perez and she feared that Escovedo would denounce them to the King, is M. Mignet's theory of the efficient cause of Escovedo's murder. Yet M. Mignet holds, and rightly, that Philip had made up his mind, as far as he ever did make up his mind, to kill Escovedo, long before that diplomatist became an inconvenient spy on the supposed lovers.

To raise matters to the tragic height of the *Phædra* of Euripides, Perez was said to be the natural son of his late employer, Gomez, the husband of his alleged mistress. Probably Perez was nothing of the sort; he was the bastard of a man of his own name, and his alleged mistress, the widow of Gomez, may even have circulated the other story to prove that her relations with Perez, though intimate, were innocent. They are a pretty set of people!

As for Escovedo, he and Perez had been friends from their youth upwards. While Perez passed from the service of Gomez to that of Philip, in 1572 Escovedo was appointed secretary to the nobly adventurous Don John of Austria. The Court believed that he was intended to play the part of spy on Don John, but he fell under the charm of that gallant heart, and readily accepted, if he did not inspire, the most daring projects of the victor of Lepanto, the Sword of Christendom. This was very inconvenient for the leaden-footed Philip, who never took time by the forelock, but always brooded over schemes and let opportunity pass. Don John, on the other hand, was all for forcing the game, and, when he was sent to temporise and conciliate in the Low Countries, and withdraw the Spanish army of occupation, his idea was to send the Spanish forces out of the Netherlands by sea. When once they were on blue water he would make a descent on England; rescue the captive Mary Stuart; marry her (he was incapable of fear!); restore the Catholic religion, and wear the English crown. A good plot, approved of by the Pope, but a plot which did not suit the genius of Philip. He placed his leaden foot upon the scheme and on various other gallant projects, conceived in the best manner of Alexandre Dumas. Now Escovedo, to whom Don John was devotedly attached, was the soul of all these chivalrous designs, and for that reason Philip regarded him as a highly dangerous person. Escovedo was at Madrid when Don John first went to the Low Countries (1576). He kept urging Philip to accept Don John's fiery proposals, though Antonio Perez entreated him to be cautious. At this date, 1576, Perez was really the friend of Escovedo. But Escovedo would not be advised; he wrote an impatient memorial to the King, denouncing his stitchless policy (*descosido*), his dilatory, shambling, idealess proceedings. So, at least, Sir William Stirling-Maxwell asserts in his *Don John of Austria*: 'the word used by Escovedo was *descosido*, "unstitched." ' But Mr. Froude says that *Philip* used the expression, later, in reference to *another* letter of Escovedo's which he also called 'a bloody letter' (January 1578). Here Mr. Froude can hardly be right, for Philip's letter containing that vulgar expression is of July 1577.

In any case, in 1576 Philip was induced, by the intercession of Perez, to overlook the fault, and Escovedo, whose presence Don John demanded, was actually sent to him in December 1576. From this date both Don John and Escovedo wrote familiarly to their friend Perez, while Perez lured them on, and showed their letters to the King. Just as Charles I. commissioned the Duke of Hamilton to spy on the Covenanted nobles, and pretend to sympathise with them, and talk in their godly style, so Philip gave Perez orders to entrap Don John and Escovedo. Perez said: 'I want no theology but my own to justify me,' and Philip wrote in reply, 'My theology takes the same view of the matter as your own.'

At this time, 1577, Perez, though a gambler and a profligate, who took presents from all hands, must have meant nothing worse, on M. Mignet's theory, than to serve Philip as he loved to be served, and keep him well informed of Don John's designs. Escovedo was not yet, according to M. Mignet, an obstacle to the amours of Perez and the King's mistress, the Princess d'Eboli. Sir William Stirling-Maxwell, on the other hand, holds that the object of Perez already was to ruin Don John; for what reason Sir William owns that he cannot discover. Indeed Perez had no such object, unless Don John confided to him projects treasonous or dangerous to the Government of his own master, the King.

Now did Don John, or Escovedo, entrust Perez with designs not merely chivalrous and impracticable, but actually traitorous? Certainly Don John did nothing of the kind. Escovedo left him and went, without being called for, to Spain, arriving in July 1577. During his absence Don John defeated the Dutch Protestants in the battle of Gemblours, on January 31, 1578. He then wrote a letter full of chivalrous loyalty to Escovedo and Perez at Madrid. He would make Philip master indeed of the Low Countries; he asked Escovedo and Perez to inspire the King with resolution. To do that was impossible, but Philip could never have desired to murder Escovedo merely because he asked help for Don John. Yet, no sooner did Escovedo announce his return to Spain, in July 1577, than Philip, in a letter to Perez, said, 'we must hasten to despatch him before he kills us.' There seems to be no doubt that the letter in which this phrase occurs is authentic, though we have it only in a copy. But is the phrase correctly translated? The words *'priesa á despacherle antes que nos mate'* certainly may be rendered, 'we must be quick and despatch *him*' (Escovedo) 'before he kills *us.*' But Mr. Froude, much more lenient to Philip than to Mary Stuart, proposes to render the phrase, 'we must despatch Escovedo quickly' (*i.e.* send him about his business) 'before he worries us to death.' Mr. Froude thus denies that, in 1577, Philip already meant to kill Escovedo. It is unlucky for Mr. Froude's theory, and for Philip's character, if the King used the phrase *twice*. In March 1578 he wrote to Perez, about Escovedo, 'act quickly *antes que nos mate,*—before he kills us. ' So Perez averred, at least, but is his date correct? This time Perez did act, and Escovedo was butchered! If Perez tells truth, in 1577, Philip meant what he said, 'Despatch him before he kills us. '

Why did Philip thus dread Escovedo? We have merely the published statements of Perez, in his account of the affair. After giving the general causes of Philip's distrust of Don John, and the ideas which a deeply suspicious monarch may very well have entertained, considering the adventurous character of his brother, Perez adds a special charge against Escovedo. He vowed, says Perez, that, after conquering England, he and Don John would attack Spain. Escovedo asked for the captaincy of a castle on a rock commanding the harbour of Santander; he was *alcalde* of that town. He and Don John would use this fortress, as Aramis and Fouquet, in the novel of Dumas, meant to use Belle Isle, against their sovereign. As a matter of fact, Escovedo had asked for the command of Mogro, the fortress commanding Santander, in the spring of 1577, and Perez told Philip that the place should be strengthened, for the protection of the harbour, but not entrusted to Escovedo. Don John's loyalty could never have contemplated the use of the place as a keep to be held in an attack on his King. But, if Perez had, in 1577, no grudge against Escovedo as being perilous to his alleged amour with the Princess d'Eboli, then the murderous plan of Philip must have sprung from the intense suspiciousness of his own nature, not from the promptings of Perez.

Escovedo reached Spain in July 1577. He was not killed till March 31, 1578, though attempts on his life were made some weeks earlier. M. Mignet argues that, till the early spring of 1578, Philip held his hand because Perez lulled his fears; that Escovedo then began to threaten to disclose the love affair of Perez to his royal rival, and that Perez, in his own private interest, now changed his tune, and, in place of mollifying Philip, urged him to the crime. But Philip was so dilatory that he could not even commit a murder with decent promptitude. Escovedo was not dangerous, even to his mind, while he was apart from Don John. But as weeks passed, Don John kept insisting, by letter, on the return of Escovedo, and for *that* reason, possibly, Philip screwed his courage to the (literally) 'sticking' point, and Escovedo was 'stuck.' Major Martin Hume, however, argues that, by this time, circumstances had changed, and Philip had now no motive for murder.

The impression of M. Mignet, and of Sir William Stirling-Maxwell, the biographer of Don John, is quite different. They hold that the Princess d'Eboli, in 1578, was Philip's mistress; that she deceived him with Perez; that Escovedo threatened to tell all, and that Perez therefore hurried on his murder. Had this been the state of affairs, would Escovedo have constantly accepted the invitations of Perez to dinner? The men would necessarily have been on the worst of terms, if Escovedo was threatening Perez, but Escovedo, in fact, kept on dining with Perez. Again, the policy of Perez would have been to send Escovedo where he wanted to go, to Flanders, well out of the way, back to Don John. It seems probable enough, though not certain, that, in 1567, the Princess and Philip were lovers. But it is, most unlikely, and it is not proved, that Philip was still devoted to the lady in 1578. Some of the Princess's family, the Mendozas, now wanted to kill Perez, as a dishonour to their blood. At the trial of Perez later, much evidence was given to show that he loved the Princess, or was suspected of doing so, but it is not shown that this was a matter about which Philip had any reason to concern himself. Thus it is not inconceivable that Escovedo disliked the relations between Perez and the Princess, but nothing tends to show that he could have made himself dangerous by revealing them to the King. Moreover, if he spoke his mind to Perez on the matter, the two would not have remained, as apparently they did, on terms of the most friendly intercourse. A squire of Perez described a scene in which Escovedo threatened to denounce the Princess, but how did the squire become a witness of the scene, in which the Princess defied Escovedo in terms of singular coarseness?

At all events, when Philip consulted the Marquis of Los Velez on the propriety of killing Escovedo rather than sending him back to Don John, the reasons, which convinced the Marquis, were mere political suspicions.

It was at that time a question of conscience whether a king might have a subject assassinated, if the royal motives, though sufficient, were not such as could be revealed with safety in a court of justice. On these principles Queen Mary had a right to take Darnley off, for excellent political causes which could not safely be made public; for international reasons. Mary, however, unlike Philip, did not consult her confessor, who believed her to be innocent of her husband's death. The confessor of Philip told him that the King had a perfect right to despatch Escovedo, and Philip gave his orders to Perez. He repeated, says Perez, in 1578, his words used in 1577: 'Make haste before he kills us.'

As to this point of conscience, the right of a king to commit murder on a subject for reasons of State, Protestant opinion seems to have been lenient. When the Ruthvens were killed at Perth, on August 5, 1600, in an affair the most mysterious of all mysteries, the Rev. Robert Bruce, a stern Presbyterian, refused to believe that James VI. had not planned their slaughter. 'But your Majesty might have secret reasons,' said Bruce to the King, who, naturally and truly, maintained his own innocence. This looks as if Mr. Bruce, like the confessor of Philip, held that a king had a right to murder a subject for secret reasons of State. The Inquisition vigorously repudiated the doctrine, when maintained by a Spanish preacher, but Knox approved of King Henry's (Darnley's) murder of Riccio. My sympathies, on this point, are with the Inquisition.

Perez, having been commissioned to organise the crime, handed on the job to Martinez, his steward. Martinez asked a ruffianly page, Enriquez, 'if I knew anybody in my country' (Murcia) 'who would stick a knife into a person.' Enriquez said, 'I will speak about it to a muleteer of my acquaintance, as, in fact, I did, and the muleteer undertook the business.' But later, hearing that a man of importance was to be knifed, Enriquez told Perez that a muleteer was not noble enough: the job 'must be entrusted to persons of more consideration.'

Enriquez, in 1585, confessed for a good reason; Perez had absurdly mismanaged the business. All sorts of people were employed, and, after the murder, they fled, and began to die punctually in an alarming manner. Naturally Enriquez thought that Perez was acting like the Mures of Auchendrane, who despatched a series of witnesses and accomplices in their murder of Kennedy. As they always needed a new accomplice to kill the previous accomplice, then another to slay the slayer, and so on, the Mures if unchecked would have depopulated Scotland. Enriquez surmised that *his* turn to die would soon come; so he confessed, and was corroborated by Diego Martinez. Thus the facts came out, and this ought to be a lesson to murderers.

As the muleteer hung fire, Perez determined to poison Escovedo. But he did not in the least know how to set about it. Science was hardly in her infancy. If you wanted to poison a man in Scotland, you had to rely on a vulgar witch, or send a man to France, at great expense, to buy the stuff, and the messenger was detected and tortured. The Court of Spain was not more scientific.

Martinez sent Enriquez to Murcia, to gather certain poisonous herbs, and these were distilled by a venal apothecary. The poison was then tried on a barndoor fowl, which was not one penny the worse. But Martinez somehow procured 'a certain water that was good to be given as a drink.' Perez asked Escovedo to dinner, Enriquez waited at table, and in each cup of wine that Escovedo drank, he, rather homœopathically, put 'a nutshellful of the water.' Escovedo was no more poisoned than the cock of the earlier experiment. 'It was ascertained that the beverage produced no effect whatever.'

A few days later, Escovedo again dined with the hospitable Perez. On this occasion they gave him some white powder in a dish of cream, and also gave him the poisoned water in his wine, thinking it a pity to waste that beverage. This time Escovedo was unwell, and again, when Enriquez induced a scullion in the royal kitchen to put more of the powder in a basin of broth in Escovedo's own house. For this the poor kitchenmaid who cooked the broth was hanged in the public square of Madrid, *sin culpa*.

Pious Philip was demoralising his subjects at a terrible rate! But you cannot make an omelet without breaking eggs. Philip slew that girl of his kitchen as surely as if he had taken a gun and shot her, but probably the royal confessor said that all was as it should be.

Historical Mysteries

In spite of the resources of Spanish science, Escovedo persisted in living, and Perez determined that he must be shot or stabbed. Enriquez went off to his own country to find a friend who was an assassin, and to get 'a stiletto with a very fine blade, much better than a pistol to kill a man with. ' Enriquez, keeping a good thing in the family, enlisted his brother: and Martinez, from Aragon, brought 'two proper kind of men, ' Juan de Nera and Insausti, who, with the King 's scullion, undertook the job. Perez went to Alcala for Holy Week, just as the good Regent Murray left Edinburgh on the morning of Darnley 's murder, after sermon. 'Have a halibi ' was the motto of both gentlemen.

The underlings dogged Escovedo in the evening of Easter Monday. Enriquez did not come across him, but Insausti did his business with one thrust, in a workmanlike way. The scullion hurried to Alcala, and told the news to Perez, who 'was highly delighted. '

We leave this good and faithful servant, and turn to Don John. When he, far away, heard the news he was under no delusions about love affairs as the cause of the crime. He wrote to his wretched brother the King 'in grief greater than I can describe. ' The King, he said, had lost the best of servants, 'a man without the aims and craft which are now in vogue. ' 'I may with just reason consider *myself* to have been the cause of his death, ' the blow was really dealt at Don John. He expressed the most touching anxiety for the wife and children of Escovedo, who died poor, because (unlike Perez) 'he had clean hands. ' He besought Philip, by the love of our Lord, 'to use every possible diligence to know whence the blow came and to punish it with the rigour which it deserves. ' He himself will pay the most pressing debts of the dead. (From Beaumont, April 20, 1578.)

Probably the royal caitiff was astonished by this letter. On September 20 Don John wrote his last letter to his brother 'desiring more than life some decision on your Majesty 's part. Give me orders for the conduct of affairs! ' Philip scrawled in the margin, 'I will not answer. ' But Don John had ended his letter 'Our lives are at stake, and all we ask is to lose them with honour. ' These are like the last words of the last letter of the great Montrose to Charles II., 'with the more alacrity and vigour I go to search my death. ' Like Montrose Don

John 'carried with him fidelity and honour to the grave. ' He died, after a cruel illness, on October 1. Brantôme says that he was poisoned by order of the King, at the instigation of Perez. 'The side of his breast was yellow and black, as if burned, and crumbled at the touch. ' These things were always said when a great personage died in his bed. They are probably untrue, but a king who could conscientiously murder his brother 's friend could as conscientiously, and for the same reasons, murder his brother.

The Princess d 'Eboli rewarded and sheltered one of the murderers of Escovedo. They were all gratified with chains of gold, silver cups, abundance of golden *écus*, and commissions in the army; all were sent out of the country, and some began to die strangely, which, as we saw, frightened Enriquez into his confession (1585).

At once Perez was suspected. He paid a visit of condolence to young Escovedo: he spoke of a love affair of Escovedo 's in Flanders; an injured husband must be the guilty man! But suspicion darkened. Perez complained to the King that he was dogged, watched, cross-examined by the *alcalde* and his son. The Escovedo family had a friend in Vasquez, another royal secretary. Knowing nothing of the King 's guilt, and jealous of Perez, he kept assuring the King that Perez was guilty: that there was an amour, detected by Escovedo: that Escovedo perished for a woman 's sake: that Philip must investigate the case, and end the scandal. The woman, of course, was the Princess d 'Eboli. Philip cared nothing for her, now at least. Mr. Froude says that Don Gaspar Moro, in his work on the Princess, 'has disproved conclusively the imagined *liaison* between the Princess and Philip II. ' On the other hand, Philip was darkly concerned in litigations about property, *against* the Princess; these affairs Vasquez conducted, while Perez naturally was on the side of the widow of his benefactor. On these points, more than a hundred letters of Vasquez exist. Meanwhile he left, and the Escovedo family left, no stone unturned to prove that Perez murdered Escovedo because Escovedo thwarted his amour with the Princess.

Philip had promised, again and again, to stand by Perez. But the affair was coming to light, and if it must come out, it suited Philip that Vasquez should track Perez on the wrong trail, the trail of the amour, not follow the right scent which led straight to the throne, and the wretch who sat on it. But neither course could be quite pleasant to the King.

Perez offered to stand his trial, knowing that evidence against him could not be found. His accomplices were far away; he would be acquitted, as Bothwell was acquitted of Darnley's death. Philip could not face the situation. He bade Perez consult the President of the Council, De Pazos, a Bishop, and tell him all, while De Pazos should mollify young Escovedo. The Bishop, a casuist, actually assured young Escovedo that Perez and the Princess 'are as innocent as myself. ' The Bishop did not agree with the Inquisition: he could say that Perez was innocent, because he only obeyed the King's murderous orders. Young Escovedo retreated: Vasquez persevered, and the Princess d 'Eboli, writing to the King, called Vasquez 'a Moorish dog. ' Philip had both Perez and the Princess arrested, for Vasquez was not to be put down; *his* business in connection with the litigations was to pursue the Princess, and Philip could not tell Vasquez that he was on the wrong trail. The lady was sent to her estates; this satisfied Vasquez, and Perez and he were bound over to keep the peace. But suspicion hung about Perez, and Philip preferred that it should be so. The secretary was accused of peculation, he had taken bribes on all hands, and he was sentenced to heavy fines and imprisonment (January 1585). Now Enriquez confessed, and a kind of secret inquiry, of which the records survive, dragged its slow course along. Perez was under arrest, in a house near a church. He dropped out of a window and rushed into the church, the civil power burst open the gates, violated sanctuary, and found our friend crouching, all draped with festoons of cobwebs, in the timber work under the roof. The Church censured the magistrates, but they had got Perez, and Philip defied the ecclesiastical courts. Perez, a prisoner, tried to escape by the aid of one of Escovedo's murderers, who was staunch, but failed, while his wife was ill treated to make him give up all the compromising letters of the King. He did give up two sealed trunks full of papers. But his ally and steward, Martinez, had first (it is said) selected and secreted the royal notes which proved the guilt of Philip.

Apparently the King thought himself safe now, and actually did not take the trouble to see whether his compromising letters were in the sealed trunks or not! At least, if he did know that they were absent, and that Perez could produce proof of his guilt, it is hard to see why, with endless doubts and hesitations, he allowed the secret process for murder against Perez to drag on, after a long interruption, into 1590. Vasquez examined and re-examined Perez, but there was still only one witness against him, the scoundrel Enriquez. One was not enough.

A new step was taken. The royal confessor assured Perez that he would be safe if he told the whole truth and declared openly that he had acted by the royal orders! Perez refused, Philip commanded again (Jan. 4, 1590). Perez must now reveal the King's motive for decreeing the murder. If Philip was setting a trap for Perez that trap only caught him if he could not produce the King's compromising letters, which, in fact, he still possessed. Mr. Froude asserts that Philip had heard from his confessor, and *he* from the wife of Perez, that the letters were still secreted and could be produced. If so, Perez would be safe, and the King's character would be lost. What was Philip's aim and motive? Would he declare the letters to be forgeries? No other mortal (of that day) wrote such an unmistakable hand as his, it was the worst in the world. He must have had some loophole, or he would never have pressed Perez to bear witness to his own crime. A loophole he had, and Perez knew it, for otherwise he would have obeyed orders, told the whole story, and been set free. He did not. Mr. Froude supposes that he did not think the royal authority would satisfy the judges. But they could not condemn Perez, a mere accessory to Philip, without condemning the King, and how could the judges do that? Perez, I think, would have taken his chance of the judges' severity, as against their King, rather than disobey the King's command to confess all, and so have to face torture. He did face the torture, which proves, perhaps, that he knew Philip could, somehow, escape from the damning evidence of his own letters. Philip's loophole, Major Martin Hume thinks, was this: if Perez revealed the King's reasons for ordering the murder, they would appear as obsolete, at the date of the deed. Pedro alone would be culpable. In any case he faced torture.

Historical Mysteries

Like most people in his circumstances, he miscalculated his own power of bearing agony. He had not the endurance of the younger Auchendrane murderer: of Mitchell, the choice Covenanting assassin: of the gallant Jacobite Nevile Payne, tortured nearly to death by the minions of the Dutch usurper, William of Orange. All of these bore the torment and kept their secrets. But 'eight turns of the rope ' opened the mouth of Perez, whose obstinacy had merely put him to great inconvenience. Yet he did not produce Philip 's letters in corroboration; he said that they had been taken from him. However, next day, Diego Martinez, who had hitherto denied all, saw that the game was up, and admitted the truth of all that Enriquez had confessed in 1585.

About a month after the torture Perez escaped. His wife was allowed to visit him in prison. She had been the best, the bravest, the most devoted of women. If she had reason for jealousy of the Princess, which is by no means certain, she had forgiven all. She had moved heaven and earth to save her husband. In the Dominican church, at high mass, she had thrown herself upon the King 's confessor, demanding before that awful Presence on the altar that the priest should refuse to absolve the King unless he set Perez free.

Admitted to her husband 's prison, she played the trick that saved Lord Ogilvy from the dungeon of the Covenanters, that saved Argyle, Nithsdale, and James Mòr Macgregor. Perez walked out of gaol in the dress of his wife. We may suppose that the guards were bribed: there is *always* collusion in these cases. One of the murderers had horses round the corner, and Perez, who cannot have been badly injured by the rack, rode thirty leagues, and crossed the frontier of Aragon.

We have not to follow his later adventures. The refusal of the Aragonese to give him up to Castile, their rescue of him from the Inquisition, cost them their constitution, and about seventy of them were burned as heretics. But Perez got clear away. He visited France, where Henry IV. befriended him; he visited England, where Bacon was his host. In 1594 (?) he published his *Relaciones* and told the world the story of Philip 's conscience. That story must not be relied on, of course, and the autograph letters of Philip as to the murder of

Escovedo are lost. But the copies of them at the Hague are regarded as authentic, and the convincing passages are underlined in red ink.

Supposing it possible that Philip after all secured the whole of the autograph correspondence, and that Perez only succeeded in preserving the copies now at the Hague, we should understand why Perez would not confess the King's crime: he had only copies of his proofs to show; and copies were valueless as evidence. But it is certain that Perez really had the letters.

'Bloody Perez,' as Bacon's mother called him, died at Paris in November 1611, outliving the wretched master whom he had served so faithfully. Queen Elizabeth tried to induce Amyas Paulet to murder Mary Stuart. Paulet, as a man of honour, refused; he knew, too, that Elizabeth would abandon him to the vengeance of the Scots. Perez ought to have known that Philip would desert him: his folly was rewarded by prison, torture, and confiscation, which were not more than the man deserved, who betrayed and murdered the servant of Don John of Austria.

NOTE.—This essay was written when I was unaware that Major Martin Hume had treated the problem in *Transactions of the Royal Historical Society*, 1894, pp. 71-107, and in *Españoles é Ingleses* (1903). The latter work doubtless represents Major Hume's final views. He has found among the Additional MSS. of the British Museum (28,269) a quantity of the contemporary letters of Perez, which supplement the copies, at the Hague, of other letters destroyed after the death of Perez. From these MSS. and other original sources unknown to Mr. Froude, and to Monsieur Mignet (see the second edition of his *Antonio Perez*; Paris, 1846), Major Hume's theory is that, for *political* reasons, Philip gave orders that Escovedo should be assassinated. This was in late October or early November, 1577. The order was not then carried out; the reason of the delay I do not clearly understand. The months passed, and Escovedo's death ceased, in altered circumstances, to be politically desirable, but he became a serious nuisance to Perez and his mistress, the Princess d'Eboli. Philip had never countermanded the murder, but Perez, according to Major Hume, falsely alleges that the King was still bent on the murder, and that other statesmen were consulted and approved of it, *shortly before the actual deed*. Perez gives this impression by a crafty manipulation of dates in his narrative. When he had Escovedo slain, he was fighting for his own hand; but Philip, who had never countermanded the murder, was indifferent, till, in 1582, when he was with Alva in Portugal. The King now learned that Perez had behaved abominably, had poisoned his mind against his brother Don Juan, had communicated State secrets to the Princess d 'Eboli, and had killed Escovedo, not in obedience to the royal order, but using that order as the shield of his private vengeance. Hence Philip 's severities to Perez; hence his final command that Perez should disclose the royal motives for the destruction of Escovedo. They would be found to have become obsolete at the date when the crime was committed, and on Perez would fall the blame.

Such is Major Hume 's theory, if I correctly apprehend it. The hypothesis leaves the moral character of Philip as black as ever: he ordered an assassination which he never even countermanded. His confessor might applaud him, but he knew that the doctors of the Inquisition, like the common sentiment of mankind, rejected the theory that kings had the right to condemn and execute, by the dagger, men who had been put to no public trial.

III

THE CAMPDEN MYSTERY

I

THE ordinary historical mystery is at least so far clear that one or other of two solutions must be right, if we only knew which. Perkin Warbeck was the rightful King, or he was an impostor. Giacopo Stuardo at Naples (1669) was the eldest son of Charles II., or he was a humbug. The Man in the Iron Mask was *certainly* either Mattioli or Eustache Dauger. James VI. conspired against Gowrie, or Gowrie conspired against James VI., and so on. There is reason and human nature at the back of these puzzles. But at the back of the Campden mystery there is not a glimmer of reason or of sane human nature, except on one hypothesis, which I shall offer. The occurrences are, to all appearance, motiveless as the events in a feverish dream. 'The whole Matter is dark and mysterious; which we must therefore leave unto Him who alone knoweth all Things, in His due Time, to reveal and to bring to Light.'

So says the author of 'A True and Perfect Account of the Examination, Confession, Trial, and Execution of *Joan Perry*, and her two Sons, *John* and *Richard Perry*, for the Supposed Murder of *Will Harrison*, Gent., Being One of the most remarkable Occurrences which hath happened in the Memory of Man. Sent in a Letter (by *Sir Thomas Overbury*, of *Burton*, in the County of *Gloucester*, Knt., and one of his Majesty's Justices of the Peace) to *Thomas Shirly*, Doctor of Physick, in London. Also Mr. *Harrison*'s Own account,' &c. (London. Printed for John Atkinson, near the Chapter House, in *St. Paul's Church-Yard*. No date, but apparently of 1676.)

Such is the vast and breathless title of a pamphlet which, by undeserved good luck, I have just purchased. The writer, Sir Thomas Overbury, 'the nephew and heir,' says Mr. John Paget, 'of the unhappy victim of the infamous Countess of Somerset ' (who had the elder Overbury poisoned in the Tower), was the Justice of the Peace who acted as *Juge d 'Instruction* in the case of Harrison 's disappearance.[5]

To come to the story. In 1660, William Harrison, Gent., was steward or 'factor ' to the Viscountess Campden, in Chipping Campden, Gloucestershire, a single-streeted town among the Cotswold hills. The lady did not live in Campden House, whose owner burned it in the Great Rebellion, to spite the rebels; as Castle Tirrim was burned by its Jacobite lord in the '15. Harrison inhabited a portion of the building which had escaped destruction. He had been for fifty years a servant of the Hickeses and Campdens, his age was seventy (which deepens the mystery), he was married, and had offspring, including Edward, his eldest son.

On a market day, in 1659, Mr. Harrison 's house was broken into, at high noon, while he and his whole family were 'at the Lecture, ' in church, a Puritan form of edification. A ladder had been placed against the wall, the bars of a window on the second story had been wrenched away with a ploughshare (which was left in the room), and 140*l.* of Lady Campden 's money were stolen. The robber was never discovered—a curious fact in a small and lonely village. The times, however, were disturbed, and a wandering Cavalier or Roundhead soldier may have 'cracked the crib. ' Not many weeks later, Harrison 's servant, Perry, was heard crying for help in the garden. He showed a 'sheep-pick, ' with a hacked handle, and declared that he had been set upon by two men in white, with naked swords, and had defended himself with his rustic tool. It is curious that Mr. John Paget, a writer of great acuteness, and for many years police magistrate at Hammersmith, says nothing of the robbery of 1659, and of Perry 's crazy conduct in the garden. Perry 's behaviour there, and his hysterical invention of the two armed men in white, give the key to his character. The two men in white were never traced of course, but, later, we meet three men not less flagitious, and even more mysterious. They appear to have been three 'men in buckram. '

At all events, in quiet Campden, adventures obviously occurred to the unadventurous. They culminated in the following year, on August 16, 1660. Harrison left his house in the morning (?) and walked the two miles to Charringworth to collect his lady's rents. The autumn day closed in, and between eight and nine o'clock old Mrs. Harrison sent the servant, John Perry, to meet his master on the way home. Lights were also left burning in Harrison's window. That night neither master nor man returned, and it is odd that the younger Harrison, Edward, did not seek for his father till very early next morning: he had the convenience, for nocturnal search, of a moon which rose late. In the morning, Edward went out and met Perry, returning alone: he had not found his master. The pair walked to Ebrington, a village half way between Campden and Charringworth, and learned that Harrison had called, on the previous evening, as he moved home through Ebrington, at the house of one Daniel. The hour is not given, but Harrison certainly disappeared when just beyond Ebrington, within less than a mile from Campden. Edward and Perry next heard that a poor woman had picked up on the highway, beyond Ebrington, near some whins or furze, a hat, band, and comb, which were Harrison's; they were found within about half a mile of his own house. The band was bloody, the hat and comb were hacked and cut. Please observe the precise words of Sir Thomas Overbury, the justice who took the preliminary examinations: 'The Hat and Comb being hacked and cut, and the Band bloody, but nothing more could there be found.' Therefore the hat and comb were not on Harrison's head when they were hacked and cut: otherwise they must have been blood-stained; the band worn about the throat was bloody, but there was no trace of blood on the road. This passage contains the key to the puzzle.

On hearing of the discovery of these objects all the people rushed to hunt for Harrison's corpse, which they did not find.

An old man like Harrison was not likely to stay at Charringworth very late, but it seems that whatever occurred on the highway happened after twilight.

Suspicion fell on John Perry, who was haled before the narrator, Sir Thomas Overbury, J.P. Perry said that after starting for

Charringworth to seek his master on the previous evening, about 8.45 P.M., he met by the way William Reed of Campden, and explained to him that as he was timid in the dark he would go back and take Edward Harrison's horse and return. Perry did as he had said, and Reed left him 'at Mr. Harrison's Court gate.' Perry dallied there till one Pierce came past, and with Pierce (he did not say why) 'he went a bow's shot into the fields,' and so back once more to Harrison's gate. He now lay for an hour in a hen house, he rose at midnight, and again—the moon having now risen and dispelled his fears—he started for Charringworth. He lost his way in a mist, slept by the road-side, proceeded in the dawn to Charringworth, and found that Harrison had been there on the previous day. Then he came back and met Edward Harrison on his way to seek his father at Charringworth.

Perry's story is like a tale told by an idiot, but Reed, Pierce, and two men at Charringworth corroborated as far as their knowledge went. Certainly Perry had been in company with Reed and Pierce, say between nine and ten on the previous night. Now, if evil had befallen Harrison it must have been before ten at night; he would not stay so late, if sober, at Charringworth. Was he usually sober? The cool way in which his wife and son took his absence suggests that he was a late-wandering old boy. They may have expected Perry to find him in his cups and tuck him up comfortably at Charringworth or at Ebrington.

Till August 24 Perry was detained in prison, or, odd to say, at the inn! He told various tales; a tinker or a servant had murdered his master and hidden him in a bean-rick, where, on search being made, *non est inventus*. Harrison, and the rents he had collected, were vanished in the azure. Perry now declared that he would tell all to Overbury, and to no other man. To him Perry averred that his mother and brother, Joan and Richard Perry, had murdered Harrison! It was his brother who, by John Perry's advice and connivance, had robbed the house in the previous year, while John 'had a Halibi,' being at church. The brother, said John, buried the money in the garden. It was sought for, but was not found. His story of the 'two men in white,' who had previously attacked him in the garden, was a lie, he said. I may add that it was not the lie of a sane man. Perry was conspicuously crazy.

He went on with his fables. His mother and brother, he declared, had often asked him to tell them when his master went to collect rents. He had done so after Harrison started for Charringworth on the morning of August 16. John Perry next gave an account of his expedition with his brother in the evening of the fatal day, an account which was incompatible with his previous tale of his doings and with the authentic evidence of Reed and Pierce. Their honest version destroyed Perry's new falsehood. He declared that Richard Perry and he had dogged Harrison, as he came home at night, into Lady Campden's grounds; Harrison had used a key to the private gate. Richard followed him into the grounds; John Perry, after a brief stroll, joined him there and found his mother (how did she come thither?) and Richard standing over the prostrate Harrison, whom Richard incontinently strangled. They seized Harrison's money and meant to put his body 'in the great sink by Wallington's Mill.' John Perry left them, and knew not whether the body was actually thrown into the sink. In fact, *non est inventus* in the sink, any more than in the bean-rick. John next introduced his meeting with Pierce, but quite forgot that he had also met Reed, and did not account for that part of his first story, which Reed and Pierce had both corroborated. The hat, comb, and band John said that he himself had carried away from Harrison's body, had cut them with his knife, and thrown them into the highway. Whence the blood on the band came he neglected to say.

On the strength of this impossible farrago of insane falsehoods, Joan and Richard Perry were arrested and brought before Overbury. Not only the 'sink' but the Campden fish-pools and the ruinous parts of the house were vainly searched in quest of Harrison's body. On August 25 the three Perrys were examined by Overbury, and Richard and the mother denied all that John laid to their charge. John persisted in his story, and Richard admitted that he and John had spoken together on the morning of the day when Harrison vanished, 'but nothing passed between them to that purpose.'

As the three were being brought back from Overbury's house to Campden an unfortunate thing happened. John was going foremost when Richard, a good way behind, dropped 'a ball of inkle from his pocket.' One of his guards picked it up, and Richard said that it 'was only his wife's hair-lace.' At one end, however, was a slip-knot. The finder took it to John, who, being a good way in front, had not seen his brother drop it. On being shown the string John shook his head, and said that 'to his sorrow he knew it, for that was the string his brother strangled his master with.' To this circumstance John swore at the ensuing trial.

The Assizes were held in September, and the Perrys were indicted both for the robbery in 1659 and the murder in 1660. They pleaded 'Guilty' to the first charge, as some one in court whispered to them to do, for the crime was covered by the Act of Pardon and Oblivion passed by Charles II. at his happy Restoration. If they were innocent of the robbery, as probably they were, they acted foolishly in pleading guilty. We hear of no evidence against them for the robbery, except John's confession, which was evidence perhaps against John, but was none against *them*. They thus damaged their case, for if they were really guilty of the robbery from Harrison's house, they were the most likely people in the neighbourhood to have robbed him again and murdered him. Very probably they tied the rope round their own necks by taking advantage of the good King's indemnity. They later withdrew their confession, and probably were innocent of the theft in 1659.

On the charge of murder they were not tried in September. Sir Christopher Turner would not proceed 'because the body of Harrison was not found.' There was no *corpus delicti*, no evidence that Harrison was really dead. Meanwhile John Perry, as if to demonstrate his lunacy, declared that his mother and brother had tried to poison him in prison! At the Spring Assizes in 1661, Sir B. Hyde, less legal than Sir Christopher Turner, did try the Perrys on the charge of murder. How he could do this does not appear, for the account of the trial is not in the Record House, and I am unable at present to trace it. In the *Arminian Magazine*, John Wesley publishes a story of a man who was hanged for murdering another man, whom he afterwards met in one of the Spanish colonies of South America. I shall not here interrupt the tale of the Perrys by explaining how a hanged man met a murdered man, but the anecdote proves that to inflict capital punishment for murder without proof that murder has been committed is not only an illegal but an injudicious proceeding. Probably it was assumed that Harrison, if alive, would have given signs of life in the course of nine or ten months.

At the trial in spring all three Perrys pleaded 'not guilty.' John's confession being proved against him, 'he told them he was then mad and knew not what he said.' There must have been *some* evidence against Richard. He declared that his brother had accused others besides him. Being asked to prove this, he answered 'that most of those that had given evidence against him knew it,' but named none. So evidence had been given (perhaps to the effect that Richard had been flush of money), but by whom, and to what effect, we do not know.

The Perrys were probably not of the best repute. The mother, Joan, was supposed to be a witch. This charge was seldom brought against popular well-living people. How intense was the fear of witches, at that date, we know from the stories and accounts of trials in Glanvil's *Sadducismus Triumphatus*. The neighbours probably held that Joan Perry would, as a witch, be 'nane the waur o' a hanging.' She was put to death first, under the belief that any hypnotic or other unholy influence of hers, which prevented her sons from confessing, would be destroyed by her death. We are not aware that post-hypnotic suggestion is removed by the death of the suggester; the experiment has not been tried. The experiment failed in Joan's case. Poor Richard, who was hanged next, could not induce the 'dogged and surly' John to clear his character by a dying declaration. Such declarations were then held irrefragable evidence, at least in Scotland, except when (as in the case of George Sprot, hanged for the Gowrie conspiracy) it did not suit the Presbyterians to believe the dying man. When John was being turned off, he said that 'he knew nothing of his master's death, nor what was become of him, but they might hereafter (possibly) hear.' Did John know something? It would not surprise me if he had an inkling of the real state of the case.

Historical Mysteries

II

They *did* hear; but what they heard, and what I have now to tell, was perfectly incredible. When 'some' years (two apparently) had passed, Will Harrison, Gent., like the three silly ewes in the folk-rhyme, 'came hirpling hame.' Where had the old man been? He explained in a letter to Sir Thomas Overbury, but his tale is as hard to believe as that of John Perry.

He states that he left his house in the afternoon (not the morning) of Thursday, August 16, 1660. He went to Charringworth to collect rents, but Lady Campden's tenants were all out harvesting. August seems an odd month for rent-collecting when one thinks of it. They came home late, which delayed Harrison 'till the close of the evening.' He only received 23 *l.*, which John Perry said, at his first examination in 1660, had been paid by one Edward Plaisterer, and Plaisterer corroborated. Harrison then walked homeward, in the dusk probably, and, near Ebrington, where the road was narrow, and bordered by whins, 'there met me one horseman who said "*Art thou there?*"' Afraid of being ridden over, Harrison struck the horse on the nose, and the rider, with a sword, struck at him and stabbed him in the side. (It was at this point of the road, where the whins grew, that the cut hat and bloody band were found, but a thrust in the side would not make a neck-band bloody.) Two other horsemen here came up, one of them wounded Harrison in the thigh. They did not now take his 23*l.*, but placed him behind one of them on horseback, handcuffed him, and threw a great cloak over him.

Now, is it likely that highwaymen would carry handcuffs which closed, says Harrison, with a spring and a snap? The story is pure fiction, and bad at that. Suppose that kidnapping, not robbery, was the motive (which would account for the handcuffs), what had any mortal to gain by kidnapping, for the purpose of selling him into slavery, a 'gent.' of seventy years of age?

In the night they took Harrison's money and 'tumbled me down a stone-pit.' In an hour they dragged him out again, and he naturally asked what they wanted with him, as they had his money already. One of these miscreants wounded Harrison again, and—stuffed his pockets full of 'a great quantity of money.' If they had a great quantity of money, what did they want with 23*l*.? We hear of no other robberies in the neighbourhood, of which misdeeds the money might have been the profits. And why must Harrison carry the money? (It has been suggested that, to win popular favour, they represented themselves as smugglers, and Harrison, with the money, as their gallant purser, wounded in some heroic adventure.)

They next rode till late on August 17, and then put Harrison down, bleeding and 'sorely bruised with the carriage of the money,' at a lonely house. Here they gave their victim broth and brandy. On Saturday they rode all day to a house, where they slept, and on Sunday they brought Harrison to Deal, and laid him down on the ground. This was about three in the afternoon. Had they wanted to make for the sea, they would naturally have gone to the *west* coast. While one fellow watched Harrison, two met a man, and 'I heard them mention seven pounds.' The man to whom seven pounds were mentioned (Wrenshaw was his name, as Harrison afterwards heard—where?) said that he thought Harrison would die before he could be put on board a ship. *Que diable allait-il faire dans cette galère?* Harrison was, however, put on board a casual vessel, and remained in the ship for six weeks.

> Where was the land to which the ship would go?
> Far, far ahead is all the sailors know!

Harrison does not say into what 'foam of perilous seas, in faery lands forlorn' the ship went wandering for six mortal weeks. Like Lord Bateman:

> He sailéd East, and he sailéd West,
> Until he came to famed Turkee,
> Where he was taken and put in prison,
> Till of his life he was wear—ee!

'Then the Master of the ship came and told me, and *the rest who were in the same condition*, that he discovered three Turkish ships.' 'The rest who were in the same condition'! We are to understand that a whole cargo of Harrisons was kidnapped and consigned captive to a vessel launched on ocean, on the off chance that the captain might meet three Turkish rovers who would snap them up. At this rate of carrying on, there must have been disappearances as strange as Harrison's, from dozens of English parishes, in August 1660. Had a crew of kidnappers been taking captives for purposes of private fiscal policy, they would have shipped them to the Virginian plantations, where Turkish galleys did not venture, and they would not have kidnapped men of seventy. Moreover, kidnappers would not damage their captives by stabbing them in the side and thigh, when no resistance was made, as was done to Harrison.

'The rest who were in the same condition' were 'dumped down' near Smyrna, where the valuable Harrison was sold to 'a grave physician.' 'This Turk he' was eighty-seven years of age, and 'preferred Crowland in Lincolnshire before all other places in England.' No inquiries are known to have been made about a Turkish medical man who once practised at Crowland in Lincolnshire, though, if he ever did, he was likely to be remembered in the district. This Turk he employed Harrison in the still room, and as a hand in the cotton fields, where he once knocked his slave down with his fist—pretty well for a Turk of eighty-seven! He also gave Harrison (whom he usually employed in the chemical department of his business) 'a silver bowl, double gilt, to drink in, and named him Boll'—his way of pronouncing bowl—no doubt he had acquired a Lincolnshire accent.

This Turk fell ill on a Thursday, and died on Saturday, when Harrison tramped to the nearest port, bowl and all. Two men in a Hamburg ship refused to give him a passage, but a third, for the price of his silver-gilt bowl, let him come aboard. Harrison was landed, without even his bowl, at Lisbon, where he instantly met a man from Wisbech, in Lincolnshire. This good Samaritan gave Harrison wine, strong waters, eight stivers, and his passage to Dover, whence he came back to Campden, much to the amazement of mankind. We do not hear the names of the ship and skipper that brought Harrison from Lisbon to Dover. Wrenshaw (the man to whom seven pounds 'were mentioned') is the only person named in this delirious tissue of nonsense.

Historical Mysteries

The editor of our pamphlet says, 'Many question the truth of this account Mr. Harrison gives of himself, and his transportation, believing he was never out of England.' I do not wonder at their scepticism. Harrison had 'all his days been a man of sober life and conversation,' we are told, and the odd thing is that he 'left behind him a considerable sum of his Lady's money in his house. 'He did not see any of the Perrys on the night of his disappearance. The editor admits that Harrison, as an article of merchandise, was not worth his freight to Deal, still less to Smyrna. His son, in his absence, became Lady Campden's steward, and behaved but ill in that situation. Some suspected that this son arranged the kidnapping of Harrison, but, if so, why did he secure the hanging of John Perry, in chains, on Broadway hill, 'where he might daily see him'?

That might be a blind. But young Harrison could not expect John Perry to assist him by accusing himself and his brother and mother, which was the most unlooked-for event in the world. Nor could he know that his father would come home from Charringworth on August 16, 1660, in the dark, and so arrange for three horsemen, in possession of a heavy weight of specie, to stab and carry off the aged sire. Young Harrison had not a great fardel of money to give them, and if they were already so rich, what had they to gain by taking Harrison to Deal, and putting him, with 'others in the same condition,' on board a casual ship? They could have left him in the 'stone-pit:' he knew not who they were, and the longer they rode by daylight, with a hatless, handcuffed, and sorely wounded prisoner, his pockets overburdened with gold, the more risk of detection they ran. A company of three men ride, in broad daylight, through England from Gloucestershire to Deal. Behind one of them sits a wounded, *and hatless,* and handcuffed captive, his pockets bulging with money. Nobody suspects anything, no one calls the attention of a magistrate to this extraordinary *démarche*! It is too absurd!

The story told by Harrison is conspicuously and childishly false. At every baiting place, at every inn, these weird riders must have been challenged. If Harrison told truth, he must have named the ship and skipper that brought him to Dover.

Dismissing Harrison's myth, we ask, what could account for his disappearance? He certainly walked, on the evening of August 16, to within about half a mile of his house. He would not have done that had he been bent on a senile amour involving his absence from home, and had that scheme of pleasure been in his mind, he would have provided himself with money. Again, a fit of 'ambulatory somnambulism,' and the emergence of a split or secondary personality with forgetfulness of his real name and address, is not likely to have seized on him at that very moment and place. If it did, as there were no railways, he could not rush off in a crowd and pass unnoticed through the country.

Once more, the theory of ambulatory somnambulism does not account for his hacked hat and bloody band found near the whins on the road beyond Ebrington. Nor does his own story account for them. He was stabbed in the side and thigh, he says. This would not cut his hat or ensanguine his band. On the other hand, he would leave pools and tracks of blood on the road— 'the high way.' 'But nothing more could there be found,' no pools or traces of blood on the road. It follows that the hacked hat and bloody band were a designed false trail, *not* left there by John Perry, as he falsely swore, but by some other persons.

The inference is that for some reason Harrison's presence at Campden was inconvenient to somebody. He had lived through most troubled times, and had come into a changed state of affairs with new masters. He knew some secret of the troubled times: he was a witness better out of the way. He may conceivably have held a secret that bore on the case of one of the Regicides; or that affected private interests, for he was the trusted servant of a great family. He was therefore spirited away: a trail certainly false—the cut hat and bloody band—was laid. By an amazing coincidence his servant, John Perry, went more or less mad—he was not sane on the evening of Thursday, August 16, and accused himself, his brother, and mother. Harrison was probably never very far from Campden during the two or three years of his disappearance. It was obviously made worth his while to tell his absurd story on his return, and to accept the situation. No other hypothesis 'colligates the facts.' What Harrison knew, why his absence was essential, we cannot hope to discover.

But he never was a captive in 'famed Turkee.' Mr. Paget writes: 'It is impossible to assign a sufficient motive for kidnapping the old man ... much profit was not likely to arise from the sale of the old man as a slave.' Obviously there was no profit, especially as the old man was delivered in a wounded and imperfect condition. But a motive for keeping Harrison out of the way is only hard to seek because we do not know the private history of his neighbours. Roundheads among them may have had excellent reasons, under the Restoration, for sequestering Harrison till the revenges of the Restoration were accomplished. On this view the mystery almost ceases to be mysterious, for such mad self-accusations as that of John Perry are not uncommon.

IV

THE CASE OF ALLAN BRECK

WHO killed the Red Fox? What was the secret that the Celts would not communicate to Mr. R.L. Stevenson, when he was writing *Kidnapped*? Like William of Deloraine, 'I know but may not tell '; at least, I know all that the Celt knows. The great-grandfather and grandfather of a friend of mine were with James Stewart of the Glens, the victim of Hanoverian injustice, in a potato field, near the road from Ballachulish Ferry to Appin, when they heard a horse galloping at a break-neck pace. 'Whoever the rider is, ' said poor James, 'he is not riding his own horse. ' The galloper shouted, 'Glenure has been shot! '

'Well, ' said James to his companion, 'whoever did it, I am the man that will hang for it. '

Hanged he was. The pit in which his gibbet stood is on the crest of a circular 'knowe, ' or hummock, on the east side of the Ballachulish Hotel, overlooking the ferry across the narrows, where the tide runs like a great swift river.

I have had the secret from two sources; the secret which I may not tell. One informant received it from his brother, who, when he came to man 's estate, was taken apart by his uncle. 'You are old enough to know now, ' said that kinsman, 'and I tell you that it may not be forgotten. ' The gist of the secret is merely what one might gather from the report of the trial, that though Allan Breck was concerned in the murder of Campbell of Glenure, he was not alone in it.

The truth is, according to tradition, that as Glenure rode on the fatal day from Fort William to his home in Appin, the way was lined with marksmen of the Camerons of Lochaber, lurking with their guns among the brushwood and behind the rocks. But their hearts failed them, no trigger was drawn, and when Glenure landed on the Appin side of the Ballachulish Ferry, he said, 'I am safe now that I am out of my mother's country, ' his mother having been of clan Cameron. But he had to reckon with the man with the gun, who was lurking in the wood of Letter More ('the great hanging coppice '), about three-quarters of a mile on the Appin side of Ballachulish Ferry. The gun was not one of the two dilapidated pieces shown at the trial of James of the Glens, nor, I am told, was it the Fasnacloich gun. The real homicidal gun was found some years ago in a hollow tree. People remember these things well in Appin and Glencoe, though the affair is a hundred and fifty years old, and though there are daily steamers bringing the newspapers. There is even a railway, not remarkable for speed, while tourists, English, French, and American, are for ever passing to view Glencoe, and to write their names in the hotel book after luncheon, then flying to other scenes. There has even been a strike of long duration at the Ballachulish Quarries, and Labour leaders have perorated to the Celts; but Gaelic is still spoken, second sight is nearly as common as short sight, you may really hear the fairy music if you bend your ear, on a still day, to the grass of the fairy knowe. Only two generations back a fairy boy lived in a now ruinous house, noted in the story of the Massacre of Glencoe, beside the brawling river: and a woman, stolen by the fairies, returned for an hour to her husband, who became very unpopular, as he neglected the means for her rescue; I think he failed to throw a dirk over her shoulder. Every now and then mysterious lights may be seen, even by the Sassenach, speeding down the road to Callart on the opposite side of the narrow sea-loch, ascending the hill, and running down into the salt water. The causes of these lights, and of the lights on the burial isle of St. Mun, in the middle of the sea strait, remain a mystery. Thus the country is still a country of prehistoric beliefs and of fairly accurate traditions. For example, at the trial of James Stewart for the murder of Glenure, one MacColl gave damaging evidence, the MacColls being a sept subordinate to the MacIans or Macdonalds of Glencoe, who, by the way, had no hand in the murder. Till recently these MacColls were still disliked for the part played by the witness, and were named 'King George's MacColls.'

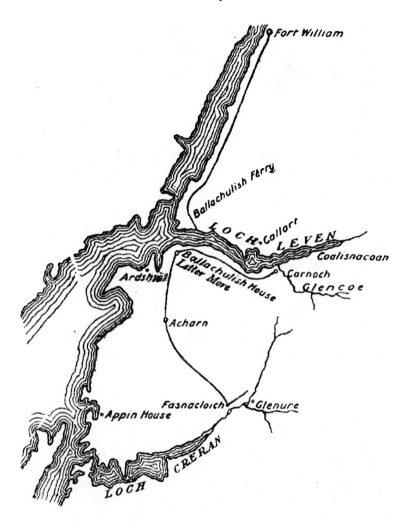

But we must come to the case of Allan Breck. To understand it, some knowledge of topography is necessary. Leaving Oban by steamer, you keep on the inside of the long narrow island of Lismore, and reach the narrow sea inlet of Loch Creran on your right. The steamer does not enter it, but, taking a launch or a boat, you go down Loch Creran. On your left is the peninsula of Appin; its famous green hills occupy the space bounded by Loch Creran on the south and Glencoe on the north. Landing near the head of Loch Creran, a walk of two miles takes you to the old house of Fasnacloich, where Allan Breck was wont to stay. Till two or three years ago it belonged to the

Historical Mysteries

Stewarts of Fasnacloich, cadets of the chief, the Laird of Appin; all Appin was a Stewart country and loyal to the King over the Water, their kinsman. About a mile from Fasnacloich, further inland, is the rather gloomy house of Glenure, the property of Campbell of Glenure, the Red Fox who was shot on the road under Letter More. Walking across the peninsula to Appin House, you pass Acharn in Duror, the farm of James Stewart of the Glens, himself an illegitimate kinsman of the Laird of Appin. To the best of my memory the cottage is still standing, and has a new roof of corrugated iron. It is an ordinary Highland cottage, and Allan, when he stayed with James, his kinsman and guardian, slept in the barn. Appin House is a large plain country house, close to the sea. Further north-east, the house of Ardshiel, standing high above the sea, is visible from the steamer going to Fort William. At Ardshiel, Rob Roy fought a sword and target duel with the laird, and Ardshiel led the Stewarts in the rising of 1745; Appin, the chief, held aloof. The next place of importance is Ballachulish House, also an old house of Stewart of Ballachulish. It is on the right hand of the road from Ballachulish Pier to Glencoe, beneath a steep wooded hill, down which runs the burn where Allan Breck was fishing on the morning of the day of Glenure's murder, done at a point on the road three-quarters of a mile to the south-west of Ballachulish House, where Allan had slept on the previous night. From the house the road passes on the south side of the salt Loch Leven (not Queen Mary's Loch Leven). Here is Ballachulish Ferry, crossing to Lochaber. Following the road you come opposite the House of Carnoch, then possessed by Macdonalds (the house has been pulled down; there is a good recent ghost story about that business), and the road now enters Glencoe. On high hills, well to the left of the road and above Loch Leven, are Corrynakeigh and Coalisnacoan (the Ferry of the Dogs), overtopping the narrows of Loch Leven. Just opposite the House of Carnoch, on the Cameron side of Loch Leven, is the House of Callart (Mrs. Cameron Lucy's). Here and at Carnoch, as at Fasnacloich, Acharn, and Ballachulish, Allan Breck was much at home among his cousins.

From Loch Leven north to Fort William, with its English garrison, all is a Cameron country. Campbell of Glenure was an outpost of Whiggery and Campbells, in a land of loyal Stewarts, Camerons, and Macdonalds or MacIans of Glencoe. Of the Camerons, the gentle

Lochiel had died in France; his son, a boy, was abroad; the interests of the clan were represented by Cameron of Fassifern, Lochiel's uncle, living a few miles west by north of Fort William. Fassifern, a well-educated man and a burgess of Glasgow, had not been out with Prince Charles, but (for reasons into which I would rather not enter) was not well trusted by Government. Ardshiel, also, was in exile, and his tenants, under James Stewart of the Glens, loyally paid rent to him, as well as to the commissioners of his forfeited estates. The country was seething with feuds among the Camerons themselves, due to the plundering by − −, of − −, of the treasure left by Prince Charles in the hands of Cluny. The state of affairs was such that the English commander in Fort William declared that, if known, it 'would shock even Lochaber consciences.' 'A great ox hath trodden on my tongue' as to *this* business. Despite the robbery of Prince Charles's gold, deep poverty prevailed.

In February, 1749, Campbell of Glenure had been appointed Factor for Government over the forfeited estates of Ardshiel (previously managed by James Stewart of the Glens), of Lochiel, and of Callart. In the summer of 1751, Glenure evicted James from a farm, and in April, 1752, took measures for evicting other farmers on Ardshiel estates. Such measures were almost unheard of in the country, and had, years before, caused some agrarian outrages among Gordons and Camerons; these were appeased by the King over the Water, James VIII. and III. James Stewart, in April, 1752, went to Edinburgh, and obtained a legal sist, or suspension of the evictions, against Glenure, which was withdrawn on Glenure's application, who came home from Edinburgh, and intended to turn the tenants out on May 15, 1752. They were assailed merely as of Jacobite name and tendencies. Meanwhile Allan Breck — who had deserted the Hanoverian army after Prestonpans, had joined Prince Charles, fought at Culloden, escaped to France, and entered the French army — was lodging about Appin among his cousins, perhaps doing a little recruiting for King Louis. He was a tall thin man, marked with smallpox.

Cruising about the country also was another Jacobite soldier, 'the Sergent More,' a Cameron, later betrayed by − −, of − −, who robbed the Prince's hoard of gold. But the Sergeant More had nothing to do, as has been fancied, with the murder of Glenure. The state of the country was ticklish; Prince Charles expected to invade with Swedish forces, under the famous Marshal Keith, by the connivance of Frederick the Great, and he had sent Lochgarry, with Dr. Archibald Cameron and others, to feel the pulse of the western clans. As Government knew all about these intrigues from Pickle the Spy, they were evicting Jacobite tenants from Ardshiel's lands, and meant to do the same, by agency of Campbell of Glenure, in Lochaber, Lochiel's country.

On Monday, May 11, Campbell, who intended to do the evictions on May 15, left Glenure for Fort William, on business; the distance is computed at sixteen miles, by the old hill road. Allan Breck, on the 11th, was staying at Fasnacloich, near Glenure, where the fishing is very good. When Glenure moved north to Fort William, Allan went to James Stewart's cottage of Acharn. Glenure's move was talked of, and that evening Allan changed his own blue coat, scarlet vest, and black velvet breeches for a dark short coat with silver buttons, a blue bonnet, and trousers (the Highlanders had been diskilted), all belonging to James Stewart. He usually did make these changes when residing with friends. In these clothes next day (Tuesday, May 12) Allan, with young Fasnacloich, walked to Carnoch, the house of Macdonald of Glencoe, situated just where the Water of Coe or Cona enters Loch Leven. The dowager of the house was natural sister of James of the Glens, and full sister of the exiled Stewart of Ardshiel. From Carnoch, Allan, on the same day, crossed the sea-strait to Callart opposite, where Mrs. Cameron was another half-sister to James of the Glens. On Wednesday Allan recrossed, called at Carnoch, and went to stay at Ballachulish House. On Thursday, when Glenure would certainly return home by Ballachulish Ferry, Allan, about mid-day, was seen to go fishing up Ballachulish burn, where he caught no trout, and I do not wonder at it.

The theory of the prosecution was that, from the high ground to the left of the burn he watched the ferry, having one or two guns, though how he got them unobserved to the place is the difficulty; he could not have walked the roads from Acharn unobserved with a gun, for the Highlanders had been disarmed. At this point he must have had the assistance and the gun of *the other man*. Allan came down from the hill, asked the ferryman if Glenure had crossed, and returned to his point of observation. About five o'clock in the afternoon, Glenure, with a nephew of his, Mungo Campbell, a 'writer' or solicitor, crossed the ferry, and was greeted and accompanied for three-quarters of a mile on his homeward way by old Stewart of Ballachulish, who turned back and went to his house. A sheriff's officer walked ahead of Glenure, who, like Mungo, was mounted. Behind both, mounted, was Campbell's servant, John Mackenzie. The old road was (and is) a rough track, through thick coppice. There came a shot, and Glenure, pierced by two balls, fell and died.

John Mackenzie, Glenure's servant, now rode onwards at a great gallop to find Campbell of Ballieveolan, and on his way came to Acharn and met James Stewart, with the two ancestors of my friend, as already described. He gave the news to James, who 'wrung his hands and expressed great concern at what had happened, as what might bring innocent people to trouble.' In fact, he had once, or oftener, when drinking, expressed a desire to have a shot at Glenure, and so had Allan. But James was a worthy, sensible man when sober, and must have known that, while he could not frighten the commissioners of forfeited estates by shooting their agent, he was certain to be suspected if their agent was shot. As a matter of fact, as we shall see, he had taken active steps to secure the presence of a Fort William solicitor at the evictions on Friday, May 15, to put in a legal protest. But he thought it unadvisable to walk three or four miles and look after Glenure's corpse; the Highlanders, to this day, have a strong dread or dislike of corpses. That night James bade his people hide his arms, four swords, a long Spanish gun, and a shorter gun, neither of which weapons, in fact, did the trick, nor could be depended on not to miss fire.

Where, meanwhile, was Allan? In the dusk, above Ballachulish House, he was seen by Kate MacInnes, a maid of the house; they talked of the murder, and she told Donald Stewart, a very young man, son-in-law of Ballachulish, where Allan was out on the hillside. Donald Stewart averred that, on hearing from Kate that Allan wanted to see him (Kate denied that she said this), he went to the hill, accused Allan of the crime, and was told, in reply, that Allan was innocent, though, as a deserter from the Hanoverian army, and likely to be suspected, he must flee the country. Other talk passed, to which we shall return. At three in the morning of Friday, May 15, Allan knocked at the window of Carnoch House (Glencoe's), passed the news, was asked no questions, refused a drink and made for the sheiling, or summer hut, high on the hill side of Coalisnacoan, whence you look down on the narrows of Loch Leven.

There we leave Allan for the moment, merely remarking that he had no money, no means of making his escape. As he is supposed by the prosecution to have planned the slaying of Glenure with James Stewart on May 11, it seems plain that James would then have given him money to use in his escape, or, if he had no money by him, would have sent at once to Fort William or elsewhere to raise it. He did not do this, and neither at Carnoch, Callart, nor Ballachulish House did Allan receive any money.

But, on May 12, when Allan went to Carnoch and Callart, James sent a servant to a very old Mr. Stewart, father of Charles Stewart, notary public. The father was a notary also, and James, who wanted a man of law to be at the evictions on May 15, and thought that Charles Stewart was absent in Moidart, conceived that the old gentleman would serve the turn. But his messenger missed the venerable sportsman, who had gone a-fishing. Learning later that Charles had returned from Moidart, James, at 8 A.M. on May 14 (the day of the murder), sent a servant to Charles at Fort William, bidding him come to the evictions on May 15, 'as everything must go wrong without a person that can act, and that I can trust.' In a postscript he added, 'As I have no time to write to William (Stewart), let him send down immediately 8*l*. to pay for four milk cows I bought for his wife at Ardshiel.' His messenger had also orders to ask William Stewart for the money.

Nothing could seem more harmless, but the prosecution might have argued that this letter was, as to the coming of the notary, a 'blind,' and that the real object was, under the plea of sending for the notary, to send the messenger for William Stewart's 8*l*., destined to aid Allan in his escape. There was no proof or even suggestion that, on May 12, James had asked old Mr. Stewart to send money for Allan's use, or had asked William Stewart, as having none by him he would have done—that is, if James had concerted the murder with Allan. If, on May 14, James was trying to raise money to help a man who, as he knew, would need it after committing a murder on that day, he showed strange want of foresight. He might not get the money, or might not be able to send it to Allan. In fact, that day James did not get the money. The prosecution argued that the money was sent for on May 14, to help Allan Breck, and did not even try to show that James had sent for money on May 12; when it would have arrived in good time. Indeed James did not, on May 12, send any message to William Stewart at Fort William, from whom, not from Charles or the old gentleman, he tried to raise the cash on May 14. A friendly or a just jury would have noted that if James planned a murder on the night of May 11, and had no money, his very first move, on May 12, would be to try to raise money for the assassin's escape. No mortal would put off that step till the morning of the crime; indeed, it is amazing that Allan, if he meant to do the deed, did not first try to obtain cash for his escape. The relations of Glenure suspected, at the time, that Allan was not the assassin, that he fled merely to draw suspicion away from the real criminal (as he does in *Kidnapped*), and they even wished to advertise a pardon for him, if he would come in and give evidence. These facts occur in a copious unpublished correspondence of the day between Glenure's brothers and kinsmen; Mr. Stevenson had never heard of these letters. Thus, up to the day of the murder, Allan may not have contemplated it; he may have been induced, unprepared, to act as accessory to *the other man.*

The point where, according to the prosecution, the evidence 'pinched' James of the Glens was his attempt to raise money on May 14. What could he want with so large a sum as 8*l.*, so suddenly, as he had no bill to meet? Well, as a number of his friends were to be thrown out of their farms, with their cattle, next day, James might need money for their relief, and it seems certain that he had made no effort to raise money at the moment when he inevitably must have done so, if guilty, that is, on May 12, immediately after concerting, as was alleged, the plot with Allan Breck. Failing to get money from William Stewart at Fort William on May 14, James did on May 15 procure a small sum from him or his wife, and did send what he could scrape together to Allan Breck at Coalisnacoan. This did not necessarily imply guilt on James's part. Allan, whether guilty or not, was in danger as a suspected man and a deserter; James was his father's friend, had been his guardian, and so, in honour, was bound to help him.

But how did he know where Allan was to be found? If both were guilty they would have arranged, on May 11, a place where Allan might lurk. If they did arrange that, both were guilty. But Donald Stewart, who went, as we have said, and saw Allan on the hillside on the night of the murder, added to his evidence that Allan had then told him to tell James of the Glens where he might be found, that is, at Coalisnacoan. These tidings Donald gave to James on the morning of May 15. James then sent a pedlar, Allan's cousin, back to William Stewart, got 3*l*., added, in the evening of the 16th, more money of his own, and sent it to Allan. There was a slight discrepancy between the story of the maid, Kate MacInnes, and that of Donald Stewart, as to what exactly passed between them, concerning Allan, on the night of the murder, and whether Allan did or did not give her a definite message to Donald. The prosecution insisted on this discrepancy, which really, as James's advocate told the jury, rather went to prove their want of collusion in the manufacture of testimony. Had their memories been absolutely coincident, we might suspect collusion— that they had been 'coached' in their parts. But a discrepancy of absolutely no importance rather suggests independent and honest testimony. If this be so, Allan and James had arranged no trysting-place on May 11, as they must have done if Allan was to murder Glenure, and James was to send him money for his escape.

But there was a discrepancy of evidence as to the hour when the pedlar sent by James to Fort William on May 15 arrived there. Was he despatched after the hour when Donald Stewart swore that he gave Allan's message to James of the Glens, or earlier, with no knowledge on James's part of the message carried by Donald? We really cannot expect certainty of memory, after five months, as to hours of the clock. Also James did not prove that he sent a message to Allan at Coalisnacoan, bidding him draw on William Stewart for money; yet on Friday, May 15, James did, by the pedlar, bid William Stewart give Allan credit, and on Saturday, May 16, Allan did make a pen from a bird's feather, and ink with powder and water, and write a letter for money, on the strength of James's credit, to William Stewart. This is certainly a difficulty for James, since he suggested John Breck MacColl, a tenant of Appin's at Coalisnacoan, for the intermediary between Allan and William Stewart, and Allan actually did employ this man to carry his letter. But Allan knew this tenant well, as did James, and there was nobody else at that desolate spot, Coalisnacoan, whom Allan could employ. So lonely is the country that a few years ago a gentleman of my acquaintance, climbing a rocky cliff, found the bones of a man gnawed by foxes and eagles; a man who never had been missed or inquired after. Remains of pencils and leather shoe strings among the bones proved that the man had been a pedlar, like James Stewart's messenger, who had fallen over the precipice in trying to cross from Coalisnacoan to the road through Glencoe. But he never was missed, nor is the date of his death known to this day.

The evidence of the lonely tenant at Coalisnacoan, as to his interviews with Allan, is familiar to readers of *Kidnapped*. The tenant had heard of the murder before he saw Allan. Two poor women, who came up from Glencoe, told the story, saying that '*two men were seen going from the spot where Glenure was killed, and that Allan Breck was one of them.*' Thus early does the mysterious figure of *the other man* haunt the evidence. The tenant's testimony was not regarded as trustworthy by the Stewart party; it tended to prove that Allan expected a change of clothes and money to be sent to him, and he also wrote the letter (with a wood-pigeon's quill, and powder and water) to William Stewart, asking for money. But Allan might do all this relying on his own message sent by Donald Stewart, on the night of the murder, to James of the Glens, and knowing, as he must have done, that William Stewart was James's agent in his large financial operations.

On the whole, then, the evidence, even where it 'pinches' James most, is by no means conclusive proof that on May 11 he had planned the murder with Allan. If so, he must have begun to try to raise money before the very day of the murder. James and his son were arrested on May 16, and taken to Fort William; scores of other persons were arrested, and the Campbells, to avenge Glenure, made the most minute examinations of hundreds of people. Meanwhile

Allan, having got 5*l*. and his French clothes by the agency of his cousin the pedlar, decamped from Coalisnacoan in the night, and marched across country to the house of an uncle in Rannoch. Thence he escaped to France, where he was seen in Paris by an informant of Sir Walter Scott's in the dawn of the French Revolution; a tall, thin, quiet old man, wearing the cross of St. Louis, and looking on at a revolutionary procession.

The activities of the Campbells are narrated in their numerous unpublished letters. We learn from a nephew of Glenure's that he had been 'several days ago forewarned,' by whom we cannot guess; tradition tells, as I have said, that he feared danger only in Lochiel's country, Lochaber, and thought himself safe in Appin. The warning, then, probably came from a Cameron in Lochaber, not from a Stewart in Appin. In coincidence with this is a dark anonymous blackmailing letter to Fassifern, as if *he* had urged the writer to do the deed:

'You will remember what you proposed on the night that Culchena was buried, betwixt the hill and Culchena. I cannot deny but that I had breathing ' (a whisper), 'and not only that, but proposal of the same to myself to do. Therefore you must excuse me, when it comes to the push, for telling the thing that happened betwixt you and me that night.... If you do not take this to heart, you may let it go as you will.' (June 6, 1752.)

Fassifern, who had no hand in the murder, 'let it go,' and probably handed the blackmailer's letter over to the Campbells. Later, — —, — — of — —, the blackest villain in the country, offered to the Government to accuse Fassifern of the murder. The writer of the anonymous letter to Fassifern is styled 'Blarmachfildich,' or 'Blarmackfildoch,' in the correspondence. I think he was a Mr. Millar, employed by Fassifern to agitate against Glenure.

In the beginning of July a man, suspected of being Allan, was arrested at Annan on the Border, by a sergeant of the Royal Welsh Fusiliers. He really seems to have changed clothes with Allan; at least he wore gay French clothes like Allan's, but he was not that hero. Young Ballachulish, at this time, knew that Allan was already across the sea. Various guesses occur as to who *the other man* was; for example, a son of James of the Glens was suspected, so there *was* another man.

The 'precognitions,' or private examinations of witnesses before the trial, extended to more than seven hundred persons. It was matter of complaint by the Stewart party that 'James Drummond's name appeared in the list of witnesses;' this is Mr. Stevenson's James More, really MacGregor, the son of Rob Roy, and father of Catriona, later Mrs. David Balfour of Shaws, in *Kidnapped* and *Catriona*. 'James More's character is reflected upon, and I believe he cannot be called worse than he deserves,' says one of the Campbells. He alleges, however, that in April, before the murder, James of the Glens visited James More, then a prisoner in Edinburgh Castle, 'caressed him,' and had a private conversation with him. The abject James More averred that, in this conversation, James of the Glens proposed that James More's brother, Robin Oig, should kill Glenure for money. James More was not examined at the trial of James of the Glens, perhaps because he had already escaped, thanks to Catriona and collusion; but his evidence appears to have reached the jury, almost all of them Campbells, who sat at Inveraray, the Duke of Argyll on the bench, and made no difficulty about finding James of the Glens 'Guilty.' To be sure, James, if guilty, was guilty as an accessory to Allan, and that Allan was guilty was not proved; he was not even before the court. It was not proved that the bullets which slew Glenure fitted the bore of James's small gun with which Allan was alleged to have perpetrated the murder, but it was proved that the lock of that gun had only one fault—it missed fire four times out of five, and, when the gun did not miss fire, it did not carry straight— missed a blackcock, sitting! *That* gun was not the gun used in the murder.

The jury had the case for James of the Glens most clearly and convincingly placed before them, in the speech of Mr. Brown for the accused. He made, indeed, the very points on which I have insisted; for example, that if James concerted a murder with Allan on May 11, he would not begin to hunt for money for Allan's escape so late as May 14, the day of the murder. Again, he proved that, without any information from James, Allan would *naturally* send for money to William Stewart, James's usual source of supply; while at

Coalisnacoan there was no man to go as messenger except the tenant, John Breck MacColl. A few women composed his family, and, as John MacColl had been the servant of James of the Glens, he was well known already to Allan. In brief, there was literally no proof of concert, and had the case been heard in Edinburgh, not in the heart of the Campbell country, by a jury of Campbells, a verdict of 'Not Guilty' would have been given: probably the jury would not even have fallen back upon 'Not Proven.' But, moved by clan hatred and political hatred, the jury, on September 24, found a verdict against James of the Glens, who, in a touching brief speech, solemnly asserted his innocence before God, and chiefly regretted 'that after ages should think me guilty of such a horrid and barbarous murder.'

He was duly hanged, and left hanging, on the little knoll above the sea ferry, close to the Ballachulish Hotel.

And *the other man*?

Tradition avers that, on the day of the execution, he wished to give himself up to justice, though his kinsmen told him that he could not save James, and would merely share his fate; but, nevertheless, he struggled so violently that his people mastered and bound him with ropes, and laid him in a room still existing. Finally, it is said that strange noises and knockings are still heard in that place, a mysterious survival of strong human passions attested in other cases, as on the supposed site of the murder of James I. of Scotland in Perth.

Do I believe in this identification of *the other man*? I have marked every trace of him in the documents, published or unpublished, and I remain in doubt. But if Allan had an accessory in the crime, who was seen at the place, an accomplice who, for example, supplied the gun, perhaps fired the shot, while Allan fled to distract suspicion, that accessory was probably the person named by legend. Though he was certainly under suspicion, so were scores of other people. The crime does not seem to me to have been the result of a conspiracy in Appin, but the act of one hot-headed man or of two hot-headed men. I hope I have kept the Celtic secret, and I defy anyone to discover *the other man* by aid of this narrative.

That James would have been quite safe with an Edinburgh jury was proved by the almost contemporary case of the murder of the English sergeant Davies. He was shot on the hillside, and the evidence against the assassins was quite strong enough to convict them. But some of the Highland witnesses averred that the phantasm of the sergeant had appeared to them, and given information against the criminals, and though there was testimony independent of the ghost's, his interference threw ridicule over the affair. Moreover the Edinburgh jury was in sympathy with Mr. Lockhart, the Jacobite advocate who defended the accused. Though undeniably guilty, they were acquitted: much more would James of the Glens have obtained a favourable verdict. He was practically murdered under forms of law, and what was thought of the Duke of Argyll's conduct on the bench is familiar to readers of *Kidnapped*. I have never seen a copy of the pamphlet put forth after the hanging by the Stewart party, and only know it through a reply in the Campbell MSS.

The tragedy remains as fresh in the memories of the people of Appin and Lochaber as if it were an affair of yesterday. The reason is that the crime of cowardly assassination was very rare indeed among the Highlanders. Their traditions were favourable to driving 'creaghs' of cattle, and to clan raids and onfalls, but in the wildest regions the traveller was far more safe than on Hounslow or Bagshot Heaths, and shooting from behind a wall was regarded as dastardly.

V

THE CARDINAL'S NECKLACE

'OH, Nature and Thackeray, which of you imitated the other?' One inevitably thinks of the old question thus travestied, when one reads, in the fifth edition, revised and augmented, of Monsieur Funck-Brentano's *L'Affaire du Collier*,[10] the familiar story of Jeanne de Valois, of Cardinal Rohan, and of the fatal diamond necklace. Jeanne de Valois might have sat, though she probably did not, for Becky Sharp. Her early poverty, her pride in the blood of Valois, recall Becky's youth, and her boasts about 'the blood of the Montmorencys.' Jeanne had her respectable friends, as Becky had the Sedleys; like Becky, she imprudently married a heavy, unscrupulous young officer; her expedients for living on nothing a year were exactly those of Mrs. Rawdon Crawley; her personal charms, her fluent tongue, her good nature, even, were those of that accomplished lady. Finally she has her Marquis of Steyne in the wealthy, luxurious Cardinal de Rohan; she robs him to a tune beyond the dreams of Becky, and, incidentally, she drags to the dust the royal head of the fairest and most unhappy of queens. Even now there seem to be people who believe that Marie Antoinette was guilty, that she cajoled the Cardinal, and robbed him of the diamonds, fateful as the jewels of Eriphyle.

That theory is annihilated by M. Funck-Brentano. But the story is so strangely complicated; the astuteness and the credulity of the Cardinal are so oddly contrasted; a momentary folly of the Queen is so astonishing and fatal; the general mismanagement of the Court is so crazy, that, had we lived in Paris at the moment, perhaps we could hardly have believed the Queen to be innocent. Even persons greatly prejudiced in her favour might well have been deceived, and the people 'loveth to think the worst, and is hardly to be moved from that opinion,' as was said of the Scottish public at the date of the Gowrie conspiracy.

An infidelity of Henri II. of France to his wedded wife, Catherine de Médicis, and the misplaced affection of Louis XV. for Madame du Barry, were the remote but real causes that helped to ruin the House of France. Without the amour of Henri II., there would have been no Jeanne de Valois; without the hope that Louis XV. would stick at nothing to please Madame du Barry, the diamond necklace would never have been woven.

Henri II. loved, about 1550, a lady named Nicole de Savigny, and by her had a son, Henri de Saint-Remy, whom he legitimated. Saint-Remy was the great, great, great, great-grandfather of Jeanne de Valois, the flower of minxes. Her father, a ruined man, dwelt in a corner of the family *château*, a predacious, poaching, athletic, broken scion of royalty, who drank and brawled with the peasants, and married his mistress, a servant-girl. Jeanne was born at the *château* of Fontette, near Bar-sur-Aube, on April 22, 1756, and she and her brother and little sister starved in their mouldering tower, kept alive by the charity of the neighbours and of the *curé*, who begged clothes for these descendants of kings. But their scutcheon was—and Jeanne never forgot the fact—argent, three *fleurs de lys* or, on a fesse azure. The *noblesse* of the family was later scrutinised by the famous d'Hozier and pronounced authentic. Jeanne, with bare feet, and straws in her hair, is said to have herded the cows, a discontented indolent child, often beaten by her peasant mother. When her father had eaten up his last acre, he and the family tramped to Paris in 1760. As Jeanne was then but four years old, I doubt if she ever 'drove the cattle home, ' as M. Funck-Brentano finds recorded in the MSS. of the advocate Target, who defended Jeanne 's victim, Cardinal Rohan.

The Valois crew lived in a village near Paris. Jeanne 's mother turned Jeanne 's father out of doors, took a soldier in his place, and sent the child to beg daily in the streets. 'Pity a poor orphan of the blood of Valois, ' she piped; 'alms, in God 's name, for two orphans of the blood of Valois! ' When she brought home little she was cruelly flogged, so she says, and occasionally she deviated into the truth. A kind lady, the Marquise de Boulainvilliers, investigated her story, found it true, and took up the Valois orphans. The wicked mother went back to Bar-sur-Aube, which Jeanne was to dazzle with her opulence, after she got possession of the diamonds.

By the age of twenty-one (1777), Jeanne was a pretty enchanting girl, with a heart full of greed and envy; two years later she and her sister fled from the convent where her protectress had placed them: a merry society convent it was. A Madame de Surmont now gave them shelter, at Bar-sur-Aube, and Jeanne married, very disreputably, her heavy admirer, La Motte, calling himself Count, and to all appearance a stupid young officer of the *gendarmerie*. The pair lived as such people do, and again made prey of Madame de Boulainvilliers, in 1781, at Strasbourg. The lady was here the guest of the sumptuous, vain, credulous, but honourable Cardinal Rohan, by this time a man of fifty, and the fanatical adorer of Cagliostro, with his philosopher's stone, his crystal gazers, his seeresses, his Egyptian mysteries, and his powers of healing diseases, and creating diamonds out of nothing.

Cagliostro doubtless lowered the Cardinal's moral and mental tone, but it does not appear that he had any connection with the great final swindle. In his supernormal gifts and graces the Cardinal did steadfastly believe. Ten years earlier, Rohan had blessed Marie Antoinette on her entry into France, and had been ambassador at the Court of Maria Theresa, the Empress. A sportsman who once fired off 1,300 cartridges in a day (can this be true?), a splendid festive churchman, who bewitched Vienna, and even the Emperor and Count Kaunitz, by his lavish entertainments, Rohan made himself positively loathed—for his corrupting luxury and his wicked wit— by the austere Empress. She procured Rohan's recall, and so worked on her daughter, Marie Antoinette, the young Queen of France, that the prelate, though Grand Almoner, was socially boycotted by the Court, his letters of piteous appeal to the Queen were not even opened, and his ambitions to sway politics, like a Tencin or a Fleury, were ruined.

So here are Rohan, Cagliostro, and Jeanne all brought acquainted. The Cardinal (and this is one of the oddest features in the affair) was to come to believe that Jeanne was the Queen's most intimate friend, and could and would make his fortune with her; while, at the same time, he was actually relieving her by little tips of from two to five louis! This he was doing, even after, confiding in Jeanne, he handed to her the diamond necklace for the Queen, and, as he believed, had himself a solitary midnight interview with her Majesty. If Jeanne was so great with the Queen as Rohan supposed, how could Jeanne also be in need of small charities? Rohan was a man of the world. His incredible credulity seems a fact so impossible to accept that it was not accepted by public opinion. The Queen, people could not but argue, must have taken his enormous gifts, and then robbed and denounced him. With the case before our eyes of Madame Humbert, who swindled scores of hard-headed financiers by the flimsiest fables, we can no longer deem the credulity of the Cardinal incredible, even though he displayed on occasion a sharpness almost as miraculous as his stupidity.

Rohan conferred a few small favours on Jeanne; her audacity was as great as that of Madame Humbert, and, late in 1781, she established herself both at Paris and in Versailles. The one card in her hand was the blood of the Valois, and for long she could not play it to any purpose. Her claims were too old and musty. If a lady of the name of Stewart were to appear to-day, able to prove that she was of royal blood, as being descended from Francis, Earl of Bothwell (who used to kidnap James VI., was forfeited, and died in exile about 1620), she could not reasonably expect to be peculiarly cherished and comforted by our royal family. Now Jeanne's claims were no better, and no nearer, in 1781, than those of our supposed Stewart adventuress in 1904. But Jeanne was sanguine. Something must be done, by hook or by crook, for the blood of the Valois. She must fasten on her great relations, the royal family. By 1783 Jeanne was pawning her furniture and dining at the expense of her young admirers, or of her servants, for, somehow, they were attached to a mistress who did not pay their wages. She bought goods on her credit as a countess, and sold them on the same day. She fainted in the crowd at Versailles, and Madame Elizabeth sent her a few louis, and had her tiny pension doubled. Jeanne fainted again under the eyes of the Queen, who never noticed her.

Her plan was to persuade small suitors that she could get them what they wanted by her backstairs influence with her royal cousin; she had a lover, Retaux de Villette, who was an expert forger, and by April 1784, relying on his skill, she began to hint to Rohan that she could win for him the Queen's forgiveness. Her Majesty had seen her faint and had been full of kindness. Nothing should be refused to the interesting daughter of the Valois. Letters from the Queen to Jeanne, forged by Villette on paper stamped with blue *fleurs de lys*, were laid before the eyes of the infatuated prelate. Villette later confessed to his forgeries; all confessed; but as all recanted their confessions, this did not impress the public. The letters proved that the Queen was relenting, as regarded Rohan. Cagliostro confirmed the fact. At a *séance* in Rohan's house, he introduced a niece of Jeanne's husband, a girl of fifteen, who played the part of crystal gazer, and saw, in the crystal, whatever Cagliostro told her to see. All was favourable to the wishes of Rohan, who was as easy of belief as any spiritualist, being entirely dominated by the Neapolitan. Cagliostro, none the less, knew nothing of the great final *coup*, despite his clairvoyance.

So far, in the summer of 1784, the great diamond fraud had not risen into Jeanne's consciousness. Her aim was merely to convince the Cardinal that she could win for him the Queen's favour, and then to work upon his gratitude. It was in July 1784 that Jeanne's husband made the acquaintance of Marie Laguay, a pretty and good-humoured but quite 'unfortunate' young woman— 'the height of honesty and dissoluteness '—who might be met in the public gardens, chaperoned solely by a nice little boy. Jeanne de Valois was not of a jealous temperament. Mademoiselle Laguay was the friend of her husband, the tawdry Count. For Jeanne that was enough. She invited the young lady to her house, and by her royal fantasy created her Baronne Gay d'Oliva (*Valoi*, an easy anagram).

She presently assured the Baronne that the Queen desired her collaboration in a practical joke, her Majesty would pay 600*l*. for the freak. This is the Baronne's own version; her innocence, she averred, readily believed that Marie Antoinette desired her assistance.

'You are only asked to give, some evening, a note and a rose to a great lord, in an alley of the gardens of Versailles. My husband will bring you hither to-morrow evening.'

Jeanne later confessed that the Baronne really was stupid enough to be quite satisfied that the whole affair was a jest.

Judged by their portraits, d'Oliva, who was to personate the Queen, in an interview with the Cardinal, was not at all like Marie Antoinette. Her short, round, buxom face bears no resemblance to the long and noble outlines of the features of the Queen. But both women were fair, and of figures not dissimilar. On August 11, 1784, Jeanne dressed up d'Oliva in the *chemise* or *gaulle*, the very simple white blouse which Marie Antoinette wears in the contemporary portrait by Madame Vigée-Lebrun, a portrait exhibited at the Salon of 1783. The ladies, with La Motte, then dined at the best restaurant in Versailles, and went out into the park. The sky was heavy, without moon or starlight, and they walked into the sombre mass of the Grove of Venus, so styled from a statue of the goddess which was never actually placed there. Nothing could be darker than the thicket below the sullen sky.

A shadow of a man appeared: *Vous voilà!* said the Count, and the shadow departed. It was Villette, the forger of the Queen's letters, the lover and accomplice of Jeanne de Valois.

Then the gravel of a path crackled under the feet of three men. One approached, heavily cloaked. D'Oliva was left alone, a rose fell from her hand, she had a letter in her pocket which she forgot to give to the cloaked man, who knelt, and kissed the skirt of her dress. She murmured something; the cloaked Cardinal heard, or thought he heard, her say: 'You may hope that the past is forgotten.'

Another shadow flitted past, whispering: 'Quick! Quick! Come on! Here are Madame and Madame d'Artois!'

They dispersed. Later the Cardinal recognised the whispering shadow that fled by, in Villette, the forger. How could he recognise a fugitive shade vaguely beheld in a dark wood, on a sultry and starless night? If he mistook the girl d'Oliva for the Queen, what is his recognition of the shadow worth?

The conspirators had a jolly supper, and one Beugnot, a friend of Jeanne, not conscious of the plot, escorted the Baronne d'Oliva back to her rooms in Paris.

The trick, the transparent trick was played, and Jeanne could extract from the Cardinal what money she wanted, in the name of the Queen that gave him a rose in the Grove of Venus. Letters from the Queen were administered at intervals by Jeanne, and the prelate never dreamed of comparing them with the authentic handwriting of Marie Antoinette.

We naturally ask ourselves, was Rohan in love with the daughter of the Valois? Does his passion account for his blindness? Most authors have believed what Jeanne later proclaimed, that she was the Cardinal's mistress. This the divine steadily denied. There was no shadow of proof that they were even on familiar terms, except a number of erotic letters, which Jeanne showed to a friend, Beugnot, saying that they were from the Cardinal, and then burned. The Cardinal believed all things, in short, and verified nothing, in obedience to his dominating idea—the recovery of the Queen's good graces.

Meanwhile, Jeanne drew on him for large sums, which the Queen, she said, needed for acts of charity. It was proved that Jeanne instantly invested the money in her own name, bought a large house with another loan, and filled it with splendid furniture. She was as extravagant as she was greedy; *alieni appetens, sui profusa.*

The Cardinal was in Alsace, at his bishopric, when in November-December 1784, Jeanne was brought acquainted with the jewellers, Böhmer and Bassenge, who could not find a customer for their enormous and very hideous necklace of diamonds, left on their hands by the death of Louis XV. The European Courts were poor; Marie Antoinette had again and again refused to purchase a bauble like a 'comforter' made of precious stones, or to accept it from the King. 'We have more need of a ship of war,' she said, and would not buy, though the jeweller fell on his knees, and threatened to drown himself. There were then no American millionaires, and the thickest and ugliest of necklaces was 'eating its head off,' for the stones had been bought with borrowed money.

In the jewellers Jeanne found new victims; they, too, believed in her credit with the Queen; they, too, asked no questions, and held that she could find them a purchaser. Jeanne imposed on them thus, while the Cardinal was still in Alsace. He arrived at Paris in January 1785. He learned, from Jeanne, that the Queen wished him to deal for her with the jewellers! She would pay the price, 60,000*l.*, by quarterly instalments.

The Cardinal could believe that the Queen, who, as he supposed, had given him a darkling interview, would entrust him with such a commission, for an article which she had notoriously refused. But there is a sane spot in every man's mind, and on examining the necklace (January 24, 1785), he said that it was in very poor taste. However, as the Queen wanted to wear it at a ceremony on February 2, he arranged the terms, and became responsible for the money. His guarantee was a document produced by Jeanne, and signed 'Marie Antoinette de France.' As Cagliostro pointed out to Rohan later, too late, the Queen could not possibly use this signature. Neither the prelate nor the tradesmen saw the manifest absurdity. Rohan carried the necklace to Jeanne, who gave it to the alleged messenger of the Queen. Rohan only saw the *silhouette* of this man, in a dusky room, through a glass door, but he later declared that in him he recognised the fleeting shade who whispered the warning to fly, in the dark Grove of Venus. It was Villette, the forger.

Naturally people asked, 'If you could not tell the Queen from Mlle. d'Oliva when you kissed her robe in the grove, how could you recognise, through a dim glass door, the man of whom you had only caught a glimpse as a fleeting shadow? If you are so clever, why, it *was* the Queen whom you met in the wood. You cannot have been mistaken in her.'

These obvious arguments told against the Queen as well as against the Cardinal.

The Queen did not wear the jewels at the feast for which she had wanted them. Strange to say, she never wore them at all, to the surprise of the vendors and of the Cardinal. The necklace was, in fact, hastily cut to pieces with a blunt heavy knife, in Jeanne's house; her husband crossed to England, and sold many stones, and bartered more for all sorts of trinkets, to Grey, of New Bond Street, and Jeffreys, of Piccadilly. Villette had already been arrested with his pockets full of diamonds, but the luck of the House of Valois, and the astuteness of Jeanne, procured his release. So the diamonds were, in part, 'dumped down' in England; many were kept by the La Mottes; and Jeanne paid some pressing debts in diamonds.

The happy La Mottes, with six carriages, a stud of horses, silver plate of great value, and diamonds glittering on many portions of their raiment, now went off to astonish their old friends at Bar-sur-Aube. The inventories of their possessions read like pages out of *The Arabian Nights*. All went merrily, till at a great ecclesiastical feast, among her friends the aristocracy, on August 17, 1785, Jeanne learned that the Cardinal had been arrested at Versailles, in full pontificals, when about to celebrate the Mass. She rushed from table, fled to Versailles, and burned her papers. She would not fly to England; she hoped to brazen out the affair.

The arrest of the Cardinal was caused thus: On July 12, 1785, the jeweller, Böhmer, went to Versailles with a letter of thanks to the Queen, dictated by Rohan. The date for the payment of the first instalment had arrived, nothing had been paid, a reduction in price had been suggested and accepted. Böhmer gave the letter of thanks to the Queen, but the Controller-General entered, and Böhmer withdrew, without waiting for a reply. The Queen presently read the letter of thanks, could not understand it, and sent for the jeweller, who had gone home. Marie Antoinette thought he was probably mad, certainly a bore, and burned his note before the eyes of Madame Campan.

'Tell the man, when you next see him, that I do not want diamonds, and shall never buy any more.'

Fatal folly! Had the Queen insisted on seeing Böhmer, all would have been cleared up, and her innocence established. Böhmer's note spoke of the recent arrangements, of the jeweller's joy that the greatest of queens possesses the handsomest of necklaces—and Marie Antoinette asked no questions!

Jeanne now (August 3) did a great stroke. She told Bassenge that the Queen's guarantee to the Cardinal was a forgery. She calculated that the Cardinal, to escape the scandal, would shield her, would sacrifice himself and pay the 60,000*l*.

But the jewellers dared not carry the news to the Cardinal. They went to Madame Campan, who said that they had been gulled: the Queen had never received the jewels. Still, they did not tell the Cardinal. Jeanne now sent Villette out of the way, to Geneva, and on August 4 Bassenge asked the Cardinal whether he was sure that the man who was to carry the jewels to the Queen had been honest? A pleasant question! The Cardinal kept up his courage; all was well, he could not be mistaken. Jeanne, with cunning audacity, did not fly: she went to her splendid home at Bar-sur-Aube.

Villette was already out of reach; d'Oliva, with her latest lover, was packed off to Brussels; there was no proof against Jeanne; her own flight would have been proof. The Cardinal could not denounce her; he had insulted the Queen by supposing that she gave him a lonely midnight tryst, a matter of high treason; the Cardinal could not speak. He consulted Cagliostro. 'The guarantee is forged,' said the sage; 'the Queen could not sign "Marie Antoinette de France." Throw yourself at the King's feet, and confess all.' The wretched Rohan now compared the Queen's forged notes to him with authentic letters of hers in the possession of his family. The forgery was conspicuous, but he did not follow the advice of Cagliostro. On August 12, the Queen extracted the whole facts, as far as known to them, from the jewellers. On August 15, the day of the Assumption, when the Cardinal was to celebrate, the King asked him: 'My cousin, what is this tale of a diamond necklace bought by you in the name of the Queen?'

The unhappy man, unable to speak coherently, was allowed to write the story, in fifteen lines.

'How could you believe,' asked the Queen with angry eyes, 'that I, who have not spoken to you for eight years, entrusted you with this commission?'

How indeed could he believe it?

He offered to pay for the jewels. The thing might still have been hushed up. The King is blamed, first for publicly arresting Rohan as he did, an enormous scandal; next for handing over the case, for public trial, to the Parlement, the hereditary foes of the Court. Fréteau de Saint-Just, one of the Bar, cried: 'What a triumph for Liberal ideas! A Cardinal a thief! The Queen implicated! Mud on the crosier and the sceptre!'

He had his fill of Liberal ideas, for he was guillotined on June 14, 1794!

Kings and queens are human beings. They like a fair and open trial. Mary Stuart prayed for it in vain, from the Estates of Scotland, and from Elizabeth. Charles I. asked for public trial in vain, from the Estates of Scotland, at the time of the unsolved puzzle of 'The Incident.' Louis XVI. and Marie Antoinette had the publicity they wanted; to their undoing. The Parlement was to acquit Rohan of the theft of the necklace (a charge which Jeanne tried to support by a sub-plot of romantic complexity), and that acquittal was just. But nothing was said of the fatal insult which he had dealt to the Queen. Villette, who had forged the royal name, was merely exiled, left free to publish fatal calumnies abroad, though high treason, as times went, was about the measure of his crime. Gay d'Oliva, whose personation of the Queen also verged on treason, was merely acquitted with a recommendation 'not to do it again.' Pretty, a young mother, and profoundly dissolute, she was the darling of Liberal and *sensible* hearts.

Jeanne de Valois, indeed, was whipped and branded, but Jeanne, in public opinion, was the scapegoat of a cruel princess, and all the mud was thrown on the face of the guiltless Queen. The friends of Rohan were all the clergy, all the many nobles of his illustrious house, all the courtly foes of the Queen (they began by the basest calumnies, the ruin that the people achieved), all the friends of Liberal ideas, who soon, like Fréteau de Saint-Just, had more of Liberalism than they liked.

These were the results which the King obtained by offering to the Cardinal his choice between the royal verdict and that of the public Court of Justice. Rohan said that, if the King would pronounce him innocent, he would prefer to abide by the royal decision. He *was* innocent of all but being a presumptuous fool; the King might, even now, have recognised the fact. Mud would have been thrown, but not all the poached filth of the streets of Paris. On the other hand, had Louis withheld the case from public trial, we might still be doubtful of the Queen 's innocence. Napoleon acknowledged it: 'The Queen was innocent, and to make her innocence the more public, she wished the Parlement to be the judge. The result was that she was taken to be guilty. ' Napoleon thought that the King should have taken the case into his own hand. This might have been wisdom for the day, but not for securing the verdict of posterity. The pyramidal documents of the process, still in existence, demonstrate the guilt of the La Mottes and their accomplices at every step, and prove the stainless character of the Queen.

La Motte could not be caught. He had fled to Edinburgh, where he lived with an aged Italian teacher of languages. This worthy man offered to sell him for 10,000*l*., and a pretty plot was arranged by the French ambassador to drug La Motte, put him on board a collier at South Shields and carry him to France. But the old Italian lost heart, and, after getting 1,000*l*. out of the French Government in advance, deemed it more prudent to share the money with the Count. Perhaps the Count invented the whole stratagem; it was worthy of the husband and pupil of Jeanne de Valois. That poor lady 's cause was lost when Villette and Gay d 'Oliva were brought back across the frontier, confessed, and corroborated each other 's stories. Yet she made a wonderfully good fight, changing her whole defence into another as plausible and futile, before the very eyes of the Court, and doing her best to ruin Rohan as a thief, and Cagliostro as the forger of the Queen 's guarantee. The bold Neapolitan was acquitted, but compelled to leave the country, and attempt England, where the phlegmatic islanders trusted him no more than they trusted Madame Humbert. We expended our main capital of credulity on Titus Oates and Bedloe, and the warming-pan lie—our imaginative innocence being most accessible in the region of religion. The French are more open to the appeal of romance, and to dissolute honesty in the person of Miss Gay d 'Oliva, to injured innocence as represented by Jeanne de Valois. That class of rogues suits a gay people, while we are well mated with such a seductive divine as Dr. Oates.

Historical Mysteries

VI

THE MYSTERY OF KASPAR HAUSER: THE CHILD OF EUROPE

THE story of Kaspar Hauser, a boy, apparently idiotic, who appeared, as if from the clouds, in Nuremberg (1828), divided Germany into hostile parties, and caused legal proceedings as late as 1883. Whence this lad came, and what his previous adventures had been, has never been ascertained. His death by a dagger-wound, in 1833—whether inflicted by his own hand or that of another—deepened the mystery. According to one view, the boy was only a waif and an impostor, who had strayed from some peasant home, where nobody desired his return. According to the other theory, he was the Crown Prince of Baden, stolen as an infant in the interests of a junior branch of the House, reduced to imbecility by systematic ill-treatment, turned loose on the world at the age of sixteen, and finally murdered, lest his secret origin might be discovered.

I state first the theory of the second party in the dispute, which believed that Kaspar was some great one: I employ language as romantic as my vocabulary affords.

Darkness in Karlsruhe! 'Tis the high noon of night: October 15, 1812. Hark to the tread of the Twelve Hours as they pass on the palace clock, and join their comrades that have been! The vast corridors are still; in the shadows lurk two burly minions of ambitious crime, Burkard and Sauerbeck. Is that a white moving shadow which approaches through the gloom? There arises a shriek, a heavy body falls, 'tis a lacquey who has seen and recognised *The White Lady of the Grand Ducal House*, that walks before the deaths of Princes. Burkard and Sauerbeck spurn the inanimate body of the menial witness. The white figure, bearing in her arms a sleeping child, glides to the tapestried wall, and vanishes through it, into the Chamber of the Crown Prince, a babe of fourteen days. She returns carrying *another* unconscious infant form, she places it in the hands of the ruffian Sauerbeck, she disappears. The miscreant speeds with the child through a postern into the park, you hear the trample of four horses, and the roll of the carriage on the road. Next day there is silence in the palace, broken but by the shrieks of a bereaved though Royal (or at least Grand Ducal) mother. Her babe lies a corpse! The Crown Prince has died in the night! The path to the throne lies open to the offspring of the Countess von Hochberg, morganatic wife of the reigning Prince, Karl Friedrich, and mother of the children of Ludwig Wilhelm August, his youngest son.

Sixteen years fleet by; years rich in Royal crimes. 'Tis four of a golden Whit Monday afternoon, in old Nuremberg, May 26, 1828. The town lies empty, dusty, silent; her merry people are rejoicing in the green wood, and among the suburban beer-gardens. One man alone, a shoemaker, stands by the door of his house in the Unschlitt Plas: around him lie the vacant streets of the sleeping city. His eyes rest on the form, risen as it were out of the earth or fallen from the skies, of a boy, strangely clad, speechless, incapable either of standing erect or of moving his limbs. That boy is the Royal infant placed of yore by the White Shadow in the hands of the cloaked ruffian. Thus does the Crown Prince of Baden return from the darkness to the daylight! He names himself KASPAR HAUSER. He is to die by the dagger of a cruel courtier, or of a hireling English Earl.

Thus briefly, and, I trust, impressively, have I sketched the history of Kaspar Hauser, 'the Child of Europe, ' as it was presented by various foreign pamphleteers, and, in 1892, by Miss Elizabeth E. Evans.[11] But, as for the 'authentic records ' on which the partisans of Kaspar Hauser based their version, they are anonymous, unauthenticated, discredited by the results of a libel action in 1883; and, in short, are worthless and impudent rubbish.

On all sides, indeed, the evidence as to Kaspar Hauser is in bewildering confusion. In 1832, four years after his appearance, a book about him was published by Paul John Anselm Von Feuerbach. The man was mortal, had been a professor, and, though a legal reformer and a learned jurist, was 'a nervous invalid ' when he wrote, and he soon after died of paralysis (or poison according to Kasparites). He was approaching a period of life in which British judges write books to prove that Bacon was Shakespeare, and his arguments were like theirs. His *Kaspar Hauser* is composed in a violently injudicial style. 'To seek the giant perpetrator of such a crime ' (as the injustice to Kaspar), 'it would be necessary ... to be in possession of Joshua 's ram 's horns, or at least of Oberon 's horn, in order, for some time at least, to suspend the activity of the powerful enchanted Colossi that guard the golden gates of certain castles, ' that is, of the palace at Karlsruhe. Such early Nuremberg records of Kaspar 's first exploits as existed were ignored by Feuerbach, who told Lord Stanhope, that any reader of these 'would conceive Kaspar to be an impostor. ' 'They ought to be burned. ' The records, which were read and in part published, by the younger Meyer (son of one of Kaspar 's tutors) and by President Karl Schmausz, have disappeared, and, in 1883, Schmausz could only attest the general accuracy of Meyer 's excerpts from the town 's manuscripts.

Taking Feuerbach 's romantic narrative of 1832, we find him averring that, about 4.30 P.M. on Whit Monday, May 26, 1828, a citizen, unnamed, was loitering at his door, in the Unschlitt Plas, Nuremberg, intending to sally out by the New Gate, when he saw a young peasant, standing in an attitude suggestive of intoxication, and apparently suffering from locomotor ataxia, 'unable to govern fully the movements of his legs. ' The citizen went to the boy, who showed him a letter directed to the captain of a cavalry regiment. The gallant captain lived near the New Gate (654 paces from the citizen 's house), and thither the young peasant walked with the citizen. So he *could* 'govern fully the movements of his legs. ' At the house, the captain being out, the boy said, 'I would be a horseman as my father was, ' also 'Don 't know. ' Later he was taken to the prison, up a steep hill, and the ascent to his room was one of over ninety steps. Thus he could certainly walk, and when he spoke of himself he said 'I ' like other people. Later he took to speaking of himself as 'Kaspar, ' in the manner of small children, and some hysterical patients under hypnotism. But this was an after-thought, for Kaspar 's line came to be that he had only learned a few words, like a parrot, words which he used to express all senses indifferently.

His eye-sight, when he first appeared, seems to have been normal, at the prison he wrote his own name as 'Kaspar Hauser,' and covered a sheet of paper with writing. Later he could see best in the dark.

So says Feuerbach, in 1832. What he does not say is whence he got his information as to Kaspar's earliest exploits. Now our earliest evidence, on oath, before a magistrate, is dated November 4, 1829. George Weichmann, shoemaker (Feuerbach's anonymous 'citizen'), then swore that, on May 26, 1828, he saw Kaspar, not making paralysed efforts to walk, but trudging down a hilly street, shouting 'Hi! ' ('or any loud cry '), and presently asking, 'with tolerable distinctness, ' 'New Gate Street? ' He took the boy that way, and the boy gave him the letter for the captain. Weichmann said that they had better ask for him at the New Gate Guard House, and the boy said 'Guard House? Guard House? New Gate no doubt just built? ' He said he came from Ratisbon, and was in Nuremberg for the first time, but clearly did not understand what Weichmann meant when he inquired as to the chances of war breaking out. In May 1834 Weichmann repeated his evidence as to Kaspar's power of talking and walking, and was corroborated by one Jacob Beck, not heard of in 1829. On December 20, 1829, Merk, the captain's servant, spoke to Kaspar's fatigue, 'he reeled as he walked, ' and would answer no questions. In 1834 Merk expanded, and said 'we had a long chat. ' Kaspar averred that he could read and write, and had crossed the frontier daily on his way to school. 'He did not know where he came from. ' Certainly Merk, in 1834, remembered much more than in 1829. Whether he suppressed facts in 1829, or, in 1834, invented fables, we do not know. The cavalry captain (November 2, 1829) remembered several intelligent remarks made by Kaspar. His dress was new and clean (denied by Feuerbach), he was tired and footsore. The evidence of the police, taken in 1834, was remote in time, but went to prove that Kaspar's eyesight and power of writing were normal. Feuerbach absolutely discredits all the sworn evidence of 1829, without giving his own sources. The early evidence shows that Kaspar could both walk and talk, and see normally, by artificial and natural light, all of which is absolutely inconsistent with Kaspar's later account of himself.

The personal property of Kaspar was a horn rosary, and several Catholic tracts with prayers to the Guardian Angel, and so forth. Feuerbach holds that these were furnished by 'devout villains'—a very sound Protestant was Feuerbach—and that Kaspar was ignorant of the being of a Deity, at least of a Protestant Deity. The letter carried by the boy said that the writer first took charge of him, as an infant, in 1812, and had never let him 'take a single step out of my house.... I have already taught him to read and write, *and he writes my handwriting exactly as I do.*' In the same hand was a letter in Latin characters, purporting to come from Kaspar's mother, 'a poor girl,' as the author of the German letter was 'a poor day-labourer.' Humbug as I take Kaspar to have been, I am not sure that he wrote these pieces. If not, somebody else was in the affair; somebody who wanted to get rid of Kaspar. As that youth was an useless, false, convulsionary, and hysterical patient, no one was likely to want to keep him, if he could do better. No specified reward was offered at the time for information about Kaspar; no portrait of him was then published and circulated. The Burgomaster, Binder, had a portrait, and a facsimile of Kaspar's signature engraved, but Feuerbach would not allow them to be circulated, heaven knows why.

How Kaspar fell, as it were from the clouds, and unseen, into the middle of Nuremberg, even on a holiday when almost every one was out of town, is certainly a puzzle. The earliest witnesses took him for a journeyman tailor lad (he was about sixteen), and perhaps nobody paid any attention to a dusty travelling tradesman, or groom out of place. Feuerbach (who did not see Kaspar till July) says that his feet were covered with blisters, the gaoler says that they were merely swollen by the tightness of his boots.

Once in prison, Kaspar, who asked to be taken home, adopted the *rôle* of 'a semi-unconscious animal,' playing with toy horses, 'blind though he saw,' yet, not long after, he wrote a minute account of all that he had then observed. He could only eat bread and water: meat made him shudder, and Lord Stanhope says that this peculiarity did occur in the cases of some peasant soldiers. He had no sense of hearing, which means, perhaps, that he did not think of pretending to be amazed by the sound of church bells till he had been in prison for some days. Till then he had been deaf to their noise. This is

Feuerbach's story, but we shall see that it is contradicted by Kaspar himself, in writing. Thus the alleged facts may be explained without recourse even to a theory of intermittent deafness. Kaspar was no more deaf than blind. He 'was all there,' and though, ten days after his arrival, he denied that he had ever seen Weichmann, in ten days more his memory for faces was deemed extraordinary, and he minutely described all that, on May 26 and later, he had observed. Kaspar was taught to write by the gaoler's little boy, though he could write when he came—in the same hand as the author of his mysterious letter. Though he had but half a dozen words on May 26, according to Feuerbach, by July 7 he had furnished Binder with his history—pretty quick work! Later in 1828 he was able to write that history himself. In 1829 he completed a work of autobiography.

Kaspar wrote that till the age of sixteen he was kept in 'a prison,' 'perhaps six or seven feet long, four broad, and five high.' There were two small windows, with closed black wooden shutters. He lay on straw, lived on bread and water, and played with toy horses, and blue and red ribbons. That he could see colours in total darkness is a proof of his inconsistent fables, or of his 'hyperæsthesia'—abnormal acuteness of the senses. 'The man' who kept him was not less hyperæsthetic, for he taught Kaspar to write in the dark. He never heard any noise, but avers that, in prison, he was alarmed by the town clock striking, on the first morning, though Feuerbach says that he did not hear the bells for several days.

Such is Kaspar's written account (1829); the published account of July 1828, derived from 'the expressions of a half-dumb animal' (as Feuerbach puts it), is much more prolix and minute in detail. The animal said that he had sat on the ground, and never seen daylight, till he came to Nuremberg. He used to be hocussed with water of an evil taste, and wake in a clean shirt. 'The man' once hit him and hurt him, for making too much noise. The man taught him his letters and the Arabic numerals. Later he gave him instructions in the art of standing. Next he took him out, and taught him about nine words. He was made by the man to walk he knew not how far, or how long, the man leading him. Nobody saw this extraordinary pair on the march. Feuerbach, who maintains that Kaspar's feet were covered with cruel blisters, from walking, also supposes that 'perhaps for the greater part of the way ' he was carried in a carriage or waggon! Whence then the cruel blisters caused by walking? There is medical evidence that his legs were distorted by confinement, but the medical *post-mortem* evidence says that this was not the case. He told Binder that his windows were shuttered: he told Hiltel, the gaoler, that from his windows he saw 'a pile of wood and above it the top of a tree.'

Obviously Kaspar's legends about himself, whether spoken in June 1828, or written in February 1829, are absurdly false. He was for three weeks in the tower, and was daily visited by the curious. Yet in these three weeks the half-conscious animal 'learned to read tolerably well, to count, to write figures ' (*that* he could do when he arrived, Feuerbach says), 'he made progress in writing a good hand, and learned a simple tune on the harpsichord, ' pretty well for a half-unconscious animal.

In July 1828, after being adopted by the excited town of Nuremberg, he was sent to be educated by and live with a schoolmaster named Daumer, and was studied by Feuerbach. They found, in Kaspar, a splendid example of the 'sensitive, ' and a noble proof of the powers of 'animal magnetism. ' In Germany, at this time, much was talked and written about 'somnambulism ' (the hypnotic state), and about a kind of 'animal magnetism ' which, in accordance with Mesmer's theory, was supposed to pass between stars, metals, magnets, and human beings. The effects produced on the patient by the hypnotist (now ascribed to 'suggestion ') were attributed to a 'magnetic efflux, ' and Reichenbach's subjects saw strange currents flowing from metals and magnets. His experiments have never, perhaps, been successfully repeated, though hysterical persons have pretended to feel the traditional effects, even when non-magnetic objects were pointed at them. Now Kaspar was really a 'sensitive, ' or feigned to be one, with hysterical cunning. Anything unusual would throw him into convulsions, or reduce him to unconsciousness. He was addicted to the tears of sensibility. Years later Meyer read to him an account of the Noachian Deluge, and he wept bitterly. Meyer thought this rather too much, the Deluge being so remote an event, and, after that, though Meyer read pathetic things in his best manner, Kaspar remained unmoved. He wrote a long account of his remarkable magnetic sensations during and before the first thunderstorm after his arrival at Nuremberg. Yet, before his appearance there, he must have heard plenty of thunderstorms, though he pretended that this was his first. The sight of the moon produced in him 'emotions of horror.' He had visions, like the Rev. Ansel Bourne, later to be described, of a beautiful male figure in a white garment, who gave him a garland. He was taken to a 'somnambulist,' and felt 'magnetic' pulls and pushes, and a strong current of air. Indeed the tutor, Daumer, shared these sensations, obviously by virtue of 'suggestion.' They are out of fashion, the doctrine of animal magnetism being as good as exploded, and nobody feels pulled or pushed or blown upon, when he consults Mrs. Piper or any other 'medium.'

From a letter of Feuerbach of September 20, 1828, we learn that Kaspar, *'without being an albino,'* can see as well in utter darkness as in daylight. Perhaps the man who taught Kaspar to write, in the dark, *was* an albino: Kaspar never saw his face. Kaspar's powers of vision abated, as he took to beef, but he remained hyperæsthetic, and could see better in a bad light than Daumer or Feuerbach. Some 'dowsers,' we know, can detect subterranean water, by the sensations of their hands, without using a twig, or divining rod, and others can 'spot' gold hidden under the carpet, with the twig. Kaspar, merely with the bare hand, detected (without touching it?) a needle under a table cloth. He gradually lost these gifts, and the theory seems to have been that they were the result of his imprisonment in the dark, and a proof of it. The one thing certain is that Kaspar had the sensitive or 'mediumistic' temperament, which usually—though not always—is accompanied by hysteria, while hysteria means cunning and fraud, whether conscious or not so conscious. Meanwhile the boy was in the hands of men credulous, curious, and, in the case of Daumer, capable of odd sensations induced by suggestion. From such a boy, in such company, the truth could not be expected, above all if, like some other persons of his class, he was subject to 'dissociation' and obliviousness as to his own past.

Rather curiously we find in Feuerbach's own published collection of Trials the case of a boy, Sörgel, who had 'paroxysms of second consciousness ... of which he was ignorant upon returning to his ordinary state of consciousness. ' We have also the famous case of the atheistic carpenter, Ansel Bourne, who was struck deaf, dumb, and blind, and miraculously healed, in a dissenting chapel, to the great comfort of 'a large and warm congregation.' Mr. Bourne then became a preacher, but later forgot who he was, strolled to a distant part of the States, called himself Browne, set up a 'notions store,' and, one day, awoke among his notions to the consciousness that he was Bourne, not Browne, a preacher, not a dealer in cheap futilities. Bourne was examined, under hypnotism, by Professor William James and others.[12]

Many such instances of 'ambulatory automatism' are given. In my view, Kaspar was, to put it mildly, an ambulatory automatist, who had strayed away, like the Rev. Mr. Bourne, from some place where nobody desired his return: rather his lifelong absence was an object of hope. The longer Kaspar lived, the more frequently was he detected in every sort of imposture that could make him notorious, or enable him to shirk work.

Kaspar had for months been the pet mystery of Nuremberg. People were sure that, like the mysterious prisoner of Pignerol, Les Exiles, and the Isle Sainte-Marguerite (1669-1703?), Kaspar was some great one, 'kept out of his own.' Now the prisoner of Pignerol was really a valet, and Kaspar was a peasant. Some thought him a son of Napoleon: others averred (as we saw) that he was the infant son of the Grand Duke Karl of Baden, born in 1812, who had not died within a fortnight of his birth, but been spirited away by a lady disguised as the spectral 'White Lady of Baden,' an aristocratic *banshie*. The subtle conspirators had bred the Grand Duke Kaspar in a dark den, the theory ran, hoping that he would prove, by virtue of such education, an acceptable recruit for the Bavarian cavalry, and that no questions would be asked. Unluckily questions were now being asked, for a boy who could only occasionally see and hear was not (though he could smell a cemetery at a distance of five hundred yards), an useful man on a patrol, at least the military authorities thought not. Had they known that Kaspar could see in the dark, they might have kept him as a guide in night attacks, but they did not know. The promising young hussar (he rode well but clumsily) was thus left in the hands of civilians: the Grand Ducal secret might be discovered, so an assassin was sent to take off the young prince.

The wonder was not unnaturally expressed that Kaspar had not smelled out the villain, especially as he was probably the educational albino, who taught him to write in the dark. On hearing of this, later, Kaspar told Lord Stanhope that he *had* smelled the man: however, he did not mention this at the time. To make a long story short, on October 17, 1829, Kaspar did not come to midday eating, but was found weltering in his gore, in the cellar of Daumer's house. Being offered refreshment in a cup, he bit out a piece of the porcelain and swallowed it. He had 'an inconsiderable wound ' on the forehead; to that extent the assassin had effected his purpose. Feuerbach thinks that the murderer had made a shot at Kaspar's throat with a razor, that Kaspar ducked cleverly, and got it on the brow, and that the assassin believed his crime to be consummated, and fled, after uttering words in which Kaspar recognised the voice of his tutor, the possible albino. No albino or other suspicious character was observed. Herr Daumer, before this cruel outrage, had remarked, in Kaspar, 'a highly regrettable tendency to dissimulation and untruthfulness, ' and, just before the attack, had told the pupil that he was a humbug. Lord Stanhope quoted a paper of Daumer's in the *Universal Gazette* of February 6, 1834 (*Allgemeine Zeitung*), in which he says that 'lying and deceit were become to Kaspar a second nature. ' When did they begin to become a second nature? In any case Daumer clove to the romantic theory of Kaspar's origin. Kaspar left Daumer's house and stayed with various good people, being accompanied by a policeman in his walks. He was sent to school, and Feuerbach bitterly complains that he was compelled to study the Latin grammar, 'and finally even Cæsar's Commentaries! ' Like other boys, Kaspar protested that he 'did not see the use of Latin, ' and indeed many of our modern authors too obviously share Kaspar's indifference to the dead languages. He laughed, in 1831, says Feuerbach, at the popish superstition 'of his early attendants ' (we only hear of one, and about *his* theological predilections we learn nothing), and he also laughed at ghosts. In his new homes Kaspar lied terribly, was angry when detected, and wounded himself—he said accidentally—with a pistol, after being reproached for shirking the Commentaries of Julius Cæsar, and for mendacity. He was very vain, very agreeable as long as no one found fault with him, very lazy, and very sentimental.

In May 1831 Lord Stanhope, who, since the attack on Kaspar in 1829, had been curious about him, came to Nuremberg, and 'took up' the hero, with fantastic fondness. Though he recognised Kaspar's mythopœic tendencies, he believed him to be the victim of some nefarious criminals, and offered a reward of 500 florins, anonymously, for information. It never was claimed.

Already had arisen a new theory, that Kaspar was the son of an Hungarian magnate. Later, Lord Stanhope averred, on oath, that inquiries made in Hungary proved Kaspar to be an impostor. In 1830, a man named Müller, who had been a Protestant preacher, and was now a Catholic priest, denounced a preacher named Wirth, and a Miss Dalbonn, a governess, as kidnappers of Kaspar from the family of a Countess, living near Pesth. Müller was exposed, his motives were revealed, and the newspapers told the story. Kaspar was therefore tried with Hungarian words, and seemed to recognise some, especially Posonbya (Pressburg). He thought that some one had said that his father was at Pressburg: and thither Lord Stanhope sent him, with Lieutenant Hickel. This was in 1831, but Kaspar recognised nothing: his companions, however, found that he pretended to be asleep in the carriage, to hear what was said about him. They ceased to speak of him, and Kaspar ceased to slumber. A later expedition into Hungary, by Hickel, in February 1832, on the strength of more Hungarian excitement on Kaspar's part, discovered that there was nothing to discover, and shook the credulity of Lord Stanhope. He could not believe Kaspar's narrative, but still hoped that he had been terrorised into falsehood. He could not believe both that the albino had never spoken to Kaspar in his prison, and also that 'the man always taught me to do what I was told.' To Lord Stanhope Kaspar averred that 'the man with whom he had always lived said nothing to him till he was on his journey.' Yet, during his imprisonment, the man had taught him, he declared, the phrases which, by his account, were all the words that he knew when he arrived at Nuremberg.

For these and other obvious reasons, Lord Stanhope, though he had relieved Nuremberg of Kaspar (November 1831), and made ample provision for him, was deeply sceptical about his narrative. The town of Nuremberg had already tried to shift the load of Kaspar on to the shoulders of the Bavarian Government. Lord Stanhope did not adopt him, but undertook to pay for his maintenance, and left him, in January 1832, under the charge of a Dr. Meyer, at Anspach. He had a curator, and a guardian, and escaped from the Commentaries of Julius Cæsar into the genial society of Feuerbach. That jurist died in May 1833 (poisoned, say the Kasparites), a new guardian was appointed, and Kaspar lived with Dr. Meyer. Finding him incurably untruthful, the doctor ceased to provoke him by comments on his inaccuracies, and Kaspar got a small clerkly place. With this he was much dissatisfied, for he, like Feuerbach, had expected Lord Stanhope to take him to England. Feuerbach, in the dedication to Lord Stanhope of his book (1832), writes, 'Beyond the sea, in fair old England, you have prepared for him a secure retreat, until the rising sun of Truth shall have dispersed the darkness which still hangs over his mysterious fate. ' If Lord Stanhope ever made this promise, his growing scepticism about Kaspar prevented him from fulfilling it. On December 9, 1833, Meyer was much provoked by Kaspar's inveterate falseness, and said that he did not know how to face Lord Stanhope, who was expected to visit Anspach at Christmas. For some weeks Kaspar had been sulky, and there had been questions about a journal which he was supposed to keep, but would not show. He was now especially resentful. On two earlier occasions, after a scene with his tutor, Kaspar had been injured, once by the assassin who cut his forehead; once by a pistol accident. On December 14, he rushed into Dr. Meyer's room, pointed to his side, and led Meyer to a place distant about five hundred yards from his house. So agitated was he that Meyer would go no further, especially as Kaspar would answer no questions. On their return, Kaspar said, 'Went Court Garden—Man—had a knife—gave a bag—struck—I ran as I could—bag must lie there. ' Kaspar was found to have a narrow wound, 'two inches and a half under the centre of the left breast, ' clearly caused by a very sharp double-edged weapon. In three or four days he died, the heart had been injured. He was able to depose, but not on oath, that on the morning of the 14th a man in a blouse (who had addressed him some days earlier) brought him a verbal message from the Court gardener, asking him to come and view some clay from a newly bored well, where, in fact, no work was being done at this time. He found no one at the well, and went to the monument of the rather forgotten poet Uz. Here a man came forward, gave him a bag, stabbed him, and fled. Of the man he gave discrepant descriptions. He became incoherent, and died.

There was snow lying, when Kaspar was stabbed, but there were no footmarks near the well, and elsewhere, only one man's track was in the Hofgarten. Was that track Kaspar's? We are not told. No knife was found. Kaspar was left-handed, and Dr. Horlacher declared that the blow must have been dealt by a left-handed man. Lord Stanhope suggested that Kaspar himself had inflicted the wound by pressure, and that, after he had squeezed the point of the knife through his wadded coat, it had penetrated much deeper than he had intended, a very probable hypothesis.

As for the bag which the assassin gave him, it was found, and Dr. Meyer said that it was very like a bag which he had seen in Kaspar's possession. It contained a note, folded, said Madame Meyer, as Kaspar folded his own notes. The writing was in pencil, in *Spiegelschrift*, that is, it had to be read in a mirror. Kaspar, on his deathbed, kept muttering incoherences about 'what is written with lead, no one can read.' The note contained vague phrases about coming from the Bavarian frontier.

After Kaspar's death, the question of 'murder or suicide?' agitated Germany, and gave birth to a long succession of pamphlets. A wild woman, Countess Albersdorf ('*née* Lady Graham,' says Miss Evans, who later calls her 'Lady Caroline Albersdorf'), saw visions, dreamed dreams, and published nonsense. Other pamphlets came out, directed against the House of Baden. In 1870 an anonymous French pamphleteer offered the Baden romance, as from the papers of a Major von Hennenhofer, the villain in chief of the White Lady plot. Lord Stanhope was named as the ringleader in the attacks on Kaspar, both at Nuremberg and Anspach. In 1883 all the fables were revived in a pamphlet produced at Ratisbon, a mere hash of the libels of 1834, 1839, 1840, and 1870. Dr. Meyer was especially attacked, his sons defended his reputation by an action for libel on the dead, an action which German law permits. There was no defence, and the publisher was fined, and ordered to destroy all the copies. In 1892 the libels were repeated, by 'Baron Alexander von Artin: ' two documents of a palpably fraudulent character were added, the rest was the old stuff. The reader may find it in Miss Evans 's *Kaspar Hauser* (1892). For example, Daumer knew a great deal. He even, in 1833, received an anonymous letter from Anspach, containing the following statement: 'Lord Daniel Alban Durteal, advocate of the Royal Court in London, said to me, "I am firmly convinced that Kaspar Hauser was murdered. It was all done by bribery. Stanhope has no money, and lives by this affair." ' Daumer and Miss Evans appear to have seen nothing odd in relying on an anonymous letter about Lord Daniel Alban Durteal!

Lord Stanhope, says Miss Evans, 'was known to have subsisted principally upon the sale of his German hymnbook, and other devotional works, for which he was a colporteur. ' Weary of piety, Lord Stanhope became a hired assassin. Perhaps this nonsense still has its believers, seduced by 'Lady Caroline Albersdorf, *née* Lady Graham, ' by Lord Daniel Alban Durteal, and by the spirit of Kaspar himself, who, summoned by Daniel Dunglas Home, at a *séance* with the Empress Eugénie, apparently, announced himself as Prince of Baden. No authority for this interesting ghost of one who disbelieved in ghosts is given.

It is quite possible that Kaspar Hauser no more knew who he was than the valet of 1669-1703 knew why he was a prisoner, no more than Mr. Browne, when a dealer in 'notions, ' knew that he was Mr. Bourne, a dissenting preacher. Nothing is certain, except that Kaspar was an hysterical humbug, whom people of sense suspected from the first, and whom believers in animal magnetism and homœopathy accepted as some great one, educated by his Royal enemies in total darkness—to fit him for the military profession.

It is difficult, of course, to account for the impossibility of finding whence Kaspar had come to Nuremberg. But, in 1887, it proved just as impossible to discover whither the Rev. Ansel Bourne had gone. Mr. Bourne 's lot was cast, not in the sleepy Royalist Bavaria of 1828, but in the midst of the admired 'hustle' of the great Western Republic. He was one of the most remarkable men in the country, not a yokel of sixteen. He was last seen at his nephew's store, 121 Broad Street, Providence, R.I., on January 17. On January 20, the hue and cry arose in the able and energetic press of his State. Mr. Bourne, as a travelling evangelist, was widely known, but, after a fortnight unaccounted for, he arrived, as A.J. Browne, at Norristown, Pa., sold notions there, and held forth with acceptance at religious meetings. On March 14 he awoke, still undiscovered, and wondered where he was. He remembered nothing since January 17, so he wired to Providence, R.I., for information. He had a whole fortnight to account for, between his departure from Providence, R.I., and his arrival at Norristown, Pa. Nobody could help him, he had apparently walked invisible, like Kaspar on his way to Nuremberg. He was hypnotised by Professor William James, and brought into his Browne condition, but could give practically no verifiable account of Browne's behaviour in that missing fortnight. He said that he went from Providence to Pawtucket, and was for some days at Philadelphia, Pa., where he really seems to have been; as to the rest 'back of that it was mixed up.' We do not hear that Kaspar was ever hypnotised and questioned, but probably he also would have been 'mixed up,' like Mr. Bourne.

The fable about a Prince of Baden had not a single shred of evidence in its favour. It is true that the Grand Duchess was too ill to be permitted to see her dead baby, in 1812, but the baby's father, grandmother, and aunt, with the ten Court physicians, the nurses and others, must have seen it, in death, and it is too absurd to suppose, on no authority, that they were all parties to the White Lady's plot. We might as well believe, as Miss Evans seems to do, on the authority of an unnamed Paris newspaper, that a Latin letter, complaining of imprisonment, was picked up in the Rhine, signed 'S. Haues Spraucio,' that the words ought to be read 'Hares Sprauka,' and that they are an anagram of Kaspar Hauser. This occurred in 1816, when Kaspar, being about four years of age, could not write Latin. No one in the secret could have hoped that the Royal infant and captive would be recognised under the name of Spraucio or even of Sprauka. Abject credulity, love of mystery, love of scandal, and political passions, produced the ludicrous mass of fables to which, as late as 1893, the Duchess of Cleveland thought it advisable to reply. In England it is quite safe to accuse a dead man of murder, or of what you please, as far as the Duchess understood the law of libel, so she had no legal remedy.

VII

THE GOWRIE CONSPIRACY

THE singular events called 'The Gowrie Conspiracy, ' or 'The Slaying of the Ruthvens, ' fell out, on evidence which nobody disputes, in the following manner. On August 5, 1600, the King, James VI., was leaving the stables at the House of Falkland to hunt a buck, when the Master of Ruthven rode up and had an interview with the monarch. This occurred about seven o 'clock in the morning. The Master was a youth of nineteen; he was residing with his brother, the Earl of Gowrie, aged twenty-two, at the family town house in Perth, some twelve or fourteen miles from Falkland. The interview being ended, the King followed the hounds, and the chase, 'long and sore, ' ended in a kill, at about eleven o 'clock, near Falkland. Thence the King and the Master, with some fifteen of the Royal retinue, including the Duke of Lennox and the Earl of Mar, rode, without any delay, to Perth. Others of the King 's company followed: the whole number may have been, at most, twenty-five.

On their arrival at Perth it appeared that they had not been expected. The Earl had dined at noon, the Royal dinner was delayed till two o 'clock, and after the scanty meal the King and the Master went upstairs alone, while the Earl of Gowrie took Lennox and others into his garden, bordering on the Tay, at the back of the house. While they loitered there eating cherries, a retainer of Gowrie, Thomas Cranstoun (brother of Sir John of that ilk), brought a report that the King had already mounted, and ridden off through the Inch of Perth. Gowrie called for horses, but Cranstoun told him that his horses were at Scone, across the Tay, two miles off. The gentlemen then went to the street door of the house, where the porter said that the King had *not* ridden away. Gowrie gave him the lie, re-entered the house, went upstairs, and returning, assured Lennox that James had certainly departed. All this is proved on oath by Lennox, Mar, Lindores, and many other witnesses.

While the company stood in doubt, outside the gate, a turret window above them opened, and the King looked forth, much agitated, shouting 'Treason! ' and crying for help to Mar. With Lennox and most of the others, Mar ran to the rescue up the main staircase of the house, where they were stopped by a locked door, which they could not break open. Gowrie had not gone with his guests to aid the King; he was standing in the street, asking, 'What is the matter? I know nothing; ' when two of the King 's household, Thomas and James Erskine, tried to seize him, the 'treason ' being perpetrated under Gowrie 's own roof. *His* friends drove the Erskines off, and some of the Murrays of Tullibardine, who were attending a wedding in Perth, surrounded him. Gowrie retreated, drew a pair of 'twin swords, ' and, accompanied by Cranstoun and others, made his way into the quadrangle of his house. At the foot of a small dark staircase they saw the body of a man lying—wounded or dead. Cranstoun now rushed up the dark stairs, followed by Gowrie, two Ruthvens, Hew Moncrieff, Patrick Eviot, and perhaps others. At the head of the narrow spiral stair they found, in a room called the Gallery Chamber, Sir Thomas Erskine, a lame Dr. Herries, a young gentleman of the Royal Household named John Ramsay, and Wilson, a servant, with drawn swords. A fight began; Cranstoun was wounded; he and his friends fled, leaving Gowrie, who had been run through the body by Ramsay. All this while the other door of the long Gallery Chamber was ringing under the hammer-strokes of Lennox and his company, and the town bell was summoning the citizens. Erskine and Ramsay now locked the door opening on the narrow stair, at which the retainers of Gowrie struck with axes. The King 's party, by means of a hammer handed by their friends through a hole in the other door of the gallery, forced the lock, and admitted Lennox, Mar, and the rest of the King 's retinue. They let James out of a small turret opening from the Gallery Chamber, and, after some dealings with the angry mob and the magistrates of Perth, they conveyed the King to Falkland after nightfall.

The whole results were the death of Gowrie and of his brother, the Master (his body it was that lay at the foot of the narrow staircase), and a few wounds to Ramsay, Dr. Herries, and some of Gowrie 's retainers.

Historical Mysteries

The death of the Master of Ruthven was explained thus:—When James cried 'Treason! ' young Ramsay, from the stable door, had heard his voice, but not his words. He had sped into the quadrangle, charged up the narrow stairs, found a door behind which was the sound of a struggle, 'dang in ' the door, and saw the King wrestling with the Master. *Behind them stood a man, the centre of the mystery, of whom he took no notice.* He drew his whinger, slashed the Master in the face and throat, and pushed him downstairs. Ramsay then called from the window to Sir Thomas Erskine, who, with Herries and Wilson, ran to his assistance, slew the wounded Master, and shut up James (who had no weapon) in the turret. Then came the struggle in which Gowrie died. No more was seen of the mysterious man in the turret, except by a townsman, who later withdrew his evidence.

Such was the whole affair, as witnessed by the King 's men, the retainers of Gowrie, and some citizens of Perth. Not a vestige of plot or plan by Gowrie and his party was discoverable. His friends maintained that he had meant, on that day, to leave Perth for 'Lothian, ' that is, for his castle at Dirleton, near North Berwick, whither he had sent most of his men and provisions. James had summoned the Master to meet him at Falkland, they said, and Gowrie had never expected the return of the Master with the King.

James 's own version was given in a public letter of the night of the events, which we only know through the report of Nicholson, the English resident at Holyrood (August 6), and Nicholson only repeated what Elphinstone, the secretary, told him of the contents of the letter, written to the King 's dictation at Falkland by David Moysie, a notary. At the end of August James printed and circulated a full narrative, practically identical with Nicholson 's report of Elphinstone 's report of the contents of the Falkland letter of August 5.

The King 's narrative is universally accepted on all hands, till we come to the point where he converses with Alexander Ruthven, at Falkland, before the buck-hunt began. There was such an interview, lasting for about a quarter of an hour, but James alone knew its nature. He says that, after an unusually low obeisance, Ruthven told the following tale:—Walking alone, on the previous evening, in the fields near Perth, he had met 'a base-like fellow, unknown to him, with a cloak cast about his mouth, ' a common precaution to avoid recognition. Asked who he was, and what his errand 'in so solitary a part, being far from all ways, ' the fellow was taken aback. Ruthven seized him, and, under his arm, found 'a great wide pot, all full of coined gold in great pieces. ' Ruthven keeping the secret to himself, took the man to Perth, and locked him in 'a privy derned house ' — that is, a room. At 4 A.M. he himself left Perth to tell the King, urging him to 'take order ' in the matter at once, as not even Lord Gowrie knew of it. When James said that it was no business of his, the gold not being treasure trove, Ruthven called him 'over scrupulous, ' adding that his brother, Gowrie, 'and other great men, ' might interfere. James then, suspecting that the gold might be foreign, brought in by Jesuits for the use of Catholic intriguers, asked what the coins and their bearer were like. Ruthven replied that the bearer seemed to be a 'Scots fellow, ' hitherto unknown to him, and that the gold was apparently of foreign mintage. Hereon James felt sure that the gold was foreign and the bearer a disguised Scots priest. He therefore proposed to send back with Ruthven a retainer of his own with a warrant to Gowrie, then Provost of Perth, and the Bailies, to take over the man and the money. Ruthven replied that, if they did, the money would be ill reckoned, and begged the King to ride over at once, be 'the first seer, ' and reward him 'at his own honourable discretion. '

The oddity of the tale and the strangeness of Ruthven 's manner amazed James, who replied that he would give an answer when the hunt was over. Ruthven said the man might make a noise, and discover the whole affair, causing the treasure to be meddled with. He himself would be missed by Gowrie, whereas, if James came at once, Gowrie and the townsfolk would be 'at the sermon. ' James made no answer, but followed the hounds. Still he brooded over the story, sent for Ruthven, and said that the hunt once ended he would accompany him to Perth.

Here James adds that, though he himself knew not that any man was with Ruthven, he had two companions, one of whom, Andrew Henderson, he now despatched to Gowrie, bidding him prepare dinner for the King. This is not part of James's direct evidence. He was *unknowing and unsuspecting that any man living had come* with Ruthven.

Throughout the chase Ruthven was ever near the King, always urging him 'to hasten the end of the hunting.' The buck was slain close to the stables, and Ruthven would not allow James to wait for a second horse: that was sent after him. So the King did not even tarry to 'brittle' the buck, and merely told the Duke of Lennox, Mar, and others that he was riding to Perth to speak with Gowrie, and would return before evening. Some of the Court went to Falkland for fresh horses, other followed slowly with weary steeds. They followed 'undesired by him,' because a report rose that the King had some purpose to apprehend the oppressive Master of Oliphant. Ruthven implored James not to bring Lennox and Mar, but only three or four servants, to which the King answered 'half angrily.'

This odd conduct roused suspicion in James. He had been well acquainted with Ruthven, who was suing for the place of a Gentleman of the Bedchamber, or Cubicular. 'The farthest that the King's suspicion could reach to was, that it might be that the Earl, his brother, had handled him so hardly, that the young gentleman, being of a high spirit, had taken such displeasure as he was beside himself;' hence his curious, agitated, and moody behaviour. James, as they rode, consulted Lennox, whose first wife had been a sister of Gowrie. Lennox had never seen anything of mental unsettlement in young Ruthven, but James bade the Duke 'accompany him into that house' (room), where the gold and the bearer of it lay. Lennox thought the story of the gold 'unlikely.' Ruthven seeing them in talk, urged that James should be secret, and bring nobody with him to the first inspection of the treasure. The King thus rode forward 'between trust and distrust.' About two miles from Perth, Ruthven sent on his other companion, Andrew Ruthven, to Gowrie. When within a mile of Perth, Ruthven himself rode forward in advance. Gowrie was at dinner, having taken no notice of the two earlier messengers.

Gowrie, with fifty or sixty men, met James 'at the end of the Inch;' the Royal retinue was then of fifteen persons, with swords alone, and no daggers or 'whingers.' Dinner did not appear till an hour had gone by (say 2 P.M.). James whispered to Ruthven that he had better see the treasure at once: Ruthven bade him wait, and not arouse Gowrie's suspicions by whispering ('rounding'). James therefore directed his conversation to Gowrie, getting from him 'but half words and imperfect sentences.' When dinner came Gowrie stood pensively by the King's table, often whispering to the servants, 'and oft-times went in and out,' as he also did before dinner. The suite stood about, as was custom, till James had nearly dined, when Gowrie took them to their dinner, separately in the hall; 'he sat not down with them as the common manner is,' but again stood silent beside the King, who bantered him 'in a homely manner.'

James having sat long enough, Ruthven whispered that he wished to be rid of his brother, so James sent Gowrie into the hall to offer a kind of grace-cup to the suite, as was usual—this by Ruthven's desire. James then rose to follow Ruthven, asking him to bring Sir Thomas Erskine with him. Ruthven requested James to 'command publicly' that none should follow at once, promising that 'he should make any one or two follow that he pleased to call for.'

The King then, expecting attendants who never came because Ruthven never summoned them, walked alone with Ruthven across the end of the hall, up a staircase, and through three or four chambers, Ruthven 'ever locking behind him every door as he passed.' We do not know whether James observed the locking of the doors, or inferred it from the later discovery that one door was locked. Then Ruthven showed 'a more smiling countenance than he had all the day before, ever saying that he had him sure and safe enough kept.' At last they reached 'a little study' (a turret chamber), where James found, 'not a bondman, but a freeman, with a dagger at his girdle,' and 'a very abased countenance.' Ruthven locked the turret door, put his hat on his head, drew the man's dagger, pointed it at the King's breast, 'avowing now that the King behoved to be in his will and used as he list,' threatening murder if James cried out, or opened the window. He also reminded the King of the death of the late Gowrie, his father (executed for treason in 1584). Meanwhile the other man stood 'trembling and quaking.' James made a long harangue on many points, promising pardon and silence if Ruthven at once let him go. Ruthven then uncovered, and promised that James 's life should be safe if he kept quiet; the rest Gowrie would explain. Then, bidding the other man ward the King, he went out, locking the door behind him. He had first made James swear not to open the window. In his brief absence James learned from the armed man that he had but recently been locked up in the turret, he knew not why. James bade him open the window 'on his right hand.' The man did as he was commanded.

Here the King 's narrative reverts to matter not within his own observation (the events which occurred downstairs during his own absence). His narrative is amply confirmed, on oath, by many nobles and gentlemen. He says (here we repeat what we began by stating) that, during his own absence, as his train was rising from dinner, one of the Earl 's servants, Cranstoun, came hastily in, assuring the Earl that the King had got to horse, and 'was away through the Inch ' (isle) of Perth. The Earl reported this to the nobles, and all rushed to the gate. The porter assured them that the King had not departed. Gowrie gave the porter the lie, but, turning to Lennox and Mar, said that he would get sure information. He then ran back across the court, and upstairs, and returned, running, with the news that 'the King was gone, long since, by the back gate, and, unless they hasted, would not be overtaken.'

The nobles, going towards the stables for their horses, necessarily passed under the window of the turret on the first floor where James was imprisoned. Ruthven by this time had returned thither, 'casting his hands abroad in a desperate manner as a man lost.' Then, saying that there was no help for it, the King must die, he tried to bind the royal hands with his garter. In the struggle James drew Ruthven towards the window, already open. At this nick of time, when the King 's friends were standing in the street below, Gowrie with them, James, 'holding out the right side of his head and his right elbow,' shouted for help. Gowrie stood 'ever asking what it meant,' but Lennox, Mar, and others, as we saw, instantly ran in, and up the chief staircase to find the King. Meanwhile James, in his agony, pushed Ruthven out of the turret, 'the said Mr. Alexander 's head under his arms, and himself on his knees,' towards the chamber door which opened on the dark staircase. James was trying to get hold of Ruthven 's sword and draw it, 'the other fellow doing nothing but standing behind the King's back and trembling all the time.' At this moment a young gentleman of the Royal Household, John Ramsay, entered from the dark *back* staircase, and struck Ruthven with his dagger. 'The other fellow' withdrew. James then pushed Ruthven down the back stairs, where he was slain by Sir Thomas Erskine and Dr. Herries, who were coming up by that way. The rest, with the death of Gowrie, followed. A tumult of the townsmen, lasting for two or three hours, delayed the return of James to Falkland.

Such is the King's published narrative. It tallies closely with the letter written by Nicholson, the English agent, to Cecil, on August 6.

James had thus his version, from which he never varied, ready on the evening of the fatal day, August 5. From his narrative only one inference can be drawn. Gowrie and his brother had tried to lure James, almost unattended, to their house. In the turret they had an armed man, who would assist the Master to seize the King. Events frustrated the conspiracy; James was well attended; the armed man turned coward, and Gowrie proclaimed the King's departure falsely to make his suite follow back to Falkland, and so leave the King in the hands of his captors. The plot, once arranged, could not be abandoned, because the plotters had no prisoner with a pot of gold to produce, so their intended treason would have been manifest.

How far is James's tale corroborated? At the posthumous trial of the Ruthvens in November, witnesses like Lennox swore to his quarter of an hour of talk with Ruthven at Falkland before the hunt. The *early* arrival of Andrew Henderson at Gowrie's house, about half-past ten, is proved by two gentlemen named Hay, and one named Moncrieff, who were then with Gowrie on business to which he at once refused to attend further, in the case of the Hays. Henderson's presence with Ruthven at Falkland is also confirmed by a manuscript vindication of the Ruthvens issued at the time. None of the King's party saw him, and their refusal to swear that they did see him shows their honesty, the point being essential. Thus the circumstance that Gowrie ordered no dinner for the King, despite Henderson's early arrival with news of his coming, shows that Gowrie meant to affect being taken by surprise. Again, the flight of

Henderson on the very night of August 5 proves that he was implicated: why else should a man fly who had not been seen by anyone (except a Perth witness who withdrew his evidence) in connection with the fatal events? No other man fled, except some of Gowrie's retainers who took open part in the fighting.

James's opinion that Ruthven was deranged, in consequence of harsh treatment by his brother, Gowrie, is explained by a dispute between the brothers about the possession of the church lands of Scone, which Gowrie held, and Ruthven desired, the King siding with Ruthven. This is quite casually mentioned in a contemporary manuscript.[13] Again, Lennox, on oath, averred that, as they rode to Perth, James told him the story of the lure, the pot of gold. Lennox was a man of honour, and he had married Gowrie's sister.

Ruthven, on his return to Gowrie's house, told a retainer, Craigingelt, that he 'had been on an errand not far off, ' and accounted for the King's arrival by saying that he was 'brought' by the royal saddler to exact payment of a debt to the man. Now James had just given Gowrie a year's immunity from pursuit of creditors, and there is no trace of the saddler's presence. Clearly Ruthven lied to Craigingelt; he had been at Falkland, *not* 'on an errand not far off.'

That Cranstoun, Gowrie's man, brought the news, or rumour, of the King's departure was admitted by himself. That Gowrie went into the house to verify the fact; insisted that it was true; gave the lie to the porter, who denied it; and tried to make the King's party take horse and follow, was proved by Lennox, Lindores, Ray (a magistrate of Perth), the porter himself, and others, on oath.

That the King was locked in by a door which could not be burst open is matter of undisputed certainty.

All these are facts that 'winna ding, and downa be disputed. ' They *were* disputed, however, when Henderson, Gowrie's factor, or steward, and a town councillor of Perth, came out of hiding between August 11 and August 20, told his story and confessed to having been the man in the turret. He said that on the night of August 4 Gowrie bade him ride very early next day with the Master of Ruthven to Falkland, and return with any message that Ruthven might send. He did return—when the Hays and Moncrieff saw him—with news that the King was coming. An hour later Gowrie bade him put on a shirt of mail and plate sleeves, as he meant to arrest a Highlander in the Shoe-gait. Later, the King arriving, Henderson was sent to Ruthven, in the gallery, and told to do whatever he was bidden. Ruthven then locked him up in the turret, giving no explanation. Presently the King was brought into the turret, and Henderson pretends that, to a faint extent, he hampered the violence of Ruthven. During the struggle between Ramsay and Ruthven he slunk downstairs, went home, and fled that night.

It was denied that Henderson had been at Falkland at all. Nobody swore to his presence there, yet it is admitted by the contemporary apologist, who accuses the King of having organised the whole conspiracy against the Ruthvens. It was said that nobody saw Henderson slink away out of the narrow stair, though the quadrangle was crowded. One Robertson, however, a notary of Perth, gave evidence (September 23) that he did see Henderson creep out of the narrow staircase and step over the Master's dead body; Robertson spoke to him, but he made no reply. If Robertson perjured himself on September 23, he withdrew his evidence, or rather, he omitted it, at the trial in November. His life would not have been worth living in Perth—where the people were partisans of the Ruthvens—if he had adhered to his first statement. In the absence of other testimony many fables were circulated as to Henderson's absence from Perth all through the day, and, on the other hand, as to his presence, in the kitchen, during the crisis. He was last seen, for certain, in the house just before the King's dinner, and then, by his account, was locked up in the turret by the Master. Probably Robertson's first story was true. Other witnesses, to shield their neighbours, denied having seen retainers of Gowrie's who most assuredly were present at the brawls in the quad rangle. It was never explained why Henderson fled at once if he was not the man in the turret. I therefore conceive that, as he certainly was at Falkland, and certainly returned early, his story is true in the main.

Given all this, only one of two theories is possible. The affair was not accidental; James did not fall into a panic and bellow 'Treason!' out of the window, merely because he found himself alone in a turret—

and why in a secluded turret?—with the Master. To that theory the locked door of the gallery is a conclusive reply. Somebody locked it for some reason. Therefore either the Ruthvens plotted against the King, or the King plotted against the Ruthvens. Both parties had good grounds for hatred, as we shall show—that is, Gowrie and James had motives for quarrel; but with the young Master, whose cause, as regards the lands of Scone, the King espoused, he had no reason for anger. If James was guilty, how did he manage his intrigue?

With motives for hating Gowrie, let us say, the King lays his plot. He chooses for it a day when he knows that the Murrays of Tullibardine will be in Perth at the wedding of one of the clan. They will defend the King from the townsfolk, clients of their Provost, Gowrie. James next invites Ruthven to Falkland (this was asserted by Ruthven's defenders): he arrives at the strangely early hour of 6.30 A.M. James has already invented the story of the pot of gold, to be confided to Lennox, as proof that Ruthven is bringing him to Perth—that he has not invited Ruthven.

Next, by secretly spreading a rumour that he means to apprehend the Master of Oliphant, James secures a large train of retainers, let us say twenty-five men, without firearms, while he escapes the suspicion that would be aroused if he ordered them to accompany him. James has determined to sacrifice Ruthven (with whom he had no quarrel whatever), merely as bait to draw Gowrie into a trap.

Having put Lennox off with a false reason for his accompanying Ruthven alone in the house of Gowrie, James privately arranges that Ruthven shall quietly summon him, or Erskine, to follow upstairs, meaning to goad Ruthven into a treasonable attitude just as they appear on the scene. He calculates that Lennox, Erskine, or both, will then stab Ruthven without asking questions, and that Gowrie will rush up, to avenge his brother, and be slain.

But here his Majesty's deeply considered plot, on a superficial view, breaks down, since Ruthven (for reasons best known to himself) summons neither Lennox nor Erskine. James, observing this circumstance, rapidly and cleverly remodels his plot, and does not begin to provoke the brawl till, being, Heaven knows why, in the turret, he hears his train talking outside in the street. He had shrewdly provided for their presence there by ordering a servant of his own to spread the false rumour of his departure, which Cranstoun innocently brought. Why did the King do this, as his original idea involved no need of such a stratagem? He had also, somehow, persuaded Gowrie to credit the rumour, in the face of the porter's denial of its possibility, and to persist in it, after making no very serious attempt to ascertain its truth. To succeed in making Gowrie do this, in place of thoroughly searching the house, is certainly the King's most striking and inexplicable success.

The King has thus two strings to his nefarious bow. The first was that Ruthven, by his orders, would bring Erskine and Lennox, and, just as they appeared, James would goad Ruthven into a treasonable attitude, whereon Lennox and Erskine would dirk him. The second plan, if this failed (as it did, because Ruthven did not obey orders), was to deceive Gowrie into bringing the retinue under the turret window, so that the King could open the window and cry 'Treason! ' as soon as he heard their voices and footsteps below. This plan succeeds. James yells out of the window. Not wanting many spectators, he has, somehow, locked the door leading into the gallery, while giving Ramsay a hint to wait outside of the house, within hearing, and to come up by the back staircase, which was built in a conspicuous tower.

The rest is easy. Gowrie may bring up as many men as he pleases, but Ramsay has had orders to horrify him by saying that the King is slain (this was alleged), and then to run him through as he gives ground, or drops his points; this after a decent form of resistance, in which three of the King's four men are wounded.

'Master of the human heart, ' like Lord Bateman, James knows that Ruthven will not merely leave him, when goaded by insult, and that Gowrie, hearing of his brother's death, will not simply stand in the street and summon the citizens.

To secure a witness to the truth of his false version of the matter James must have begun by artfully bribing Henderson, Gowrie's steward, either simply to run away, and then come in later with corroboration, or actually to be present in the turret, and then escape.

Or perhaps the King told his man-in-the-turret tale merely 'in the air;' and then Henderson, having run away in causeless panic, later 'sees money in it,' and appears, with a string of falsehoods. 'Chance loves Art,' says Aristotle, and chance might well befriend an artist so capable and conscientious as his Majesty. To be sure Mr. Hill Burton says 'the theory that the whole was a plot of the Court to ruin the powerful House of Gowrie must at once, after a calm weighing of the evidence, be dismissed as beyond the range of sane conclusions. Those who formed it had to put one of the very last men in the world to accept of such a destiny into the position of an unarmed man who, without any preparation, was to render himself into the hands of his armed adversaries, and cause a succession of surprises and acts of violence, which, by his own courage and dexterity, he would rule to a determined and preconcerted plan.'[14]

If there was a royal plot, *without a plan*, then James merely intended to raise a brawl and 'go it blind.' This, however, is almost beyond the King's habitual and romantic recklessness. We must prefer the theory of a subtly concerted and ably conducted plan, constructed with alternatives, so that, if one string breaks, another will hold fast. That plan, to the best of my poor powers, I have explained.

To drop the figure of irony, all this hypothesis is starkly incredible. James was not a recklessly adventurous character to go weaponless with Ruthven, who wore a sword, and provoke him into insolence. If he had been ever so brave, the plot is of a complexity quite impossible; no sane man, still less a timid man, could conceive and execute a plot at the mercy of countless circumstances, not to be foreseen. Suppose the Master slain, and Gowrie a free man in the street. He had only to sound the tocsin, summon his devoted townsmen, surround the house, and ask respectfully for explanations.

Take, on the other hand, the theory of Gowrie's guilt. Here the motives for evil will on either side may be briefly stated. Since the murder of Riccio (1566) the Ruthvens had been the foes of the Crown. Gowrie's grandfather and father were leaders in the attack on Mary and Riccio; Gowrie's father insulted Queen Mary, while caged in Loch Leven Castle, by amorous advances—so she declares.

In 1582 Gowrie's father captured James and held him in degrading captivity. He escaped, and was reconciled to his gaoler, who, in 1584, again conspired, and was executed, while the Ruthven lands were forfeited. By a new revolution (1585-1586) the Ruthvens were reinstated. In July 1593 Gowrie's mother, by an artful ambuscade, enabled the Earl of Bothwell again to kidnap the King. In 1594 our Gowrie, then a lad, joined Bothwell in open rebellion. He was pardoned, and in August 1594 went abroad, travelled as far as Rome, studied at Padua, and, summoned by the party of the Kirk, came to England in March 1600. Here he was petted by Elizabeth, then on almost warlike terms with James. For thirty years every treason of the Ruthvens had been backed by Elizabeth; and Cecil, ceaselessly and continuously, had abetted many attempts to kidnap James. These plots were rife as late as April 1600. The object always was to secure the dominance of the Kirk over the King, and Gowrie, as the natural noble leader of the Kirk, was recalled to Scotland, in 1600, by the Rev. Mr. Bruce, the chief of the political preachers, whom James had mastered in 1596-97. Gowrie, arriving, instantly headed the Opposition, and, on June 21, 1600, successfully resisted the King's request for supplies, rendered necessary by his hostile relations with England. Gowrie then left the Court, and about July 20 went to hunt in Atholl; his mother (who had once already lured James into a snare) residing at his Perth house. On August 1 Gowrie warned his mother of his return, and she went to their strong castle of Dirleton, near North Berwick and the sea, while Gowrie came to his Perth house on August 3, it being understood that he was to ride to Dirleton on August 5. Thither he had sent on most of his men and provisions. On August 5, we know he went on a longer journey.

We have shown that a plot by James is incredible. There is no evidence to prove a plot by Gowrie, beyond the whole nature of the events, and the strange conduct of himself and his brother. But, if plot he did, he merely carried out, in the interests of his English friends, the traditional policy of his grandfather, his father, his mother, and his ally, Bothwell, at this time an exile in Spain, maturing a conspiracy in which he claimed Gowrie as one of his confederates. While the King was a free man, Gowrie could not hope to raise the discontented Barons, and emancipate the preachers—yet more bitterly discontented—who had summoned him home. Let the

King vanish, and the coast was clear; the Kirk's party, the English party, would triumph.

The inference is that the King was to be made to disappear, and that Gowrie undertook to do it. Two witnesses—Mr. Cowper, minister of Perth, and Mr. Rhynd, Gowrie's old tutor—averred that he was wont to speak of the need of extreme secrecy 'in the execution of a high and dangerous purpose.' Such a purpose as the trapping of the King by a secret and sudden onfall was the mere commonplace of Scottish politics. Cecil's papers, at this period and later, are full of such schemes, submitted by Scottish adventurers. That men so very young as the two Ruthvens should plan such a device, romantic and perilous, is no matter for marvel.

The plot itself must be judged by its original idea, namely, to lure James to Perth, with only two or three servants, at an early hour in the day. Matters fell out otherwise; but, had the King entered Gowrie House early, and scantly attended, he might have been conveyed across Fife, disguised, in the train of Gowrie as he went to Dirleton. Thence he might be conveyed by sea to Fastcastle, the impregnable eyrie of Gowrie's and Bothwell's old ally, the reckless intriguer, Logan of Restalrig. The famous letters which Scott, Tytler, and Hill Burton regarded as proof of that plot, I have shown, by comparison of handwritings, to be all forged; but one of them, claimed by the forger as his model for the rest, is, I think, a feigned copy of a genuine original. In that letter (of Logan to Gowrie) he is made to speak of their scheme as analogous to one contrived against 'a nobleman of Padua,' where Gowrie had studied. This remark, in a postscript, can hardly have been invented by the forger, Sprot, a low country attorney, a creature of Logan's. All the other letters are mere variations on the tune set by this piece.

A plot of this kind is, at least, not impossible, like the quite incredible conspiracy attributed to James. The scheme was only one of scores of the same sort, constantly devised at that time. The thing next to impossible is that Henderson was left, as he declared, in the turret, by Ruthven, without being tutored in his *rôle*. The King's party did not believe that Henderson here told truth; he had accepted the *rôle*, they said, but turned coward. This is the more likely as, in December

1600, a gentleman named Robert Oliphant, a retainer of Gowrie, fled from Edinburgh, where certain revelations blabbed by him had come into publicity. He had said that, in Paris, early in 1600, Gowrie moved him to take the part of the armed man in the turret; that he had 'with good reason dissuaded him; that the Earl thereon left him and dealt with Henderson in that matter; that Henderson undertook it and yet fainted '—that is, turned craven. Though nine years later, in England, the Privy Council acquitted Oliphant of concealing treason, had he not escaped from Edinburgh in December 1600 the whole case might have been made clear, for witnesses were then at hand.

We conclude that, as there certainly was a Ruthven plot, as the King could not possibly have invented and carried out the affair, and that as Gowrie, the leader of the Kirk party, was young, romantic, and 'Italianate,' he did plan a device of the regular and usual kind, but was frustrated, and fell into the pit which he had digged. But the Presbyterians would never believe that the young leader of the Kirk party attempted what the leaders of the godly had often done, and far more frequently had conspired to do, with the full approval of Cecil and Elizabeth. The plot was an orthodox plot, but, to this day, historians of Presbyterian and Liberal tendencies prefer to believe that the King was the conspirator. The dead Ruthvens were long lamented, and even in the nineteenth century the mothers, in Perthshire, sang to their babes, 'Sleep ye, sleep ye, my bonny Earl o' Gowrie.'[15]

A lady has even written to inform me that she is the descendant of the younger Ruthven, who escaped after being stabbed by Ramsay and Erskine, fled to England, married, and had a family. I in vain replied that young Ruthven's body was embalmed, exhibited in the Scottish Parliament, and hacked to pieces, which were set on spikes in public places, and that after these sufferings he was unlikely to marry. The lady was not to be shaken in her belief.

In *The Athenæum* for August 28, 1902, Mr. Edmund Gosse recognises Ramsay the Ruthven slayer as author of a Century of English Sonnets (1619), of which Lord Cobham possesses a copy apparently unique. The book was published at Paris, by Réné Giffart. The

Scottish name, Gifford, was at that time spelled 'Giffart,' so the publisher was of Scottish descent.

VIII

THE STRANGE CASE OF DANIEL DUNGLAS HOME

THE case of Daniel Dunglas Home is said, in the *Dictionary of National Biography*, to present a curious and unsolved problem. It really presents, I think, two problems equally unsolved, one scientific, and the other social. How did Mr. Home, the son of a Scottish mother in the lower middle class at highest, educated (as far as he was educated at all) in a village of Connecticut, attain his social position? I do not ask why he was 'taken up' by members of noble English families: 'the caresses of the great' may be lavished on athletes, and actors, and musicians, and Home's remarkable performances were quite enough to make him welcome in country houses. Moreover, he played the piano, the accordion, and other musical instruments. For his mysterious 'gift' he might be invited to puzzle and amuse royal people (not in England), and continental emperors, and kings. But he did much more than what Houdin or Alexis, a conjuror and a clairvoyant, could do. He successively married, with the permission and good will of the Czar, two Russian ladies of noble birth, a feat inexplicable when we think of the rules of the continental *noblesse*. A duc, or a prince, or a marquis may marry the daughter of an American citizen who has made a fortune in lard. But the daughters of the Russian *noblesse* do not marry poor American citizens with the good will of the Czar. By his marriages Home far outwent such famous charlatans as Cagliostro, Mesmer, and the mysterious Saint Germain the deathless. Cagliostro and Saint Germain both came on the world with an appearance of great wealth and display. The source of the opulence of Saint Germain is as obscure as was the source of the sudden enrichment of Beau Wilson, whom Law, the financier, killed in a duel. Cagliostro, like Law, may have acquired his diamonds by gambling or swindling. But neither these two men nor Mesmer, though much in the society of princes, could have hoped, openly and with the approval of Louis XV. or Louis XVI., to wed a noble lady. Yet Home did so twice, though he had no wealth at all.

Cagliostro was a low-born Neapolitan ruffian. But he had a presence! In the Memoirs of Madame d'Oberkirch she tells us how much she disliked and distrusted Cagliostro, always avoiding him, and warning Cardinal Rohan against him — in vain. But she admits that the man dominated her, or would have dominated her, by something inexplicable in his eyes, his bearing, and his unaccountable knowledge, as when he publicly announced, on a certain day, the death of the great Empress, Maria Theresa, of which the news did not arrive till five days later. Now Home had none of this dominating personality. He has been described to me, by a lady who knew him in his later years, when he had ceased to work drawing-room miracles in society, as a gentle, kindly, quiet person, with no obvious fault, unless a harmless and childlike vanity be a fault. Thus he struck an observer not of his intimate circle. He liked to give readings and recitations, and he played the piano with a good deal of feeling. He was a fair linguist, he had been a Catholic, he was of the middle order of intelligence, he had no 'mission' except to prove that disembodied spirits exist, if that were a legitimate inference from the marvels which attended him.

Mr. Robert Bell in *The Cornhill Magazine*, Vol. II., 1860, described Home's miracles in an article called 'Stranger than Fiction.' His account of the man's personality is exactly like what I have already given. Home was 'a very mild specimen of familiar humanity.' His health was bad. 'The expression of his face in repose' (he was only twenty-seven) 'is that of physical suffering.... There is more kindliness and gentleness than vigour in the character of his features.... He is yet so young that the playfulness of boyhood has not passed away, and he never seems so thoroughly at ease with himself and others as when he is enjoying some light and temperate amusement.'

Thus there was nothing in Home to dominate, or even to excite personal curiosity. He and his more intimate friends, not marchionesses but middle-class people, corresponded in a style of rather distasteful effusiveness. He was a pleasant young man in a house, not a Don Juan. I have never heard a whisper about light loves—unless Mr. Hamilton Aïdé, to be quoted later, reports such a whisper—not a word against his private character, except that he allowed a terribly vulgar rich woman to adopt him, and give him a very large sum of money, later withdrawn. We shall see that she probably had mixed motives both for giving and for withdrawing the gift, but it was asserted, though on evidence far from sound, that 'the spirits' had rapped out a command to give Home some thirty thousand pounds. Spirits ought not to do these things, and, certainly, it would have been wiser in Home to refuse the widow's gold even if they did. Beyond this one affair, and an alleged case of imposture at a *séance*, Home's private character raised no scandals that have survived into our knowledge. It is a very strange thing, as we shall see, that the origin of Home's miracles in broad daylight or artificial light, could never be traced to fraud, or, indeed, to any known cause; while the one case in which imposture is alleged on first-hand evidence occurred under conditions of light so bad as to make detection as difficult as belief in such circumstances, ought to have been impossible. It is not easy to feel sure that we have certainly detected a fraud in a dim light; but it is absurd to believe in a miracle, when the conditions of light are such as to make detection difficult.

Given this mild young musical man, the problems of how he achieved his social successes, and how he managed to escape exposure, if he did his miracles by conjuring, are almost equally perplexing. The second puzzle is perhaps the less hard of the two, for Home did not make money as a medium (though he took money's worth), and in private society few seized and held the mystic hands that moved about, or when they seized they could not hold them. The hands melted away, so people said.

A sketch of Home's life must now be given.[16] He was born in 1833, at Currie, a village near Edinburgh. In his later years he sent to his second wife a photograph of the street of cottages beside the burn, in one of which he first saw the light. His father had a right to bear the arms of the Earls of Home, with a *brisure*, being the natural son of Alexander, tenth Earl of Home.[17] The Medium's ancestor had fought, or, according to other accounts, had shirked fighting, at

Flodden Field, as is popularly known from the ballad *The Sutors of Selkirk*. The maiden name of Home's mother was Macneil. He was adopted by an aunt, who, about 1842, carried the wondrous child to America. He had, since he was four years old, given examples of second sight; it was in the family. Home's mother, who died in 1850, was second-sighted, as were her great-uncle, an Urquhart, and her uncle, a Mackenzie. So far there was nothing unusual or alarming in Home's case, at least to any intelligent Highlander. Not till 1850, after his mother's death, did Home begin to hear 'loud blows on the head of my bed, as if struck by a hammer.' The Wesley family, in 1716-17, had been quite familiar with this phenomenon, and with other rappings, and movements of objects untouched. In fact all these things are of world-wide diffusion, and I know no part of the world, savage or civilised, where such events do not happen, according to the evidence.

In no instance, as far as I am informed, did anything extraordinary occur in connection with Home which cannot be paralleled in the accounts of Egyptian mediums in Iamblichus.[18]

In 1850 America was interested in 'The Rochester Knockings,' and the case of the Fox girls, a replica of the old Cock Lane case which amused Dr. Johnson and Horace Walpole. The Fox girls became professional mediums, and, long afterwards, confessed that they were impostors. They were so false that their confession is of no value as evidence, but certainly they were humbugs. The air was full of talk about them, and other people like them, when Home, aged seventeen, was so constantly attended by noises of rappings that his aunt threw a chair at him, summoned three preachers, an Independent, a Baptist, and a Wesleyan (Home was then a Wesleyan), and plunged into conflict with the devil. The furniture now began to move about, untouched by man, and Home's aunt turned him out of the house. Home went to a friend in another little town, people crowded to witness the phenomena, and the press blazoned the matter abroad. Henceforth, Home was a wonder worker; but once, for a whole year—February 1856 to February 1857— 'the power' entirely deserted him, and afterwards, for shorter periods.

In 1852 he was examined by the celebrated American poet, Bryant, by a professor of Harvard, and others, who reported the usual physical phenomena, and emphatically declared that 'we know we were not imposed upon or deceived.' 'Spirits' spoke through the voice of the entranced Home, or rapped out messages, usually gushing, and Home floated in the air, at the house of Mr. Ward Cheney, at South Manchester, Connecticut. This phenomenon is constantly reported in the Bible, in the Lives of the Saints by the Bollandists, in the experiences of the early Irvingites, in witch trials, in Iamblichus, and in savage and European folklore. Lord Elcho, who was out with Prince Charles in the Forty-Five, writes in his unpublished Memoirs that, being at Rome about 1767, he went to hear the evidence in the process of canonising a saint, recently dead, and heard witnesses swear that they had seen the saint, while alive, floating about in the air, like Home. St. Theresa was notorious for this accomplishment. Home's first feat of this kind occurred 'in a darkened room,' a very dark room indeed, as the evidence shows. It had been darkened on purpose to try an experiment in seeing 'N rays,' which had been recently investigated by Reichenbach. Science has brought them recently back into notice. The evidence for the fact, in this case, was that people felt Home's feet in mid air. 'I have been lifted in the light of day only once, and that was in America;' also, in the light of four gas lamps 'in a room in Sloane Street.'

After attracting a good deal of notice in New York, Home, on April 9, 1855, turned up at Cox's Hotel, Jermyn Street, where Mr. Cox gave him hospitality as a *non-* 'paying guest.' Now occurred the affair of Sir David Brewster and Lord Brougham. Both were capable of hallucinations. Lord Brougham published an account of a common death-bed wraith, which he saw once while in a bath (the vision coincided with the death of the owner of the wraith), and Sir David's daughter tells how that philosopher saw that of the Rev. Mr. Lyon, in St. Leonard's College, St. Andrews, a wraith whose owner was in perfect health. Sir David sent letters, forming a journal, to his family, and, in June (no day given) 1855, described his visit to Home. He says that he, Lord Brougham, Mr. Cox, and Home sat down 'at a moderately sized table, *the structure of which we were invited to examine.* In a short time the table shuddered and a tremulous motion ran up our arms.... The table actually rose from the ground, when no hand was upon it. A larger table was produced, and exhibited similar movements. An accordion was held in Lord Brougham's hand, and gave out a single note.... A small hand-bell was then laid with its mouth on the carpet, and after lying for some time, it actually rang when nothing could have touched it. The bell was then placed upon the other side, still upon the carpet, and it came over to me, and placed itself in my hand. It did the same to Lord Brougham. These were the principal experiments: we could give no explanation of them, and could not conjecture how they could be produced by any kind of mechanism.... We do not believe that it was the work of spirits.'

So Sir David wrote in a private letter of June 1855, just after the events. But the affair came to be talked about, and, on September 29, 1855, Sir David wrote to *The Morning Advertiser*. He had seen, he said, 'several mechanical effects which I was unable to explain.... But I saw enough to convince myself that they could all be produced by human feet and hands, ' though he also, in June, 'could not conjecture how they could be produced by any kind of mechanism.' Later, October 9, Sir David again wrote to the newspaper. This time he said that he might have discovered the fraud, had he 'been permitted to take a peep beneath the drapery of the table.' But in June he said that he 'was invited to examine the structure of the table.' He denied that 'a large table was moved about in a most extraordinary way.' In June he had asserted that this occurred. He declared that the bell did not ring. In June he averred that it rang 'when nothing could have touched it.' In October he suggested that machinery attached to 'the lower extremities of Mr. Home's body' could produce the effects: in June 'we could not conjecture how they could be produced by any kind of mechanism.' On Sir David's death, his daughter and biographer, Mrs. Gordon, published (1869) his letter of June 1855. Home then scored rather freely, as the man of science had denied publicly, in October 1855, what he had privately written to his family in June 1855, when the events were fresh in his memory. This was not the only case in which 'a scientist of European reputation did not increase his reputation ' for common veracity in his attempts to put down Home.

Historical Mysteries

The adventures of Home in the Courts of Europe, his desertion of the errors of Wesleyan Methodism for those of the Church of Rome, his handsome entertainment by diamond-giving emperors, his expulsion from Rome as a sorcerer, and so forth, cannot be dealt with here for lack of space. We come to the great Home-Browning problem.

In 1855, Home met Mr. and Mrs. Browning at the house of a Mr. Rymer, at Ealing, the first of only two meetings.[19] On this occasion, says Home, a wreath of clematis rose from the table and floated towards Mrs. Browning, behind whom her husband went and stood. The wreath settled on the lady's head, not on that of Mr. Browning, who, Home thought, was jealous of the favour. This is manifestly absurd. Soon after, all but Mr. Rymer were invited to leave the room. Two days later, Mr. Browning asked to be allowed to bring a friend for another *séance*, but the arrangements of the Rymers, with whom Home was staying, made this impossible. Later, Home, with Mrs. Rymer, called on the Brownings in town, and Mr. Browning declined to notice Home; there was a scene, and Mrs. Browning (who was later a three-quarters believer in 'spirits') was distressed. In 1864, after Mrs. Browning's death, Mr. Browning published *Mr. Sludge, the Medium*, which had the air of a personal attack on Home as a detected and confessing American impostor. Such is Home's account. It was published in 1872, and was open to contradiction. I am not aware that Mr. Browning took any public notice of it.

In July 1889 the late Mr. F.W.H. Myers and Professor W.F. Barrett published, in the *Journal of the Society for Psychical Research*, p. 102, the following statement: 'We have found no allegations of *fraud*' (in Home) 'on which we should be justified in laying much stress. Mr. Robert Browning has told to one of us' (Mr. Myers) 'the circumstances which mainly led to that opinion of Home which was expressed in *Mr. Sludge, the Medium*.' It appears that a lady (since dead) repeated to Mr. Browning a statement made to her by a lady and gentleman (since dead) as to their finding Home in the act of experimenting with phosphorus on the production of 'spirit lights,' 'which (so far as Mr. Browning remembers) were to be rubbed round the walls of the room, near the ceiling, so as to appear when the room was darkened. This piece of evidence powerfully impressed

Mr. Browning; but it comes to us at third hand, without written record, and at a distance of nearly forty years.'

Clearly this story is not evidence against Home.

But, several years ago, an eminent writer, whom I need not name, published in a newspaper another version. Mr. Browning had told him, he said, that, sitting with Home and Mrs. Browning (apparently alone, these three) in a darkened room, he saw a white object rise above the table. This Home represented as the phantasm of a child of Mr. and Mrs. Browning, which died in infancy. Mr. Browning seized the phantasm, which was Home's naked foot.

But it must be remembered that (1) Mr. and Mrs. Browning had no child which died in infancy; and (2) Mrs. Browning's belief survived the shock. On December 5, 1902, in the *Times Literary Supplement*, a letter by Mr. R. Barrett Browning appeared. He says: 'Mr. Hume, who subsequently changed his name to Home' ('Home' is pronounced 'Hume' in Scotland), 'was detected in a "vulgar fraud," for I have heard my father repeatedly describe how he caught hold of his foot *under* the table.' In the other story the foot was *above* the table; in the new version no infant phantasm occurs. Moreover, to catch a man's foot under a table in itself proves nothing. What was the foot doing, and why did Mr. Browning not tell this, but quite a different story, to Mr. Myers? We 'get no forrarder.'

On November 28, 1902, Mr. Merrifield, in the *Times Literary Supplement*, published a letter on August 30 (?), 1855, from Mrs. Browning to Miss De Gaudrion, as to the *séance* with the Brownings at Ealing. Mrs. Browning enclosed a letter from Mr. Browning, giving his impressions. '*Mine, I must frankly say, were entirely different*,' wrote Mrs. Browning; and Home says: 'Mrs. Browning was much moved, and she not only then but ever since expressed her entire belief and pleasure in what occurred.' In her letter, Mrs. Browning adds: 'For my own part, and in my own conscience, I find no reason for considering the medium in question responsible for anything seen or heard on that occasion.' But 'I consider that the seeking for intercourse with any particular spirit would be apt to end either in disappointment or delusion, ' and she uses the phrase 'the supposed spirits. '

This lady who wrote thus at the time cannot conceivably have been looking for the ghost of a child that never was born, and been deceived by Home 's white foot, which Mr. Browning then caught hold of—an incident which Mrs. Browning could not have forgotten by August 30, 1855, if it occurred in July of that year. Yet Mr. —— has published the statement that Mr. Browning told him that story of Home 's foot, dead child, and all, and Mr. —— is a man of undoubted honour, and of the acutest intelligence.

Mr. Browning (August 30, 1855) assured Miss De Gaudrion that he held 'the whole display of hands, ' 'spirit utterances, ' &c., to be 'a cheat and imposture. ' He acquitted the Rymers (at whose house the *séance* was held) of collusion, and spoke very highly of their moral character. But he gave no reason for his disbelief, and said nothing about catching hold of Home 's foot either under or above the table. He simply states his opinion; the whole affair was 'melancholy stuff. ' How can we account for the story of Mr. Browning and Home 's foot? Can poets possess an imagination too exuberant, or a memory not wholly accurate?

But Mr. Merrifield had written, on August 18, 1855, a record of an Ealing *séance* of July 1855. About fourteen people sat round a table, in a room of which two windows opened on the lawn. The nature of the light is not stated. There was 'heaving up of the table, tapping, playing an accordion under the table, and so on. ' No details are given; but there were no visible hands. Later, by such light as exists when the moon has set on a July night, Home gave another *séance*. 'The outlines of the windows we could well see, and the form of any large object intervening before them, though not with accuracy of outline. ' In these circumstances, in a light sufficient, he thinks, Mr. Merrifield detected 'an object resembling a child 's hand with a long white sleeve attached to it ' and also attached to Home 's shoulder and arm, and moving as Home moved. A lady, who later became Mrs. Merrifield, corroborated.[20]

This is the one known alleged case of detection of fraud, on Home 's part, given on first-hand evidence, and written only a few weeks after the events. One other case I was told by the observer, very many years after the event, and in this case fraud was not necessarily implied. It is only fair to remark that Mr. F.W.H. Myers thought these 'phantasmal arms instructive in more than one respect, ' as supplying 'a missing link between mere phantasms and ectoplastic phenomena. '[21]

Now this is the extraordinary feature in the puzzle. There are many attested accounts of hands seen, in Home's presence, in a good light, with no attachment; and no fraud is known ever to have been detected in such instances. The strange fact is that if we have one record of a detection of Home in a puerile fraud in a faint light, we have none of a detection in his most notable phenomena in a good light. To take one example. In *The Nineteenth Century* for April 1896 Mr. Hamilton Aïdé published the following statement, of which he had made the record in his Diary, 'more than twenty years ago.' Mr. Aïdé also told me the story in conversation. He was 'prejudiced' against Home, whom he met at Nice, 'in the house of a Russian lady of distinction. ' 'His *very* physical manifestations, I was told, had caused his expulsion from more than one private house. ' Of these aberrations one has not heard elsewhere. Mr. Aïdé was asked to meet M. Alphonse Karr, 'one of the hardest-headed, the wittiest, and most sceptical men in France ' (a well-merited description), at a *séance* with Home. Mr. Aïdé 's prejudice, M. Karr 's hard-headed scepticism, prove them witnesses not biassed in favour of hocus-pocus.

The two arrived first at the villa, and were shown into a very large, uncarpeted, and brilliantly lighted salon. The furniture was very heavy, the tables were 'mostly of marble, *and none of them had any cloths upon them.*' There were about twenty candles in sconces, all lit, and a moderator lamp in the centre of 'the ponderous round rosewood table at which we were to sit. ' Mr. Aïdé 'examined the room carefully, ' and observed that wires could not possibly be attached to the heavy furniture ranged along the walls, and on the polished floor wires could not escape notice. The number present, including Home, was nine when all had arrived. All hands were on the table, but M. Alphonse Karr insisted on being allowed to break the circle, go under the table, or make any other sort of search whenever he pleased. 'This Home made no objection to. ' Raps 'went *round* under the table, fluttering hither and thither in a way difficult to account for by the dislocation of the medium 's toe ' (or knee), 'the common explanation. ' (I may remark that this kind of rapping is now so rare that I think Mr. Frederick Myers, with all his experience, never heard it.) Mr. Aïdé was observant enough to notice that a lady had casually dropped her bracelet, though she vowed that it 'was snatched from her by a spirit. ' 'It was certainly removed from her lap, and danced about under the table.... '

Then suddenly 'a heavy armchair, placed against the wall at the further end of the *salotto*, ran violently out into the middle of the room towards us. ' Other chairs rushed about 'with still greater velocity. ' The heavy table then tilted up, and the moderator lamp, with some pencils, slid to the lower edge of the table, but did not fall off. Mr. Aïdé looked under the table: Home 's legs were inactive. Home said that he thought the table would 'ascend, ' and Alphonse Karr dived under it, and walked about on all fours, examining everybody 's feet—the others were standing up. The table rose 'three or four feet, ' at highest, and remained in air 'from two to three minutes. ' It rose so high that 'all could see Karr, and see also that no one 's legs moved. ' M. Karr was not a little annoyed; but, as 'Sandow could not have lifted the table evenly, ' even if allowed to put his hands beneath it, and as Home, at one side, had his hands above it, clearly Home did not lift it.

All alike beheld this phenomenon, and Mr. Aïdé asks 'was I hypnotised? ' Were all hypnotised? People have tried to hypnotise Mr. Aïdé, never with success, and certainly no form of hypnotism known to science was here concerned. No process of that sort had been gone through, and, except when Home said that he thought the table would ascend, there had been no 'verbal suggestion; ' nobody was told what to look out for. In hypnotic experiment it is found that A. (if told to see anything not present) will succeed, B. will fail, C. will see something, and so on, though these subjects have been duly hypnotised, which Mr. Aïdé and the rest had not. That an unhypnotised company (or a company wholly unaware that any hypnotic process had been performed on them) should all be subjected by any one to the same hallucination, by an unuttered command, is a thing unknown to science, and most men of science would deny that even one single person could be hallucinated by a special suggestion not indicated by outward word, gesture, or otherwise. We read of such feats in tales of 'glamour,' like that of the Goblin Page in *The Lay of the Last Minstrel*, but to psychological science, I repeat, they are absolutely unknown. The explanation is not what is technically styled a *vera causa*. Mr. Aïdé's story is absolutely unexplained, and it is one of scores, attested in letters to Home from people of undoubted sense and good position. Mr. Myers examined and authenticated the letters by post marks, handwriting, and other tests.[22]

In one case the theory of hallucination induced by Home, so that people saw what did not occur, was asserted by Dr. Carpenter, F.R.S.[23] Dr. Carpenter, who was a wondrously superior person, wrote: 'The most diverse accounts of a *séance* will be given by a believer and a sceptic. One will declare that a table rose in the air, while another (who had been watching its feet) is confident that it never left the ground.' Mr. Aïdé's statement proves that this explanation does not fit *his* case. Dr. Carpenter went on to say what was not true: 'A whole party of believers will affirm that they saw Mr. Home float in at one window and out at another, whilst a single honest sceptic declares that Mr. Home was sitting in his chair all the time.'[24] This was false. Dr. Carpenter referred to the published statement of Lord Adare (Dunraven) and Lord Lindsay (the Earl of Crawford), that they saw Home float into a window of the room where they were sitting, out of the next room, where Home was, *and float back again*, at Ashley Place, S.W., December 16, 1868. No 'honest sceptic' was present and denied the facts. The other person present, Captain Wynne, wrote to Home, in a letter printed (with excisions of some contemptuous phrases) by Madame Home, and read in the original MS. by Mr. Myers. He said: 'I wrote to the *Medium* to say I was present as a witness. I don't think that any one who knows me would for one moment say that I was a victim to hallucination or any humbug of that kind.' Dr. Carpenter, in 1871, writing in the *Quarterly Review* (Vol. 131, pp. 336, 337), had criticised Lord Lindsay's account of what occurred on December 16, 1868. He took exception to a point in Lord Lindsay's grammar, he asked why Lord Lindsay did not cite the two other observers, and he said (what I doubt) that the observations were made by moonlight. So Lord Lindsay had said; but the curious may consult the almanack. Even in a fog, however, people in a room can see a man come in by the window, and go out again, 'head first, with the body rigid,' at a great height above the ground.

Mr. Podmore has suggested that Home thrust his head and shoulders out of the window, and that the three excited friends fancied the rest; but they first saw him in the air outside of the window of their room.[25] Nothing is explained, in this case, by Dr. Carpenter's explanation. Dr. Carpenter (1871) discredited the experiments made on Home by Sir William Crookes and attested by Sir William Huggins, because the latter was only 'an amateur in a branch of research which tasks the keenest powers of observation,' not of experiment; while, in the chemical experiments of Sir William Crookes, 'the ability he displayed was purely *technical*.' Neither gentleman could dream 'that there are *moral* sources of error.'[26]

Alas, Dr. Carpenter, when he boldly published (in 1876) the thing that was not, proved that a 'scientist' may be misled by 'moral sources of error'!

In 1890, in *Proceedings of the S.P.R.*, Sir William Crookes published full contemporary accounts, noted by himself, of his experiments on Home in 1871, with elaborate mechanical tests as to alteration of weights; and recorded Home's feats in handling red-hot coals, and communicating the power of doing so to others, and to a fine cambric handkerchief on which a piece of red-hot charcoal lay some time. Beyond a hole of half an inch in diameter, to which Home drew attention, the cambric was unharmed. Sir William tested it: it had undergone no chemical preparation.

Into the details of the mechanical tests as to alterations of weights I cannot go. Mr. Angelo Lewis (Professor Hoffman), an expert in conjuring, says that, accepting Sir William's veracity, and that he was not hallucinated, the phenomena 'seem to me distinctly to be outside the range of trick, and therefore to be good evidence, so far as we can trust personal evidence at all, of Home's power of producing motion, without contact, in inanimate bodies.' Sir William himself writes (1890): 'I have discovered no flaw in the experiments, or in the reasoning I based upon them. '[27] The notes of the performances were written while they were actually in course of proceeding. Thus 'the table rose completely off the ground several times, whilst the gentlemen present took a candle, and, kneeling down, deliberately examined the position of Mr. Home's knees and feet, and saw the three feet of the table quite off the ground.' Every observer in turn satisfied himself of the facts; they could not all be hallucinated.

I have not entered on the 'spiritual' part of the puzzle, the communications from 'spirits' of matters not *consciously* known to persons present, but found to be correct. That is too large a subject. Nor have I entered into the case of Mrs. Lyon's gift to Home, for the evidence only proved, as the judge held, that the gift was prompted, at least to some extent, by what Home declared to be spiritual rappings. But the only actual witness to the fact, Mrs. Lyon herself, was the reverse of a trustworthy witness, being a foolish capricious underbred woman. Hume's mystery, as far as the best of the drawing-room miracles are concerned, is solved by no theory or combination of theories, neither by the hypothesis of conjuring, nor of collective hallucination, nor of a blend of both. The cases of Sir David Brewster and of Dr. Carpenter prove how far some 'scientists' will go, rather than appear in an attitude of agnosticism, of not having a sound explanation.[28]

> NOTE.—Since this paper was written, I have been obliged by several interesting communications from a person very intimate with Home. Nothing in these threw fresh light on the mystery of his career, still less tended to confirm any theory of dishonesty on his part. His legal adviser, a man of honour, saw no harm in his accepting Mrs. Lyon's proffered gift, though he tried, in vain, to prevent her from increasing her original present.

IX

THE CASE OF CAPTAIN GREEN

'PLAY on Captain Green 's wuddie, '[29] said the caddy on Leith Links; and his employer struck his ball in the direction of the Captain 's gibbet on the sands. Mr. Duncan Forbes of Culloden sighed, and, taking off his hat, bowed in the direction of the unhappy mariner 's monument.

One can imagine this little scene repeating itself many a time, long after Captain Thomas Green, his mate, John Madder or Mather, and another of his crew were taken to the sands at Leith on the second Wednesday in April 1705, being April 11, and there hanged within the floodmark upon a gibbet till they were dead. Mr. Forbes of Culloden, later President of the Court of Session, and, far more than the butcher Cumberland, the victor over the rising of 1745, believed in the innocence of Captain Green, wore mourning for him, attended the funeral at the risk of his own life, and, when the Porteous Riot was discussed in Parliament, rose in his place and attested his conviction that the captain was wrongfully done to death.

Green, like his namesake in the Popish Plot, was condemned for a crime of which he was probably innocent. Nay more, he died for a crime which was not proved to have been committed, though it really may have been committed by persons with whom Green had no connection, while Green may have been guilty of other misdeeds as bad as that for which he was hanged. Like the other Green, executed for the murder of Sir Edmund Berry Godfrey during the Popish Plot, the captain was the victim of a fit of madness in a nation, that nation being the Scottish. The cause of their fury was not religion—the fever of the Covenant had passed away—but commerce.

'Twere long to tell and sad to trace the origin of the Caledonian frenzy. In 1695 the Scottish Parliament had passed, with the royal assent, an Act granting a patent to a Scottish company dealing with Africa, the Indies, and, incidentally, with the globe at large. The Act committed the occupant of the Scottish throne, William of Orange, to backing the company if attacked by alien power. But it was unlucky that England was then an alien power, and that the Scots Act infringed the patent of the much older English East India Company. Englishmen dared not take shares, finally, in the venture of the Scots; and when the English Board of Trade found out, in 1697, the real purpose of the Scottish company—namely, to set up a factory in Darien and anticipate the advantages dreamed of by France in the case of M. de Lesseps 's Panama Canal— 'a strange thing happened. ' The celebrated philosopher, Mr. John Locke, and the other members of a committee of the English Board of Trade, advised the English Government to plagiarise the Scottish project, and seize the section of the Isthmus of Panama on which the Scots meant to settle. This was not done; but the Dutch Usurper, far from backing the Scots company, bade his colonies hold no sort of intercourse with them. The Scots were starved out of their settlement. The few who remained fled to New York and Jamaica, and there, perishing of hunger, were refused supplies by the English colonial governors. A second Scottish colony succumbed to a Spanish fleet and army, and the company, with a nominal capital of 400,000*l.* and with 220,000*l.* paid up, was bankrupt. Macaulay calculates the loss at about the same as a loss of forty millions would have been to the Scotland of his own day; let us say twenty-two millions.

We remember the excitement in France over the Panama failure. Scotland, in 1700, was even more furious, and that led to the hanging of Captain Green and his men. There were riots; the rioters were imprisoned in the Heart of Midlothian—the Tolbooth—the crowd released them; some of the crowd were feebly sentenced to the pillory, the public pelted them—with white roses; and had the Chevalier de St. George not been a child of twelve, he would have had a fair chance of recovering his throne. The trouble was tided over; William III. died in 1702. Queen Anne came to the Crown. But the bankrupt company was not dead. Its charter was still legal, and, with borrowed money, it sent out vessels to trade with the Indies. The company had a vessel, the 'Annandale, ' which was seized in the Thames, at the instance of the East India Company, and condemned for a breach of that company's privileges.

This capture awakened the sleeping fury among my fiery countrymen (1704). An English ship, connected with either the English East India Company or the rival Million Company, put into Leith Road to repair. Here was a chance; for the charter of the Scots company authorised them 'to make reprisals and to seek and take reparation of damage done by sea and land.' On the strength of this clause, which was never meant to apply to Englishmen in Scottish waters, but to foreigners of all kinds on the Spanish Main, the Scottish Admiralty took no steps. But the company had a Celtic secretary, Mr. Roderick Mackenzie, and the English Parliament, in 1695, had summoned Mr. Mackenzie before them, and asked him many questions of an impertinent and disagreeable nature. This outrageous proceeding he resented, for he was no more an English than he was a Japanese subject. The situation of the 'Worcester' in Scottish waters gave Roderick his chance. His chief difficulty, as he informed his directors, was 'to get together a sufficient number of such genteel, pretty fellows as would, of their own free accord, on a sudden advertisement, be willing to accompany me on this adventure' (namely, the capture of the 'Worcester'), 'and whose dress and behaviour would not render them suspected of any uncommon design in going aboard.' A scheme more sudden and daring than the seizure, by a few gentlemen, of a well-armed English vessel had not been executed since the bold Buccleuch forced Carlisle Castle and carried away Kinmont Willie. The day was Saturday, and Mr. Mackenzie sauntered to the Cross in the High Street, and invited genteel and pretty fellows to dine with him in the country. They were given an inkling of what was going forward, and some dropped off, like the less resolute guests in Mr. Stevenson's adventure of the hansom cabs. When they reached Leith, Roderick found himself at the head of eleven persons, of whom 'most be as good gentlemen, and (I must own) much prettier fellows than I pretend to be.' They were of the same sort as Roy, Middleton, Haliburton, and Dunbar, who, fourteen years earlier, being prisoners on the Bass Rock, seized the castle, and, through three long years, held it for King James against the English navy.

Historical Mysteries

The eleven chose Mr. Mackenzie as chief, and, having swords, pistols, 'and some with bayonets, too, ' set out. Mackenzie, his servant, and three friends took a boat at Leith, with provision of wine, brandy, sugar, and lime juice; four more came, as a separate party, from Newhaven; the rest first visited an English man-of-war in the Firth, and then, in a convivial manner, boarded the 'Worcester. ' The punch-bowls were produced, liquor was given to the sailors, while the officers of the 'Worcester ' drank with the visitors in the cabin. Mackenzie was supposed to be a lord. All was festivity, 'a most compleat scene of a comedy, acted to the life, ' when, as a Scottish song was being sung, each officer of the 'Worcester ' found a pistol at his ear. The carpenter and some of the crew rushed at the loaded blunderbusses that hung in the cabin; but there were shining swords between them and the blunderbusses. By nine at night, on August 12, Mackenzie 's followers were masters of the English ship, and the hatches, gunroom, chests, and cabinets were sealed with the official seal of the Scottish African and East India Company. In a day or two the vessel lay without rudder or sails, in Bruntisland Harbour, 'as secure as a thief in a mill. ' Mackenzie landed eight of the ship 's guns and placed them in an old fort commanding the harbour entry, manned them with gunners, and all this while an English man-of-war lay in the Firth!

For a peaceful secretary of a commercial company, with a scratch eleven picked up in the street on a Saturday afternoon, to capture a vessel with a crew of twenty-four, well accustomed to desperate deeds, was 'a sufficient camisado or onfall. ' For three or four days and nights Mr. Mackenzie had scarcely an hour 's sleep. By the end of August he had commenced an action in the High Court of Admiralty for condemning the 'Worcester ' and her cargo, to compensate for the damages sustained by his company through the English seizure of their ship, the 'Annandale. ' When Mackenzie sent in his report on September 4, he added that, from 'very odd expressions dropt now and then from some of the ship 's crew, ' he suspected that Captain Green, of the 'Worcester, ' was 'guilty of some very unwarrantable practices. '

The Scottish Privy Council were now formally apprised of the affair, which they cautiously handed over to the Admiralty. The Scottish company had for about three years bewailed the absence of a ship of their own, the 'Speedy Return, ' which had never returned at all. Her skipper was a Captain Drummond, who had been very active in the Darien expedition; her surgeon was Mr. Andrew Wilkie, brother of James Wilkie, tailor and burgess of Edinburgh. The pair were most probably descendants of the Wilkie, tailor in the Canongate, who was mixed up in the odd business of Mr. Robert Oliphant, in the Gowrie conspiracy of 1600. Friends of Captain Drummond, Surgeon Wilkie, and others who had disappeared in the 'Speedy Return, ' began to wonder whether the crew of the 'Worcester, ' in their wanderings, had ever come across news of the missing vessel. One George Haines, of the 'Worcester, ' hearing of a Captain Gordon, who was the terror of French privateers, said: 'Our sloop was more terrible upon the coast of Malabar than ever Captain Gordon will be to the French. ' Mackenzie asking Haines if he had ever heard of the 'Speedy Return, ' the missing ship, Haines replied: 'You need not trouble your head about her, for I believe you won 't see her in haste. ' He thought that Captain Drummond had turned pirate.

Haines now fell in love with a girl at Bruntisland, aged nineteen, named Anne Seaton, and told her a number of things, which she promised to repeat to Mackenzie, but disappointed him, though she had blabbed to others. It came to be reported that Captain Green had pirated the 'Speedy Return, ' and murdered Captain Drummond and his crew. The Privy Council, in January 1705, took the matter up. A seal, or forged copy of the seal, of the Scottish African and East India Company was found on board the 'Worcester, ' and her captain and crew were judicially interrogated, after the manner of the French *Juge d 'Instruction*.

On March 5, 1705, the Scottish Court of Admiralty began the trial of Green and his men. Charles May, surgeon of the 'Worcester, ' and two negroes, Antonio Ferdinando, cook 's mate, and Antonio Francisco, captain 's man, were ready to give evidence against their comrades. They were accused of attacking, between February and May, 1703, off the coast of Malabar a vessel bearing a red flag, and having English or Scots aboard. They pursued her in their sloop, seized and killed the crew, and stole the goods.

Everyone in Scotland, except resolute Whigs, believed the vessel attacked to have been Captain Drummond's 'Speedy Return.' But there was nothing definite to prove the fact; there was no *corpus delicti*. In fact the case was parallel to that of the Campden mystery, in which three people were hanged for killing old Mr. Harrison, who later turned up in perfect health. In Green's, as in the Campden case, some of the accused confessed their guilt, and yet evidence later obtained tends to prove that Captain Drummond and his ship and crew were all quite safe at the date of the alleged piracy by Captain Green. None the less, it does appear that Captain Green had been pirating somebody, and perhaps he was 'none the waur o' a hanging,' though, as he had an English commission to act against pirates, it was argued that, if he had been fighting at all, it was against pirates that he had been making war. Now Haines's remark that Captain Drummond, as he heard, had turned pirate, looks very like a 'hedge' to be used in case the 'Worcester' was proved to have attacked the 'Speedy Return.'

There was a great deal of preliminary sparring between the advocates as to the propriety of the indictment. The jury of fifteen contained five local skippers. Most of the others were traders. One of them, William Blackwood, was of a family that had been very active in the Darien affair. Captain Green had no better chance with these men than James Stewart of the Glens in face of a jury of Campbells. The first witness, Ferdinando, the black sea cook, deponed that he saw Green's sloop take a ship under English colours, and that Green, his mate, Madder, and others, killed the crew of the captured vessel with hatchets. Ferdinando's coat was part of the spoil, and was said to be of Scottish cloth. Charles May, surgeon of the 'Worcester,' being on shore, heard firing at sea, and, later, dressed a wound, a gunshot he believed, on the arm of the black cook; dressed wounds, also, of two sailors, of the 'Worcester,' Mackay and Cuming—Scots obviously, by their names. He found the deck of the 'Worcester,' when he came on board, lumbered with goods and chests. He remarked on this, and Madder, the mate, cursed him, and bade him 'mind his plaister box.' He added that the 'Worcester,' before his eyes, while he stood on shore, was towing another vessel, which, he heard, was sold to a native dealer—Coge Commodo—who told the witness that the 'Worcester' 'had been fighting.' The

'Worcester' sprang a leak, and sailed for five weeks to a place where she was repaired, as if she were anxious to avoid inquiries.

Antonio Francisco, Captain Green's black servant, swore that, being chained and nailed to her forecastle, he heard the 'Worcester' fire six shots. Two days later a quantity of goods was brought on board (captured, it would seem, by the terrible sloop of the 'Worcester'), and Ferdinando then told this witness about the killing of the captured crew, and showed his own wounded arm. Francisco himself lay in chains for two months, and, of course, had a grudge against Captain Green. It was proved that the 'Worcester' had a cipher wherein to communicate with her owners, who used great secrecy; that her cargo consisted of arms, and was of such slight value as not to justify her voyage, unless her real business was piracy. The ship was of 200 tons, twenty guns, thirty-six men, and the value of the cargo was but 1,000*l*. Really, things do not look very well for the enterprise of Captain Green! There was also found a suspicious letter to one of the crew, Reynolds, from his sister-in-law, advising him to confess, and referring to a letter of his own in which he said that some of the crew 'had basely confessed.' The lady's letter and a copy of Reynolds's, admitted by him to be correct, were before the Court.

Again, James Wilkie, tailor, had tried at Bruntisland to 'pump' Haines about Captain Drummond; Haines swore profane, but later said that he heard Drummond had turned pirate, and that off the coast of Malabar they had manned their sloop, lest Drummond, whom they believed to be on that coast, should attack them. Other witnesses corroborated Wilkie, and had heard Haines say that it was a wonder the ground did not open and swallow them for the wickedness 'that had been committed during the last voyage on board of that old I omit a nautical term of endearment] *Bess.*' Some one telling Haines that the mate's uncle had been 'burned in oil' for trying to burn Dutch ships at Amsterdam, 'the said George Haines did tell the deponent that if what Captain Madder [the mate] had done during his last voyage were known, he deserved as much as his uncle had met with.' Anne Seaton, the girl of Haines's heart, admitted that Haines had told her 'that he knew more of Captain Drummond than he would express at that time,' and she had heard his expressions of remorse. He had blabbed to many witnesses of a precious something hidden aboard the 'Worcester;' to Anne he said that he had now thrown it overboard. We shall see later what this object was. Anne was a reluctant witness. Glen, a goldsmith, had seen a seal of the Scots East India Company in the hands of Madder, the inference being that it was taken from the 'Speedy Return.'

Sir David Dalrymple, for the prosecution, made the most he could of the evidence. The black cook's coat, taken from the captured vessel, 'in my judgment appears to be Scots rugg.' He also thought it a point in favour of the cook's veracity that he was very ill, and forced to lie down in court; in fact, the cook died suddenly on the day when Captain Green was condemned, and the Scots had a high opinion of dying confessions. The white cook, who joined the 'Worcester' after the sea-fight, said that the black cook told him the whole story at that time. Why did the 'Worcester' sail for thirty-five days to repair her leak, which she might have done at Goa or Surat, instead of sailing some 700 leagues for the purpose? The jury found that there was 'one clear witness to robbery, piracy, and murder,' and accumulative corroboration.

The judges ordered fourteen hangings, to begin with those of Green, Madder, and three others on April 4. On March 16, at Edinburgh, Thomas Linsteed made an affidavit that the 'Worcester' left him on shore, on business, about January 1703; that fishing crews reported the fight of the sloop against a vessel unknown; they left before the fight ended; that the Dutch and Portuguese told him how the 'Worcester's' men had sold a prize, and thought but little of it, 'because it is what is ordinary on that coast,' and that the 'Worcester's' people told him to ask them no questions. On March 27 George Haines made a full confession of the murder of a captured crew, he being accessory thereto, at Sacrifice Rock, between Tellicherry and Calicut; and that he himself, after being seized by Mackenzie, threw his journal of the exciting events overboard. Now, in his previous blabbings before the trial, as we have seen, Haines had spoken several times about something on board the 'Worcester' which the Scots would be very glad to lay hands on, thereby indicating this journal of his; and he told Anne Seaton, as she deponed at the trial, that he had thrown the precious something overboard. In his confession of March 27 he explained what the mysterious something was. He also declared (March 28) that the victims of the piracy 'spoke the Scots language.' A sailor named Bruckley also made full confession. These men were reprieved, and doubtless expected to be; but Haines, all the while remorseful, I think, told the truth. The 'Worcester' had been guilty of piracy.

But had she pirated the Scottish ship, the 'Speedy Return,' Captain Drummond? As to that point, on April 5, in England, two of the crew of the 'Worcester,' who must somehow have escaped from Mackenzie's raid, made affidavit that the 'Worcester' fought no ship during her whole voyage. This would be more satisfactory if we knew more of the witnesses. On March 21, at Portsmouth, two other English mariners made affidavit that they had been of the crew of the 'Speedy Return;' that she was captured by pirates, while Captain Drummond and Surgeon Wilkie were on shore, at Maritan in Madagascar; and that these two witnesses 'went on board a Moca ship called the "Defiance,"' escaped from her at the Mauritius, and returned to England in the 'Raper' galley. Of the fate of Drummond and Wilkie, left ashore in Madagascar, they naturally knew nothing. If they spoke truth, Captain Green certainly did not seize the 'Speedy Return,' whatever dark and bloody deeds he may have done off the coast of Malabar.

In England, as Secretary Johnstone, son of the caitiff Covenanter, Waristoun, wrote to Baillie of Jerviswoode, the Whigs made party capital out of the proceedings against Green: they said it was a Jacobite plot. I conceive that few Scottish Whigs, to be sure, marched under Roderick Mackenzie.

In Scotland the Privy Council refused Queen Anne's demand that the execution of Green should be suspended till her pleasure was known, but they did grant a week's respite. On April 10 a mob, partly from the country, gathered in Edinburgh; the Privy Council, between the mob and the Queen, let matters take their course. On April 11 the mob raged round the meeting-place of the Privy Council, rooms under the Parliament House, and chevied the Chancellor into a narrow close, whence he was hardly rescued. However, learning that Green was to swing after all, the mob withdrew to Leith sands, where they enjoyed the execution of an Englishman. The whole affair hastened the Union of 1707, for it was a clear case of Union or war between the two nations.

As for Drummond, many years later, on the occasion of the Porteous riot, Forbes of Culloden declared in the House of Commons that a few months after Green was hanged letters came from Captain Drummond, of the 'Speedy Return,' 'and from the very ship for whose capture the unfortunate person suffered, informing their friends that they were all safe.' But the 'Speedy Return' was taken by pirates, two of her crew say, off Madagascar, and burned. What was the date of the letters from the 'Speedy Return' to which, long afterwards, Forbes, and he alone, referred? What was the date of the capture of the 'Speedy Return,' at Maritan, in Madagascar? Without the dates we are no wiser.

Now comes an incidental and subsidiary mystery. In 1729 was published *Madagascar, or Robert Drury's Journal during Fifteen Years' Captivity on that Island, written by Himself, digested into order, and now published at the Request of his Friends.* Drury says, as we shall see, that he, a lad of fifteen, was prisoner in Madagascar from *about* 1703 to 1718, and that there he met Captain Drummond, late of the 'Speedy Return.' If so, Green certainly did not kill Captain Drummond. But Drury's narrative seems to be about as authentic and historical as the so-called *Souvenirs of Madame de Créquy.* In the edition of 1890[30] of Drury's book, edited by Captain Pasfield Oliver, R.A., author of *Madagascar,* the Captain throws a lurid light on Drury and his volume. Captain Pasfield Oliver first candidly produces what he thinks the best evidence for the genuineness of Drury's story; namely a letter of the Rev. Mr. Hirst, on board H.M.S. 'Lenox,' off Madagascar, 1759. This gentleman praises Drury's book as the best and most authentic, for Drury says that he was wrecked in the 'Degrave,' East Indiaman, and his story 'exactly agrees, as far as it goes, with the journal kept by Mr. John Benbow,' second mate of the 'Degrave.' That journal of Benbow's was burned, in London, in 1714, but several of his friends remembered that it tallied with Drury's narrative. But, as Drury's narrative was certainly 'edited,' probably by Defoe, that master of fiction may easily have known and used Benbow's journal. Otherwise, if Benbow's journal contained the same references to Captain Drummond in Madagascar as Drury gives, then the question is settled: Drummond died in Madagascar after a stormy existence of some eleven years on that island. As to Drury, Captain Pasfield Oliver thinks that his editor, probably Defoe, or an imitator of Defoe, 'faked' the book, partly out of De Flacourt's *Histoire de Madagascar* (1661), and a French authority adds another old French source, Dapper's *Description de l 'Afrique.* Drury was himself a pirate, his editor thinks: Defoe picked his brains, or an imitator of Defoe did so, and Defoe, or whoever was the editor, would know the story that Drummond really lost the 'Speedy Return' in Madagascar, and could introduce the Scottish adventurer into Drury's romance.

We can never be absolutely certain that Captain Drummond lost his ship, but lived on as a kind of *condottiere* to a native prince in Madagascar. Between us and complete satisfactory proof a great gulf has been made by fire and water, 'foes of old' as the Greek poet says, which conspired to destroy the journal kept by Haines and the journal kept by Benbow. The former would have told us what piratical adventures Captain Green achieved in the 'Worcester;' the latter, if it spoke of Captain Drummond in Madagascar, would have proved that the captain and the 'Speedy Return' were not among the 'Worcester's' victims. If we could be sure that Benbow's journal corroborated Drury's romance, we could not be sure that the editor of the romance did not borrow the facts from the journal of Benbow, and we do not know that this journal made mention of Captain Drummond, for the only valid testimony as to the captain's appearance in Madagascar is the affidavit of Israel Phippany and Peter Freeland, at Portsmouth, March 31, 1705, and these mariners may have perjured themselves to save the lives of English seamen condemned by the Scots.

Yet, as a patriotic Scot, I have reason for believing in the English affidavit at Portsmouth. The reason is simple, but sufficient. Captain Drummond, if attacked by Captain Green, was the man to defeat that officer, make prize of his ship, and hang at the yardarm the crew which was so easily mastered by Mr. Roderick Mackenzie and eleven pretty fellows. Hence I conclude that the 'Worcester' really had been pirating off the coast of Malabar, but that the ship taken by

Captain Green in these waters was not the 'Speedy Return,' but another, unknown. If so, there was no great miscarriage of justice, for the indictment against Captain Green did not accuse him of seizing the 'Speedy Return,' but of piracy, robbery, and murder, though the affair of the 'Speedy Return' was brought in to give local colour. This fact and the national excitement in Scotland probably turned the scale with the jury, who otherwise would have returned a verdict of 'Not Proven.' That verdict, in fact, would have been fitted to the merits of the case; but 'there was mair tint at Shirramuir' than when Captain Green was hanged.[31] That Green was deeply guilty, I have inferred from the evidence. To Mr. Stephen Ponder I owe corroboration. He cites a passage from Hamilton's *New Account of the East Indies* (1727), chap. 25, which is crucial.

'The unfortunate Captain Green, who was afterwards hanged in Scotland, came on board my ship at sunset, very much overtaken in drink and several of his men in the like condition (at Calicut, February 1703). He wanted to sell Hamilton some arms and ammunition, and told me that they were what was left of a large quantity that he had brought from England, but had been at Madagascar and had disposed of the rest to good advantage among the pirates. I told him that in prudence he ought to keep these as secrets lest he might be brought in trouble about them. He made but little account of my advice, and so departed. About ten in the night his chief mate Mr. Mather came on board of my ship and seemed to be very melancholy.... He burst out in tears and told me he was afraid that he was undone, that they had acted such things in their voyage that would certainly bring them to shame and punishment, if they should come to light; and he was assured that such a company of drunkards as their crew was composed of could keep no secret. I told him that I had heard at Coiloan (Quilon) that they had not acted prudently nor honestly in relation to some Moors' ships they had visited and plundered *and in sinking a sloop with ten or twelve Europeans in her* off Coiloan. Next day I went ashore and met Captain Green and his supercargo Mr. Callant, who had sailed a voyage from Surat to Sienly with me. Before dinner-time they were both drunk, and Callant told me that he did not doubt of making the greatest voyage that ever was made from England on so small a stock as 500*l*.

'In the evening their surgeon accosted me and asked if I wanted a surgeon. He said he wanted to stay in India, for his life was uneasy on board of his ship, that though the captain was civil enough, yet Mr. Mather had treated him with blows for asking a pertinent question of some wounded men, who were hurt in the engagement with the sloop. I heard too much to be contented with their conduct, and so I shunned their conversation for the little time I staid at Calicut.

'Whether Captain Green and Mr. Mathew had justice impartially in their trial and sentence I know not. I have heard of as great innocents condemned to death as they were.'

The evidence of Hamilton settles the question of the guilt of Green and his crew, as regards some unfortunate vessel, or sloop. Had the 'Speedy Return' a sloop with her?

X

QUEEN OGLETHORPE

(*In collaboration with* MISS ALICE SHIELD).

'HER Oglethorpe majesty was kind, acute, resolute, and of good counsel. She gave the Prince much good advice that he was too weak to follow, and loved him with a fidelity which he returned with an ingratitude quite Royal.'

So writes Colonel Henry Esmond, describing that journey of his to Bar-le-Duc in Lorraine, whence he brought back 'Monsieur Baptiste,' all to win fair Beatrix Esmond. We know how 'Monsieur Baptiste' stole his lady-love from the glum Colonel, and ran after the maids, and drank too much wine, and came to the King's Arms at Kensington the day after the fair (he was always 'after the fair'), and found Argyll's regiment in occupation, and heard King George proclaimed.

Where in the world did Thackeray pick up the materials of that brilliant picture of James VIII., gay, witty, reckless, ready to fling away three crowns for a fine pair of eyes or a neat pair of ankles? His Majesty's enemies brought against him precisely the opposite kind of charges. There is a broad-sheet of 1716, *Hue and Cry after the Pretender*, which is either by Swift or by one of 'the gentlemen whom,' like Captain Bobadil, he 'had taught to write almost or altogether as well as himself.' As to gaiety in James, 'you tell him it is a fine day, and he weeps, and says he was unfortunate from his mother's womb.' As to ladies, 'a weakness for the sex remarked in many popular monarchs' (as Atterbury said to Lady Castlewood), our pamphleteer tells the opposite tale. Two Highland charmers being introduced 'to comfort him after the comfort of a man,' James displayed 'an incredible inhumanity to beauty and clean linen,' merely asking them 'whether they thought the Duke of Argyll would stand another battle?' It is hard on a man to be stamped by history as recklessly gay and amorous, also as a perfect Mrs. Gummidge for tearful sentiment, and culpably indifferent to the smiles of beauty. James is greatly misunderstood: the romance of his youth—sword and cloak and disguise, pistol, dagger and poison, prepared for him; story of true love blighted by a humorous cast of destiny; voyages, perils, shipwrecks, dances at inns—all is forgotten or is unknown.

Meanwhile, who was her 'Oglethorpean majesty,' and why does the pamphleteer of 1716 talk of 'James Stuart, *alias* Oglethorpe'? By a strange combination of his bad luck, James is called Miss Oglethorpe 's ungrateful lover by Thackeray, and Miss Oglethorpe 's brother by the pamphleteer, and by Whig slander in general. Thackeray, in fact, took Miss Oglethorpe from the letter which Bolingbroke wrote to Wyndham, after St. Germains found him out, as St. James 's had done, for a traitor. Bolingbroke merely mentions Fanny Oglethorpe as a busy intriguer. There is no evidence that she ever was at Bar-le-Duc in her life, none that she ever was 'Queen Oglethorpe.' We propose to tell, for the first time, the real story of this lady and her sisters.

The story centres round The Meath Home for Incurables! This excellent institution occupies Westbrook Place, an old house at Godalming, close to the railway, which passes so close as to cut off one corner of the park, and of the malodorous tanyard between the remnant of grounds and the river Wey that once washed them. On an October day, the Surrey hills standing round about in shadowy distances, the silence of two centuries is scarcely broken by the rustle of leaves dropping on their own deep carpet, and the very spirit of a lost cause dwells here, slowly dying. The house stands backed by a steep wooded hill, beyond which corn-fields 'clothe the wold and meet the sky;' the mansion is a grey, two-storied parallelogram flanked by square towers of only slighter elevation; their projecting bays surmounted by open-work cornices of leafy tracery in whiter stone.

The tale used to run (one has heard it vaguely in conversation) that the old house at Godalming is haunted by the ghost of Prince

Charlie, and one naturally asks, 'What is *he* doing there? ' What he was doing there will appear later.

In 1688, the year of the *Regifugium*, Westbrook Place was sold to Theophilus Oglethorpe, who had helped to drive

>   the Whigs
>   Frae Bothwell Brigs,

and, later, to rout Monmouth at Sedgemoor. This gentleman married Eleanor Wall, of an Irish family, a Catholic— 'a cunning devil, ' says Swift. The pair had five sons and four daughters, about whom county histories and dictionaries of biography blunder in a helpless fashion. We are concerned with Anne Henrietta, born, probably, about 1680-83, Eleanor (1684), James (June 1, 1688, who died in infancy), and Frances Charlotte, Bolingbroke 's 'Fanny Oglethorpe. ' The youngest brother, James Edward, born 1696, became the famous philanthropist, General Oglethorpe, governor of Georgia, patron of the Wesleys, and, in extreme old age, the 'beau ' of Hannah More, and the gentleman who remembered shooting snipe on the site of Conduit Street.

After the Revolution Sir Theophilus was engaged with Sir John Fenwick, was with him when he cocked his beaver in the face of the Princess of Orange, had to fly to France, after the failure at La Hogue, and in 1693 was allowed to settle peacefully at Westbrook Place. Anne and Eleanor were left in France, where they were brought up as Catholics at St. Germains, and befriended by the exiled James and Mary of Modena. Now in 1699 Theophilus, one of the Oglethorpe boys, was sent out to his father 's old friend Mr. Pitt, Governor of Fort St. George in India, the man of the Pitt Diamond. His outfit had to be prepared in a hurry, and a young gentlewoman, Frances Shaftoe, was engaged to help with the sewing of his several dozens of linen shirts, 'the flourishing of neckcloths and drawing of cotton stripes; ' as young gentlewomen of limited means were used to do before they discovered hospitals and journalism. This girl, who developed a political romance of her own, was of good Northumberland family, related to Sir John Fenwick and the Delavals. Her father, a merchant in Newcastle, had educated her 'in a civil and virtuous manner, ' and she had lived there about eighteen years, behaving herself discreetly, modestly, and honestly, as nine Northumbrian justices of the peace were ready to testify under their hand. The strange story she later told of her experiences at Westbrook and afterwards cannot, therefore, be wholly dismissed as a tale trumped up for political purposes, though its most thrilling incident is so foolish a lie as to discredit the whole.

On the Saturday before Christmas 1699 (so ran her later 'revelations, '[32] made in 1707) she took the coach from Godalming, obedient to instructions by letter from Sir Theophilus. A little way down the Strand he joined her in the coach, accompanied by two young ladies—friends, she was told, of Lady Oglethorpe; and for some time she knew no more of who they were and whence they came. They were very secret, appeared in no company, but made themselves useful in the pleasant, homely ways of English country life of that time: helped with the sewing, made their own bed, swept their chamber, dressed the two little girls, Mary and Fanny, and waited on each other. Presently it turned out that they were Anne and Eleanor Oglethorpe, who had been eleven years in France, at the Court of James II., where they were known as Anne and Eleanor Barkly. They had taken advantage of the peace to come secretly 'over a long sea, ' and had waited at the house of their mother 's brother-in-law, Mr. Cray the City wine-merchant, until Parliament was up and their father could take them home for Christmas. A member of Parliament must not be compromised by the presence of Catholic daughters from St. Germains, whom it was treason even to harbour.

Fanny Shaftoe was admitted into the family, she says, on quite familiar terms, but 'always behaved very meek and humble, ready to help any of the servants to make beds or to take care of the little boy ' (the General) 'when his nurse was busy helping in the garden. ' Anne and Eleanor were merry, friendly girls, and chatted only too freely with Fanny Shaftoe over the sewing. She certainly heard a great deal of 'treason ' talked. She heard how Sir Theophilus and his wife went back and forward, disguised, between England and St. Germains; how Lady Oglethorpe had taken charge of the Queen 's diamonds when she fled from Whitehall and safely returned them three years later, travelling as an old doctor-woman in a riding-hood, selling powders and plasters in a little basket. There was unseemly jubilation over the death of Queen Anne's son, the little Duke of Gloucester, in July 1700—though Fanny admits they were sorry at first—and somewhat partisan comparisons were drawn between him, 'a poor, soft child who had no wit' (he was really a very promising, spirited boy), and the little Prince of Wales, 'who was very witty.'

To this careless chatter Fanny Shaftoe added exaggerations and backstairs gossip, and an astounding statement which lived as the feeblest lie *can* live. Anne Oglethorpe, she said, informed her that the real Prince of Wales (born June 10, 1688) had died at Windsor of convulsions when five or six weeks old; that Lady Oglethorpe hurried up to town with her little son James, born a few days before the Prince, and that the Oglethorpe baby died, or *was lost on the road*. The truth was a secret between her mother and the Queen! All they knew was that their little brother never turned up again. Anne added, confusing the story by too much detail, as all accounts of the royal fraud are confused, that the children had been sick together; that the Prince had then died, and her brother had been substituted for him.

In November 1700 Frances Shaftoe (according to her later revelations) left Westbrook: her mother had written from Newcastle to say her sister was dying. Anne and Eleanor were very sympathetic—they were really nice girls. Lady Oglethorpe was very kind, and gave her four guineas for her eleven months' services; and she seems to have been satisfied with it as handsome remuneration. She asserts, inconsistently, that she had much ado to get away; but she never went to Newcastle. Three months later, being still in London, she was sent for to a house in the Strand, where she met Anne Oglethorpe. Anne gave her a letter from her mother, which had been kept back because Anne had expected to come up sooner to town, otherwise she would have sent it. Anne had a cold and a swelled face. She and Eleanor were going to France, and she persuaded Fanny to go with them. To make a long tale short, they shut her up in a convent lest she should blab the great secret, 'James Stuart is really James Oglethorpe!'

Historical Mysteries

In September 1701 James II. died, and Lady Oglethorpe carried to the Princess Anne the affecting letter of farewell he wrote to her, commending his family to her care. Anne and Eleanor went to England in November 1702, and from that date until Easter 1706 Fanny Shaftoe says she heard no more about them. In April 1702 Sir Theophilus died, and was buried in St. James's, Piccadilly, where the memorial erected by his widow may be seen.

Theophilus, the heir, probably remained a while in the far East with Pitt; but there were Oglethorpes nearer home to dabble in the Scots plot of that year (1704). In June several Scottish officers—Sir George Maxwell, Captain Livingstone, and others, amounting to fifteen or sixteen, with three ladies, one of whom was Anne Oglethorpe, embarked at the Hague for Scotland. Sir George had tried in vain to procure a passport from Queen Anne's envoy, so, though it was in war-time, they sailed without one. Harley informed by Captain Lacan, late of Galway's Foot in Piedmont, told Lord Treasurer Godolphin, who had the party arrested on landing. The Queen, who plotted as much as anybody on behalf of her brother, was indulgent to fellow-conspirators, and, though it was proved their purpose had been 'to raise commotions in Scotland,' they were soon set at liberty, and the informer sent back to Holland with empty pockets.[33]

Anne Oglethorpe, nevertheless, having crossed without a pass, lay at the mercy of the Government, but, as with Joseph in Egypt, her misfortune turned into her great opportunity. The late Mr. H. Manners, in an article in the *Dictionary of National Biography*,[34] supposes she had been King James's mistress before she left St. Germains. Now, see how Thackeray has misled historians! *He* makes *Fanny* Oglethorpe, James's mistress, 'Queen Oglethorpe,' at Bar-le-Duc in 1714. And, resting on this evidence, Mr. Manners represents *Anne* Oglethorpe as James's mistress at St. Germains in 1704! Anne left St. Germains before James was sixteen, and her character is blasted by the easy plan of mistaking her for her younger sister, who was no more Queen Oglethorpe than *she* was.

Poor Anne did not 'scape calumny, perhaps deserved it. Boyer says that Godolphin and Harley quarrelled for her smiles, which beamed on Harley (Lord Oxford, Swift's 'Dragon'), and 'an irreconcilable enmity' arose. In 1713 Schutz describes Anne Oglethorpe as Oxford's mistress, but she had troubles of her own before that date. She arrived in England, a Jacobite conspirator, in 1704. Her wit and beauty endeared her to Harley, and she probably had a foot in both camps, Queen Anne's and King James's.

But in 1706 strange rumours came from the North. Mrs. Shaftoe had, after five years' silence, received letters from her daughter Fanny, the sempstress, by a secret hand, and was filling Newcastle with lamentations over trepanning, imprisonment, and compulsory conversion, with the object of making Fanny a nun. A young English priest, agent for supplying the Catholic squires of Northumberland with chaplains, was sent to France by her Catholic cousin, Mrs. Delaval, to find out the truth. The consequence of his inquiries was that Anne Oglethorpe was arrested in England, and charged before the Queen and Council with trepanning and trying to force Fanny Shaftoe to become a nun. Anne flung herself at the Queen's feet and implored mercy. She escaped being sent to Newgate, but was imprisoned in a Messenger's house to await further proceedings, and ordered to produce Fanny Shaftoe as a witness.

Eleanor Oglethorpe was in France, and rushed to the convent where Fanny Shaftoe was held captive, told her how Anne was in prison on her account, and entreated her to sign a statement that she had come to France and become a Catholic of her own free will. But Fanny refused. Her long detailed story was printed and published for the prosecution in 1707, at the moment when the Chevalier's chances in Scotland were most promising. Had he landed only with his valet, says Ker of Kersland, Scotland would have been his. Cameronians and Cavaliers alike would have risen. But the French Admiral would not put him on shore. As for Anne she was discharged, having great allies; but Fanny Shaftoe's story did its work. James Stuart, for Whig purposes, was 'James Oglethorpe,' Anne's brother. Fanny's narrative was republished in 1745, to injure Prince Charlie.

Restored to society and Harley, Anne queened it royally. If we believe old Tom Hearne, whose MSS. are in the Bodleian, Anne practically negotiated the Treaty of Utrecht. She found a French priest, whose sister was in the household of Madame de Maintenon, she wrote mysterious letters to him, he showed them to Louis XIV., and the priest was presently lurking in Miss Oglethorpe's town house. Harley visited his Egeria; she introduced the abbé; Gauthier (the abbé himself?) and Messager were appointed by France to treat. Harley insisted on the surrender of Dunkirk! Louis offered Anne Oglethorpe 2,000,000 livres if she would save Dunkirk for France. Her Oglethorpean majesty refused the gold, but did Louis's turn, on condition that he would restore King James! For all this magnanimity we have only Tom Hearne's word. Swift, for example, was not likely to reveal these romantic circumstances about the Lady and the Dragon.

Swift does not mention Anne in his letters, but being so deep in the greatest intrigues of the day and in the smallest, she was a valuable source of information to Thomas Carte, the nonjuring historian and her lifelong correspondent, when he was gathering materials for his Life of the first Duke of Ormond and his *History of England*. In 1713, Nairne, James's secretary, desires Abram (Menzies) to inquire if Mrs. *Oglethorpe* had credit with Honyton (Harley), and how far?[35] Schutz, the Hanoverian envoy, writes to Bothmar, November 21, 1713: 'Miss Oglethorpe, the Lord Treasurer's mistress, said that the Pretender was to travel, and she said it on the very day the news came from Holland that the Bishop of London had declared to the plenipotentiaries who are there, that the Queen entreated their masters not to receive the Pretender in their dominions.'[36] She knew all the particulars of Harley's opposition to the Duke of Ormond's schemes for improving the army, and what the Exchequer could and could not supply to back them.[37] She knew all about Lady Masham's quarrel with her cousin, Lord Oxford, in 1713, over the 100,000*l.* in ten per cents which Lady Masham had expected to make out of the Quebec expedition and Assiento contract, had not his lordship so 'disobliged her.' Anne acted as intermediary, hunting up her friend the Duke of Ormond, with whom her mother had great influence, and fetching him to meet Lady Masham at Kensington—who told him how ill the Queen was, and how uneasy at nothing being done for her brother, the Chevalier. If Ormond would but secure Lady Masham 30,000*l.* of the 100,000*l.*, she would join with him, and he should have the modelling of the army as he pleased. Ormond also failed to oblige Lady Masham, but Bolingbroke, whom she hated, snatched his opportunity in the quarrel and got her the money; in return for which service, Lady Masham had Harley turned out of office and Bolingbroke set in his place. And then Queen Anne died.

Miss Oglethorpe also knew that Sir Thomas Hanmer and Bishop Atterbury were the two persons who sent the messenger (mentioned only as Sir C.P. in the Carte Papers) to warn Ormond to escape to France in 1715. Women seem to have managed the whole political machine in those days, as the lengthy and mysterious letters of 'Mrs. White,' 'Jean Murray,' and others in the Carte MSS. testify.

We are not much concerned with the brothers of the Oglethorpe girls, but the oldest, Theophilus, turned Jacobite. That he had transferred his allegiance and active service to King James is proved by his letters from Paris to James, and to Gualterio in 1720 and 1721.[38] According to the second report on the Stuart Papers at Windsor, he was created a baron by James III in 1717. In 1718 he was certainly outlawed, for his younger brother, James Edward (the famous General Oglethorpe), succeeded to the Westbrook property in that year.

In July 1714 Fanny Oglethorpe, now about nineteen, turns up as an active politician. The Chevalier at Bar and his adherents in Paris, Scotland, and London, were breathlessly waiting for the death of Queen Anne, which was expected to restore him to the throne of his ancestors. Fanny had been brought up a Protestant by her mother in England, under whose auspices she had served her apprenticeship to plotting. Then she came to France, but Fanny cannot have been Thackeray's 'Queen Oglethorpe' at Bar-le-Duc. In the first place, she was not there; in the second, a lady of Lorraine was reigning monarch.[39]

With the fall of Oxford in 1714 ended Anne's chief opportunity of serving her King. The historian therefore turns to her sister Eleanor, who had been with her in the Fanny Shaftoe affair, but remained in France. Penniless as she was, Eleanor's beauty won the heart of the Marquis de Mézières, a great noble, a man over fifty, ugly, brave, misshapen. Theirs, none the less, was a love match, as the French

Court admiringly proclaimed. 'The frog-faced ' Marquis, the vainest of men, was one of the most courageous. Their daughters became the Princesses de Montauban and de Ligne, whose brilliant marriages caused much envy. Of their sons we shall hear later. Young Fanny Oglethorpe, a girl of twenty in 1715, resided with her sister Eleanor (Madame de Mézières), and now Bolingbroke, flying from the Tower, and become the Minister of James, grumbles at the presence of Fanny, and of Olive Trant, among the conspirators for a Restoration. Olive, the Regent 's mistress, was 'the great wheel of the machine, ' in which Fanny 'had her corner, ' at Saint Germains. 'Your female teazers, ' James calls them in a letter to Bolingbroke. Not a word is said of a love affair.

How the Fifteen ended we all know. Ill-managed by Mar, perhaps betrayed by Bolingbroke, the rising collapsed. Returning to France, James dismissed Bolingbroke and retired to Avignon, thence to Urbino, and last to Rome. In 1719 he describes 'Mrs. Oglethorpe 's letters ' as politically valueless, and full of self-justifications, and 'old stories. ' He answers them only through his secretary; but in 1722 he consoled poor Anne by making her a Countess of Ireland. Anne 's bolt was shot, she had had her day, but the day of her fair sisters was dawning. Mr. John Law, of Lauriston *soi-disant*, had made England too hot to hold him. His great genius for financial combinations was at this time employed by him in gleek, trick-track, quadrille, whist, loo, ombre, and other pastimes of mingled luck and skill. In consequence of a quarrel about a lady, Mr. Law fought and slew Beau Wilson, that mysterious person, who, from being a poverty-stricken younger son, hanging loose on town, became in a day, no man knows how, the richest and most splendid of blades. The Beau 's secret died with him; but Law fled to France with 100,000 crowns in his valise. Here the swagger, courage, and undeniable genius of Mr. Law gained the favour of the Regent d 'Orléans, the Bank and the Mississippi Scheme were floated, the Rue Quincampoix was crowded, France swam in a dream of gold, and the friends of Mr. Law, 'coming in on the ground-floor, ' or buying stock before issue at the lowest prices, sold out at the top of the market.

Historical Mysteries

Paris was full of Jacobites from Ireland and Scotland—Seaforth, Tullibardine, Campbell of Glendaruel, George Kelly (one of the Seven Men of Moidart), Nick Wogan, gayest and bravest of Irishmen, all engaged in a pleasing plan for invading England with a handful of Irish soldiers in Spanish service. The Earl Marischal and Keith his brother (the Field-Marshal) came into Paris broken men, fleeing from Glenshiel. *They* took no Mississippi shares, but George Kelly, Fanny Oglethorpe, and Olive Trant, all *liés* with Law and Orléans, 'plunged, ' and emerged with burdens of gold. Fanny for her share had 800,000 livres, and carried it as her dowry to the Marquis des Marches, whom she married in 1719, and so ceased conspiring. The Oglethorpe girls, for penniless exiles, had played their cards well. Fanny and Eleanor had won noble husbands. Poor Anne went back to Godalming, where—in the very darkest days of the Jacobite party, when James was a heart-broken widower, and the star of Prince Charles's natal day shone only on the siege of Gaeta— she plotted with Thomas Carte, the historian.

The race of 1715 was passing, the race of 1745 was coming on, and touching it is to read in the brown old letters the same loyal names— Floyds, Wogans, Gorings, Trants, Dillons, Staffords, Sheridans, the Scots of course, and the French descendants of the Oglethorpe girls. Eleanor's infants, the de Mézières family, had been growing up in beauty and honour, as was to be expected of the children of the valiant Marquis and the charming Eleanor. Their eldest daughter, Eléonore Eugénie, married Charles de Rohan, Prince de Montauban, younger brother of the Duc de Montbazon, whose wife was the daughter of the Duc de Bouillon and Princess Caroline Sobieska, and so first cousin to the sons of James III. That branch of Oglethorpes thus became connected with the royal family, which would go far towards rousing their hereditary Jacobitism when the Forty-Five cast its shadow before.

In May 1740, Madame de Mézières took it into her head to run over to England, and applied to Newcastle for a pass, through Lady Mary Herbert of Powis—a very *suspect* channel! The Minister made such particular inquiries as to the names of the servants she intended to bring, that she changed her mind and did not go. One wonders what person purposed travelling in her suite whose identity dared not stand too close scrutiny. There was a brave and eager Prince of Wales over the water, nearly twenty, who had some years ago fleshed his maiden sword with honour, and who was in secret correspondence on his own account with his father's English supporters. Could he have had some such plan even then of putting fate to the touch? He is reported in Coxe's *Walpole* to have been in Spain, in disguise, years before.

In 1742 Eleanor had the sorrow of losing a daughter in a tragic way. She had recently become a canoness of Povesay, a very noble foundation, indeed, in Lorraine, where the Sisters wore little black ribbons on their heads which they called 'husbands.' She was twenty-five, very pretty, and most irreligiously devoted to shooting and hunting. Though these chapters of noble canonesses are not by any means strict after the use of ordinary convents, there were serious expostulations made when the novice insisted upon constantly carrying a gun and shooting. She fell one day when out with her gun as usual. It went off and killed her on the spot.

Whatever Eleanor aimed at in 1740 by a journey to England, was baulked by Newcastle's caution. In 1743 the indefatigable lady, 'and a Scottish lord,' submitted a scheme to Louis XV., but it was thwarted by de Noailles. Then Prince Charles rode secretly out of Rome, landed, like Napoleon, at Fréjus, and at the expedition of Dunkirk met the Earl Marischal and young Glengarry.

The Chevalier de Mézières, too, Eleanor's son, went to Dunkirk with Saxe to embark for England. There was a great storm, and the ships went aground. Several officers and soldiers jumped into the sea, and some were drowned. The Chevalier de Mézières came riding along the shore, to hear that a dear friend was drowning. The sea was going back, but very heavy, and de Mézières rode straight into the raging waters to seek his friend. The waves went over his head and carried away his hat, but he persevered until he had seized a man. He dragged him ashore, to find it was a common soldier. He hastened back, and saved several soldiers and two or three officers. His friend, after all, had never been in danger.

The Saxe expedition never sailed, so Eugène de Mézières went to beat Hanoverians elsewhere, and was wounded at Fontenoy.

Consequently he could not follow the Prince to Scotland. His mother, Eleanor, plunged into intrigue for the forward party (Prince Charlie's party), distrusted by James at Rome. 'She is a mad woman,' said James. She and Carte, the historian, were working up an English rising to join the Prince's Scottish adventure, but were baffled by James's cautious, helpless advisers. Then came the Forty-Five. Eleanor was not subdued by Culloden: the undefeated old lady was a guest at the great dinner, with the splendid new service of plate, which the Prince gave to the Princesse de Talmond and his friends in 1748. He was braving all Europe, in his hopeless way, and refusing to leave France, in accordance with the Treaty of Aix-la-Chapelle. When he was imprisoned at Vincennes, Eleanor was threatened. Catholic as she was, she frankly declared that Prince Charles had better declare himself a Protestant, and marry a German Protestant Princess. He therefore proposed to one, a day or two before he disappeared from Avignon, in February 1749, and he later went over to London, and embraced the Anglican faith.

It was too late; but Eleanor Oglethorpe was not beaten. In October 1752 'the great affair' was being incubated again. Alexander Murray, of the Elibank family, exasperated by his imprisonment for a riot at the Westminster election, had taken service with Prince Charles. He had arranged that a body of young Jacobite officers in foreign service, with four hundred Highlanders under young Glengarry, should overpower the Guards, break into St. James's Palace, and seize King George; while the Westminster mob, Murray's lambs, should create an uproar. Next day Glengarry would post north, the Highlanders would muster at the House of Touch, and Charles would appear among his beloved subjects. The very medal to commemorate the event was struck, with its motto, *Laetamini Cives*. The Prince was on the coast in readiness—nay, if we are not mistaken, the Prince was in Westbrook House at Godalming!

This we conjecture because, in that very budding time of the Elibank Plot, Newcastle suddenly discovered that the unwearied Eleanor Oglethorpe, Marquise de Mézières, was in England,—had arrived secretly, without any passport. He tracked her down at Westbrook House, that lay all desolate and deserted, the windows closed, the ight-of-way through the grounds illegally shut up. General

Oglethorpe after 1746 had abandoned his home, for he had been court-martialled on a charge of not attacking Cluny and Lord George Murray, when the Highlanders stood at bay, at Clifton, and defeated Cumberland 's advanced-guard. The general was acquitted, but, retiring to his wife's house at Carham, he deserted Westbrook Place.

The empty house, retired in its woodlands, on the Portsmouth road, convenient for the coast, was the very place for Prince Charles to lurk in, while Murray and Glengarry cleared the way to the throne. And so, in fact, we find Eleanor Oglethorpe secretly ensconced at Westbrook Place while the plot ripened, and local tradition still shows the vault in which 'the Pretender ' could take refuge if the house was searched. All this, again, coincides with the vague legend of the tall, brown-haired ghost who haunts Westbrook Place,—last home of a last hope.

The young Glengarry, as we know, carried all the tale of the plot to the English Prime Minister, while he made a merit of his share in it with James at Rome. Eleanor, too, was run to earth at Westbrook Place. She held her own gallantly. As to having no passport, she reminded Newcastle that she *had* asked for a passport twelve years ago, in 1740. She was now visiting England merely to see her sister Anne, who 'could not outlast the winter, ' but who did so, none the less. Nor could Anne have been so very ill, for on arriving at Dover in October Eleanor did not hasten to Anne 's sick-bed. Far from that, she first spent an agreeable week—with whom? With my Lady Westmoreland, at Mereworth, in Kent. Now, Lord Westmoreland was the head of the English Jacobites, and at Mereworth, according to authentic family tradition, Prince Charles held his last Council on English ground. The whole plot seems delightfully transparent, and it must be remembered that in October Newcastle knew nothing of it; he only received Glengarry 's information early in November.

The letter of Madame de Mézières, with her account of her innocent proceedings, is written in French exactly like that of the Dowager Countess of Castlewood, in *Esmond*. She expressed her special pleasure in the hope of making Newcastle 's personal acquaintance. She went to Bath; she made Lady Albemarle profoundly uncomfortable about her lord 's famous mistress in Paris, and no doubt she plunged, on her return, into the plots with Prussia for a Restoration. In the Privy Council, in November 1753, her arrest was decided on. Newcastle jots down, on a paper of notes: 'To seize Madame de Mézières with her papers. No expense to be spared to find the Pretender's son. Sir John Gooderich to be sent after him. Lord Anson to have frigates on the Scotch and Irish coasts.'

By 1759 Eleanor was, perhaps, weary of conspiring. Her daughter, the Princesse de Ligne, was the fair patroness of that expedition which Hawke crushed in Quibéron Bay, while Charles received the news at Dunkirk.

All was ended. For seventy-two years the Oglethorpe women had used their wit and beauty, through three generations, for a lost cause. They were not more lucky, with the best intentions, than Eleanor's grandson, the Prince de Lambesc. With hereditary courage he rescued an old woman from a burning cottage, and flung her into a duck-pond to extinguish her blazing clothes. The old woman was drowned!

Not long ago a lady of much wit, but of no occult pretensions, and wholly ignorant of the Oglethorpes, looked over Westbrook Place, then vacant, with the idea of renting it. On entering it she said, 'I have a feeling that very interesting things have happened here'! Probably they had.[40]

XI

THE CHEVALIER D 'ÉON

THE mystery of the Chevalier d 'Éon (1728-1810), the question of his sex, on which so many thousand pounds were betted, is no mystery at all. The Chevalier was a man, and a man of extraordinary courage, audacity, resource, physical activity, industry, and wit. The real mystery is the problem why, at a mature age (forty-two) did d 'Éon take upon him, and endure for forty years, the travesty of feminine array, which could only serve him as a source of notoriety—in short, as an advertisement? The answer probably is that, having early seized opportunity by the forelock, and having been obliged, after an extraordinary struggle, to leave his hold, he was obliged to clutch at some mode of keeping himself perpetually in the public eye. Hence, probably, his persistent assumption of feminine costume. If he could be distinguished in no other way, he could shine as a mystery; there was even lucre in the pose.[41]

Charles d 'Éon was born on October 7, 1728, near Tonnerre. His family was of *chétive noblesse*, but well protected, and provided for by 'patent places. ' He was highly educated, took the degree of doctor of law, and wrote with acceptance on finance and literature. His was a studious youth, for he was as indifferent to female beauty as was Frederick the Great, and his chief amusements were fencing, of which art he was a perfect master, and society, in which his wit and gaiety made the girlish-looking lad equally welcome to men and women. All were fond of 'le petit d 'Éon, ' so audacious, so ambitious, and so amusing.

The Prince de Conti was his chief early patron, and it was originally in support of Conti 's ambition to be King of Poland that Louis XV. began his incredibly foolish 'secret '—a system of foreign policy conducted by hidden agents behind the backs of his responsible ministers at Versailles and in the Courts of Europe. The results naturally tend to recall a Gilbert and Sullivan comic opera of diplomacy. We find magnificent ambassadors gravely trying to carry out the royal orders, and thwarted by the King's secret agents. The King seems to have been too lazy to face his ministers, and compel them to take his own line, while he was energetic enough to work like Tiberius or Philip II. of Spain at his secret Penelope's task of undoing by night the warp and woof which his ministers wove by day. In these mysterious labours of his the Comte de Broglie, later a firm friend of d'Éon, was, with Tercier, one of his main assistants.

The King thus enjoyed all the pleasures and excitements of a conspirator in his own kingdom, dealing in ciphered despatches, with the usual cant names, carried in the false bottoms of snuff-boxes, precisely as if he had been a Jacobite plotter. It was entertaining, but it was not diplomacy, and, sooner or later, Louis was certain to be 'blackmailed' by some underling in his service. That underling was to be d'Éon.

In 1755 Louis wished to renew relations, long interrupted, with Elizabeth, Empress of Russia, the lady whom Prince Charlie wanted to marry, and from whose offered hand the brave James Keith fled as fast as horses could carry him. Elizabeth, in 1755, was an ally of England, but was known to be French in her personal sympathies, though she was difficult of access. As a messenger, Louis chose a Scot, described by Captain Buchan Telfer as a Mackenzie, a Jesuit, calling himself the Chevalier Douglas, and a Jacobite exile. He is not to be found in the *Dictionary of National Biography*. A Sir James and a Sir John Douglas—if both were not the same man—were employed as political agents between the English and Scottish Jacobites in 1746, and, in 1749, between the Prince and the Landgrave of Hesse. Whatever the true name of the Douglas of Louis XV., I suspect that he was one or the other of these dim Jacobites of the Douglas clan. In June 1755 this Chevalier Douglas was sent by Louis to deal with Elizabeth. He was certainly understood by Louis to be a real Douglas, a fugitive Jacobite, and he was to use in ciphered despatches precisely the same silly sort of veiled language about the fur trade as Prince Charles's envoys had just been using about 'the timber trade' with Sweden.

Douglas set forth, disguised as an intellectual British tourist, in the summer of 1755, and it is Captain Buchan Telfer's view that d'Éon joined him, also as a political agent, in female apparel, on the road, and that, while Douglas failed and left Russia by October 1755, d'Éon remained at St. Petersburg, attired as a girl, Douglas's niece, and acting as the *lectrice* of the Empress, whom he converted to the French alliance! This is the traditional theory, but is almost certainly erroneous. Sometimes, in his vast MSS., d'Éon declares that he went to Russia disguised in 1755. But he represents himself as then aged twenty, whereas he was really twenty-seven, and this he does in 1773, before he made up his mind to pose for life as a woman. He had a running claim against the French government for the expenses of his first journey to Russia. This voyage, in 1776, he dates in 1755, but in 1763, in an official letter, he dates his journey to Russia, of which the expenses were not repaid, in 1756. That is the true chronology. Nobody denies that he did visit Russia in 1756 attired as a male diplomatist, but few now believe that in 1755 he accompanied Douglas as that gentleman's pleasing young niece.

MM. Homberg and Jousselin, in their recent work,[42] declare that among d'Éon's papers, which lay for a century in the back shop of a London bookseller, they find letters to him, from June 1756, written by Tercier, who managed the secret of Louis XV. There are no known proofs of d'Éon's earlier presence in Russia, and in petticoats, in 1755.

He did talk later of a private letter of Louis XV., of October 4, 1763, in which the King wrote that he 'had served him usefully in the guise of a female, and must now resume it, ' and that letter is published, but all the evidence, to which we shall return, tends to prove that this paper is an ingenious deceptive 'interpolation. ' If the King did write it, then he was deceiving the manager of his secret policy— Tercier—for, in the note, he bids d'Éon remain in England, while he was at the same time telling Tercier that he was uneasy as to what d'Éon might do in France, when he obeyed his *public* orders to return.[43] If, then, the royal letter of October 4, 1763, testifying to d'Éon's feminine disguise in Russia, be genuine, Louis XV. had three strings to his bow. He had his public orders to ministers, he had his private conspiracy worked through Tercier, and he had his secret intrigue with d'Éon, of which Tercier was allowed to know nothing. This hypothesis is difficult, if not impossible, and the result is that d'Éon was not current in Russia as Douglas's pretty French niece and as reader to the Empress Elizabeth in 1755.

In 1756, in his own character as a man and a secretary, he did work under Douglas, then on his second visit, public and successful, to gain Russia to the French alliance; for, dismissed in October 1755, Douglas came back and publicly represented France at the Russian Court in July 1756. This was, to the highest degree of probability, d'Éon's first entrance into diplomacy, and he triumphed in his mission. He certainly made the acquaintance of the Princess Dashkoff, and she, as certainly, in 1769-1771, when on a visit to England, gave out that d'Éon was received by Elizabeth in a manner more appropriate to a woman than a man. It is not easy to ascertain precisely what the tattle of the Princess really amounted to, but d'Éon represents it so as to corroborate his tale about his residence at Elizabeth's Court, as *lectrice*, in 1755. The evidence is of no value, being a biassed third-hand report of the Russian lady's gossip. There is a mezzotint, published in 1788, from what professes to be a copy, by Angelica Kauffmann, of a portrait of d'Éon in female costume, at the age of twenty-five. If these attributions are correct, d'Éon was masquerading as a girl three years before he went to Russia, and, if the portrait is exact, was wearing the order of St. Louis ten years before it was conferred on him. The evidence as to this copy of an alleged portrait of d'Éon is full of confusions and anachronisms, and does not even prove that he thus travestied his sex in early life.

In Russia, when he joined Douglas there in the summer of 1756, d'Éon was a busy secretary of legation. In April 1757, he went back to Versailles bearing rich diplomatic sheaves with him, and one of those huge presents of money in gold, to Voltaire, which no longer come in the way of men of letters. While he was at Vienna, on his way back to St. Petersburg, tidings came of the battle of Prague; d'Éon hurried to Versailles with the news, and, though he broke his leg in a carriage accident, he beat the messenger whom Count Kaunitz officially despatched, by thirty-six hours. This unladylike proof of energy and endurance procured for d'Éon a gold snuff-box (Elizabeth only gave him a trumpery snuff-box in tortoiseshell), with the King's miniature, a good deal of money, and a commission in the dragoons, for the little man's heart was really set on a military rather than a diplomatic career. However, as diplomat he ferreted out an important secret of Russian internal treachery, and rejected a bribe of a diamond of great value. The money's worth of the diamond was to be paid to him by his own Government, but he no more got that than he got the 10,000 livres for his travelling expenses.

Thus early was he accommodated with a grievance, and because d'Éon had not the wisdom to see that a man with grievances is a ruined man, he overthrew, later, a promising career, in the violence of his attempts to obtain redress. This was d'Éon's bane, and the cause of the ruinous eccentricities for which he is remembered. In 1759 he ably seconded the egregious Louis XV. in upsetting the policy which de Choiseul was carrying on by the King's orders. De Choiseul's duty was to make the Empress mediate for peace in the Seven Years' War. The duty of d'Éon was to secure the failure of de Choiseul, without the knowledge of the French ambassador, the Marquis de l'Hospital, of whom he was the secretary. Possessed of this pretty secret, d'Éon was a man whom Louis could not safely offend and snub, and d'Éon must therefore have thought that there could scarcely be a limit to his success in life. But he disliked Russia, and left it for good in August 1760.

He received a life pension of 2,000 livres, and was appointed aide-de-camp to the Maréchal de Broglie, commanding on the Upper Rhine. He distinguished himself, in August 1761, by a very gallant piece of service in which, he says, truly or not, he incurred the ill-will of the Comte de Guerchy. The pair were destined to ruin each other a few years later. D'Éon also declares that he led a force which 'dislodged the Highland mountaineers in a gorge of the mountain at Einbeck.' I know not what Highland regiment is intended, but D'Éon's orders bear that he was to *withdraw* troops opposed to the Highlanders, and a certificate in his favour from the Duc and the Comte de Broglie does not allude to the circumstance that, instead of retreating before the plaids, he drove them back to the English camp. It may therefore be surmised that, though D'Éon often distinguished himself, and was wounded in the thigh at Ultrop, his claim of a victory over a Highland regiment is— 'an interpolation.' De Broglie writes, 'we purpose retreating. I send M. d 'Éon to withdraw the Swiss and Grenadiers of Champagne, who are holding in check the Scottish Highlanders lining the wood on the crest of the mountain, whence they have caused us much annoyance. ' The English outposts were driven in; but, after that was done, the French advance was checked by the plaided Gael: d 'Éon did not

> quell the mountaineer
> As their tinchel quells the game.

Not a word is said about his triumph even in the certificate of the two de Broglies which d 'Éon published in 1764.

In 1762, France and England, weary of war, began the preliminaries of peace, and d 'Éon was attached as secretary of legation to the French negotiator in London, the Duc de Nivernais, who was on terms so intimate with Madame de Pompadour that she addressed him, in writing, as *petit époux*. In the language of the affections as employed by the black natives of Australia, this would have meant that de Nivernais was the recognised rival of Louis XV. in the favour of the lady; but the inference must not be carried to that length. There are different versions of a trick which d 'Éon, as secretary, played on Mr. Robert Wood, author of an interesting work on Homer, and with the Jacobite *savant*, Jemmy Dawkins, the explorer of Palmyra. The story as given by Nivernais is the most intelligible account. Mr. Wood, as under secretary of state, brought to Nivernais, and read to him, a diplomatic document, but gave him no copy. D 'Éon, however, opened Wood 's portfolio, while he dined with Nivernais, and had the paper transcribed. To this d 'Éon himself adds that he had given Wood more than his 'whack, ' during dinner, of a heady wine grown in the vineyards of his native Tonnerre.

In short, the little man was so serviceable that, in the autumn of 1762, de Nivernais proposed to leave him in England, as interim Minister, after the Duc 's own return to France. 'Little d 'Éon is very active, very discreet, never curious or officious, neither distrustful nor a cause of distrust in others. ' De Nivernais was so pleased with him, and so anxious for his promotion, that he induced the British Ministers, contrary to all precedent, to send d 'Éon, instead of a British subject, to Paris with the treaty, for ratification. He then received from Louis XV. the order of St. Louis, and, as de Nivernais was weary of England, where he had an eternal cold, and resigned, d 'Éon was made minister plenipotentiary in London till the arrival of the new ambassador, de Guerchy.

Now de Guerchy, if we believe d 'Éon, had shown the better part of valour in a dangerous military task, the removal of ammunition under fire, whereas d 'Éon had certainly conducted the operation with courage and success. The two men were thus on terms of jealousy, if the story is true, while de Nivernais did not conceal from d 'Éon that he was to be the brain of the embassy, and that de Guerchy was only a dull figure-head. D 'Éon possessed letters of de Broglie and de Praslin, in which de Guerchy was spoken of with pitying contempt; in short, his despatch-boxes were magazines of dangerous diplomatic combustibles. He also succeeded in irritating de Praslin, the French minister, before returning to his new post in London, for d 'Éon was a partisan of the two de Broglies, now in the disgrace of Madame de Pompadour and of Louis XV.; though the Comte de Broglie, 'disgraced' as he was, still managed the secret policy of the French King.

D 'Éon's position was thus full of traps. He was at odds with the future ambassador, de Guerchy, and with the minister, de Praslin; and would not have been promoted at all, had it been known to the minister that he was in correspondence with, and was taking orders from, the disgraced Comte de Broglie. But, by the fatuous system of the King, d 'Éon, in fact, was doing nothing else. De Broglie, exiled from Court, was d 'Éon's real master, he did not serve de Guerchy and de Praslin, and Madame de Pompadour, who was not in the secret of her royal lover.

The King's secret now (1763) included a scheme for the invasion of England, which d 'Éon and a military agent were to organise, at the very moment when peace had been concluded. There is fairly good evidence that Prince Charles visited London in this year, no doubt with an eye to mischief. In short, the new minister plenipotentiary to St. James's, unknown to the French Government, and to the future ambassador, de Guerchy, was to manage a scheme for the ruin of the country to which he was accredited. If ever this came out, the result would be, if not war with England, at least war between Louis XV., his minister, and Madame de Pompadour, a result which frightened Louis XV. more than any other disaster.

The importance of his position now turned d 'Éon 's head, in the opinion of Horace Walpole, who, of course, had not a guess at the true nature of the situation. D 'Éon, in London, entertained French visitors of eminence, and the best English society, it appears, with the splendour of a full-blown ambassador, and at whose expense? Certainly not at his own, and neither the late ambassador, de Nivernais, nor the coming ambassador, de Guerchy, a man far from wealthy, had the faintest desire to pay the bills. Angry and tactless letters, therefore, passed between d 'Éon in London and de Guerchy, de Nivernais, and de Praslin in Paris. De Guerchy was dull and clumsy; d 'Éon used him as the whetstone of his wit, with a reckless abandonment which proves that he was, as they say, 'rather above himself, ' like Napoleon before the march to Moscow. London, in short, was the Moscow of little d 'Éon. When de Guerchy arrived, and d 'Éon was reduced to *secrétariser*, and, indeed, was ordered to return to France, and not to show himself at Court, he lost all self-control. The recall came from the minister, de Praslin, but d 'Éon, as we know, though de Praslin knew it not, was secretly representing the King himself. He declares that, at this juncture (October 11, 1763), Louis XV. sent him the extraordinary private autograph letter, speaking of his previous services in female attire, and bidding him remain with his papers in England disguised as a woman. The improbability of this action by the King has already been exposed. (Pp. 242, 243 *supra*.)

But when we consider the predicament of Louis, obliged to recall d 'Éon publicly, while all his ruinous secrets remained in the hands of that disgraced and infuriated little man, it seems not quite impossible that he may have committed the folly of writing this letter. For the public recall says nothing about the secret papers of which d 'Éon had quantities. What was to become of them, if he returned to France in disgrace? If they reached the hands of de Guerchy they meant an explosion between Louis XV. and his mistress, and his ministers. To parry the danger, then, according to d 'Éon, Louis privately bade him flee disguised, with his cargo of papers, and hide in female costume. If Louis really did this (and d 'Éon told the story to the father of Madame de Campan), he had three strings to his bow, as we have shown, and one string was concealed, a secret within a secret, even from Tercier. Yet what folly was so great as to be beyond the capacity of Louis?

Meanwhile d 'Éon simply refused to obey the King 's public orders, and denied their authenticity. They were only signed with a *griffe*, or stamp, not by the King 's pen and hand. He would not leave London. He fought de Guerchy with every kind of arm, accused him of suborning an assassin, published private letters and his own version of the affair, fled from a charge of libel, could not be extradited (by virtue of what MM. Homberg and Jousselin call 'the law of *Home Rule*! '), fortified his house, and went armed. Probably there really were designs to kidnap him, just as a regular plot was laid for the kidnapping of de la Motte, at Newcastle, after the affair of the Diamond Necklace. In 1752 a Marquis de Fratteau was collared by a sham marshal court officer, put on board a boat at Gravesend, and carried to the Bastille!

D 'Éon, under charge of libel, lived a fugitive and cloistered existence till the man who, he says, was to have assassinated him, de Vergy, sought his alliance, and accused de Guerchy of having suborned him to murder the little daredevil. A grand jury brought in a true bill against the French ambassador, and the ambassador 's butler, accused of having drugged d 'Éon, fled. But the English Government, by aid of what the Duc de Broglie calls a *noli prosequi* (*nolle* being usual), tided over a difficulty of the gravest kind. The granting of the *nolle prosequi* is denied.[44] The ambassador was mobbed and took leave of absence, and Louis XV., through de Broglie, offered to d 'Éon terms humiliating to a king. The Chevalier finally gave up the warrant for his secret mission in exchange for a pension of 12,000 livres, but he retained all other secret correspondence and plans of invasion. As for de Guerchy, he resigned (1767), and presently died of sheer annoyance, while his enemy, the Chevalier, stayed in England as London correspondent of Louis XV. He reported, in 1766, that Lord Bute was a Jacobite, and de Broglie actually took seriously the chance of restoring, by Bute 's aid,

Charles III., who had just succeeded, by the death of the Old Chevalier, to 'a kingdom not of this world.'

The death of Louis XV., in 1774, brought the folly of the secret policy to an end, but in the same year rumours about d 'Éon 's dubious sex appeared in the English newspapers on the occasion of his book, *Les Loisirs du Chevalier d 'Éon*, published at Amsterdam. Bets on his sex were made, and d 'Éon beat some bookmakers with his stick. But he persuaded Drouet, an envoy from France, that the current stories were true, and this can only be explained, if explained at all, by his perception of the fact that, his secret employment being gone, he felt the need of an advertisement. Overtures for the return of the secret papers were again made to d 'Éon, but he insisted on the restoration of his diplomatic rank, and on receiving 14,000*l*. on account of expenses. He had aimed too high, however, and was glad to come to a compromise with the famous Beaumarchais. The extraordinary bargain was struck that d 'Éon, for a consideration, should yield the secret papers, and, to avoid a duel with the son of de Guerchy, and the consequent scandal, should pretend to be a woman, and wear the dress of that sex. In his new capacity he might return to France and wear the cross of the Order of St. Louis.

Beaumarchais was as thoroughly taken in as any dupe in his own comedies. In d 'Éon he 'saw a blushing spinster, a kind of Jeanne d 'Arc of the eighteenth century, pining for the weapons and uniform of the martial sex, but yielding her secret, and forsaking her arms, in the interest of her King. On the other side the blushless captain of dragoons listened, with downcast eyes, to the sentimental compliments of Beaumarchais, and suffered himself, without a smile, to be compared to the Maid of Orleans,' says the Duc de Broglie. 'Our manners are obviously softened,' wrote Voltaire. 'D 'Éon is a Pucelle d 'Orléans who has not been burned.' To de Broglie, d 'Éon described himself as 'the most unfortunate of unfortunate females!' D 'Éon returned to France, where he found himself but a nine days ' wonder. It was observed that this *pucelle* too obviously shaved; that in the matter of muscular development she was a little Hercules; that she ran upstairs taking four steps at a stride; that her hair, like that of Jeanne d 'Arc, was *coupé en rond*, of a military shortness; and that she wore the shoes of men, with low heels, while she spoke like a grenadier! At first d 'Éon had all the social advertisement which was now his one desire, but he became a nuisance, and, by his quarrels with Beaumarchais, a scandal. In drawing-room plays he acted his English adventures with the great play-writer, whose part was highly ridiculous. Now d 'Éon pretended to desire to 'take the veil ' as a nun, now to join the troops being sent to America. He was consigned to retreat in the Castle of Dijon (1779); he had become a weariness to official mankind. He withdrew (1781-85) to privacy at Tonnerre, and then returned to London in the semblance of a bediamonded old dame, who, after dinner, did not depart with the ladies. He took part in fencing matches with great success, and in 1791 his library was sold at Christie 's, with his swords and jewels. The catalogue bears the motto, from Juvenal,

Quale decus rerum, si virginis auctio fiat,

no doubt selected by the learned little man. The snuff-box of the Empress Elizabeth, a gift to the diplomatist of 1756, fetched 2*l*. 13*s*. 6*d*.! The poor old boy was badly hurt at a fencing match in his sixty-eighth year, and henceforth lived retired from arms in the house of a Mrs. Cole, an object of charity. He might have risen to the highest places if discretion had been among his gifts, and his career proves the *quantula sapientia* of the French Government before the Revolution. In no other time or country could 'the King 's Secret ' have run a course far more incredible than even the story of the Chevalier d 'Éon.

XII

SAINT-GERMAIN THE DEATHLESS

AMONG the best brief masterpieces of fiction are Lytton 's *The Haunters and the Haunted*, and Thackeray 's *Notch on the Axe* in *Roundabout Papers*. Both deal with a mysterious being who passes through the ages, rich, powerful, always behind the scenes, coming no man knows whence, and dying, or pretending to die, obscurely— you never find authentic evidence of his decease. In other later times, at other courts, such an one reappears and runs the same course of luxury, marvel, and hidden potency.

Lytton returned to and elaborated his idea in the Margrave of *A Strange Story*, who has no 'soul, ' and prolongs his physical and intellectual life by means of an elixir. Margrave is not bad, but he is inferior to the hero, less elaborately designed, of *The Haunters and the Haunted*. Thackeray 's tale is written in a tone of mock mysticism, but he confesses that he likes his own story, in which the strange hero, through all his many lives or reappearances, and through all the countless loves on which he fatuously plumes himself, retains a slight German-Jewish accent.

It appears to me that the historic original of these romantic characters is no other than the mysterious Comte de Saint-Germain—not, of course, the contemporary and normal French soldier and minister, of 1707-1778, who bore the same name. I have found the name, with dim allusions, in the unpublished letters and MSS. of Prince Charles Edward Stuart, and have not always been certain whether the reference was to the man of action or to the man of mystery. On the secret of the latter, the deathless one, I have no new light to throw, and only speak of him for a single reason. Aristotle assures us, in his *Poetics*, that the best known myths dramatised on the Athenian stage were known to very few of the Athenian audience. It is not impossible that the story of Saint-

Germain, though it seems as familiar as the myth of Œdipus or Thyestes, may, after all, not be vividly present to the memory of every reader. The omniscient Larousse, of the *Dictionnaire Universel*, certainly did not know one very accessible fact about Saint-Germain, nor have I seen it mentioned in other versions of his legend. We read, in Larousse, 'Saint-Germain is not heard of in France before 1750, when he established himself in Paris. No adventure had called attention to his existence; it was only known that he had moved about Europe, lived in Italy, Holland, and in England, and had borne the names of Marquis de Montferrat and of Comte de Bellamye, which he used at Venice. '

Lascelles Wraxall, again, in *Remarkable Adventures* (1863), says: 'Whatever truth there may be in Saint-Germain's travels in England and the East Indies, it is indubitable that, for from 1745 to 1755, he was a man of high position in Vienna, ' while in Paris he does not appear, according to Wraxall, till 1757, having been brought from Germany by the Maréchal de Belle-Isle, whose 'old boots, ' says Macallester the spy, Prince Charles freely damned, 'because they were always stuffed with projects. ' Now we hear of Saint-Germain, by that name, as resident, not in Vienna, but in London, at the very moment when Prince Charles, evading Cumberland, who lay with his army at Stone, in Staffordshire, marched to Derby. Horace Walpole writes to Mann in Florence (December 9, 1745):

'We begin to take up people ... the other day they seized an odd man who goes by the name of Count Saint-Germain. He has been here these two years, and will not tell who he is, or whence, but professes that he does not go by his right name. He sings, plays on the violin wonderfully, composes, is mad, and not very sensible. He is called an Italian, a Spaniard, a Pole; a somebody that married a great fortune in Mexico, and ran away with her jewels to Constantinople; a priest, a fiddler, a vast nobleman. The Prince of Wales has had unsatiated curiosity about him, but in vain. However, nothing has been made out against him; he is released, and, what convinces me he is not a gentleman, stays here, and talks of his being taken up for a spy. '

Here is our earliest authentic note on Saint-Germain; a note omitted by his French students. He was in London from 1743 to 1745, under a name not his own, but that which he later bore at the Court of France. From the allusion to his jewels (those of a deserted Mexican bride?), it appears that he was already as rich in these treasures as he was afterwards, when his French acquaintances marvelled at them. As to his being 'mad,' Walpole may refer to Saint-Germain's way of talking as if he had lived in remote ages, and known famous people of the past.

Having caught this daylight glimpse of Saint-Germain in Walpole, having learned that in December 1745 he was arrested and examined as a possible Jacobite agent, we naturally expect to find contemporary official documents about his examination by the Government. Scores of such records exist, containing the questions put to, and the answers given by, suspected persons. But we vainly hunt through the Newcastle MSS. and the State Papers, Domestic, in the Record Office, for a trace of the examination of Saint-Germain. I am not aware that he has anywhere left his trail in official documents; he lives in more or less legendary memoirs, alone.

At what precise date Saint-Germain became an intimate of Louis XV., the Duc de Choiseul, Madame de Pompadour, and the Maréchal de Belle-Isle, one cannot ascertain. The writers of memoirs are the vaguest of mortals about dates; only one discerns that Saint-Germain was much about the French Court, and high in the favour of the King, having rooms at Chambord, during the Seven Years' War, and just before the time of the peace negotiations of 1762-1763. The art of compiling false or forged memoirs of that period was widely practised; but the memoirs of Madame du Hausset, who speaks of Saint-Germain, are authentic. She was the widow of a poor man of noble family, and was one of two *femmes de chambre* of Madame de Pompadour. Her manuscript was written, she explains, by aid of a brief diary which she kept during her term of service. One day M. Senac de Meilhan found Madame de Pompadour's brother, M. de Marigny, about to burn a packet of papers. 'It is the journal,' he said, 'of a *femme de chambre* of my sister, a good kind woman.' De Meilhan asked for the manuscript, which he later gave to Mr. Crawford, one of the Kilwinning family, in Ayrshire, who later helped in the escape of Louis XVI. and Marie Antoinette to Varennes, where they were captured. With the journal of Madame du Hausset were several letters to Marigny on points of historical anecdote.[45]

Crawford published the manuscript of Madame du Hausset, which he was given by de Meilhan, and the memoirs are thus from an authentic source. The author says that Louis XV. was always kind to her, but spoke little to her, whereas Madame de Pompadour remarked, 'The King and I trust you so much that we treat you like a cat or a dog, and talk freely before you.'

As to Saint-Germain, Madame du Hausset writes: 'A man who was as amazing as a witch came often to see Madame de Pompadour. This was the Comte de Saint-Germain, who wished to make people believe that he had lived for several centuries. One day Madame said to him, while at her toilet, "What sort of man was Francis I., a king whom I could have loved?" "A good sort of fellow," said Saint-Germain; "too fiery—I could have given him a useful piece of advice, but he would not have listened." He then described, in very general terms, the beauty of Mary Stuart and La Reine Margot. "You seem to have seen them all," said Madame de Pompadour, laughing. "Sometimes," said Saint-Germain, "I amuse myself, not by making people believe, but by letting them believe, that I have lived from time immemorial." "But you do not tell us your age, and you give yourself out as very old. Madame de Gergy, who was wife of the French ambassador at Venice fifty years ago, I think, says that she knew you there, and that you are not changed in the least." "It is true, madame, that I knew Madame de Gergy long ago." "But according to her story you must now be over a century old." "It may be so, but I admit that even more possibly the respected lady is in her dotage." '

At this time Saint-Germain, says Madame du Hausset, looked about fifty, was neither thin nor stout, seemed clever, and dressed simply, as a rule, but in good taste. Say that the date was 1760, Saint-Germain looked fifty; but he had looked the same age, according to Madame de Gergy, at Venice, fifty years earlier, in 1710. We see how pleasantly he left Madame de Pompadour in doubt on that point.

He pretended to have the secret of removing flaws from diamonds. The King showed him a stone valued at 6,000 francs—without a flaw it would have been worth 10,000. Saint-Germain said that he could remove the flaw in a month, and in a month he brought back the diamond—flawless. The King sent it, without any comment, to his jeweller, who gave 9,600 francs for the stone, but the King returned the money, and kept the gem as a curiosity. Probably it was not the original stone, but another cut in the same fashion, Saint-Germain sacrificing 3,000 or 4,000 francs to his practical joke. He also said that he could increase the size of pearls, which he could have proved very easily—in the same manner. He would not oblige Madame de Pompadour by giving the King an elixir of life: 'I should be mad if I gave the King a drug. ' There seems to be a reference to this desire of Madame de Pompadour in an unlikely place, a letter of Pickle the Spy to Mr. Vaughn (1754)! This conversation Madame du Hausset wrote down on the day of its occurrence.

Both Louis XV. and Madame de Pompadour treated Saint-Germain as a person of consequence. 'He is a quack, for he says he has an elixir, ' said Dr. Quesnay, with medical scepticism. 'Moreover, our master, the King, is obstinate; he sometimes speaks of Saint-Germain as a person of illustrious birth. '

The age was sceptical, unscientific, and, by reaction, credulous. The *philosophes*, Hume, Voltaire, and others, were exposing, like an ingenious American gentleman, 'the mistakes of Moses. ' The Earl Marischal told Hume that life had been chemically produced in a laboratory, so what becomes of Creation? Prince Charles, hidden in a convent, was being tutored by Mlle. Luci in the sensational philosophy of Locke, 'nothing in the intellect which does not come through the senses '—a queer theme for a man of the sword to study. But, thirty years earlier, the Regent d 'Orléans had made crystal-gazing fashionable, and stories of ghosts and second-sight in the highest circles were popular. Mesmer had not yet appeared, to give a fresh start to the old savage practice of hypnotism; Cagliostro was not yet on the scene with his free-masonry of the ancient Egyptian school. But people were already in extremes of doubt and of belief; there might be something in the elixir of life and in the philosopher 's stone; it might be possible to make precious stones chemically, and

Saint-Germain, who seemed to be over a century old at least, might have all these secrets.

Whence came his wealth in precious stones, people asked, unless from some mysterious knowledge, or some equally mysterious and illustrious birth?

He showed Madame de Pompadour a little box full of rubies, topazes, and diamonds. Madame de Pompadour called Madame du Hausset to look at them; she was dazzled, but sceptical, and made a sign to show that she thought them paste. The Count then exhibited a superb ruby, tossing aside contemptuously a cross covered with gems. 'That is not so contemptible, ' said Madame du Hausset, hanging it round her neck. The Count begged her to keep the jewel; she refused, and Madame de Pompadour backed her refusal. But Saint-Germain insisted, and Madame de Pompadour, thinking that the cross might be worth forty louis, made a sign to Madame du Hausset that she should accept. She did, and the jewel was valued at 1,500 francs—which hardly proves that the other large jewels were genuine, though Von Gleichen believed that they were, and thought the Count's cabinet of old masters very valuable.

The fingers, the watch, the snuff-box, the shoe buckles, the garter studs, the solitaires of the Count, on high days, all burned with diamonds and rubies, which were estimated, one day, at 200,000 francs. His wealth did not come from cards or swindling—no such charges are ever hinted at; he did not sell elixirs, nor prophecies, nor initiations. His habits do not seem to have been extravagant. One might regard him as a clever eccentric person, the unacknowledged child, perhaps, of some noble, who had put his capital mainly into precious stones. But Louis XV. treated him as a serious personage, and probably knew, or thought he knew, the secret of his birth. People held that he was a bastard of a king of Portugal, says Madame du Hausset. Perhaps the most ingenious and plausible theory of the birth of Saint-Germain makes him the natural son, not of a king of Portugal, but of a queen of Spain. The evidence is not evidence, but a series of surmises. Saint-Germain, on this theory, 'wrop his buth up in a mistry ' (like that of Charles James Fitzjames de la Pluche), out of regard for the character of his royal mamma. I believe this about as much as I believe that a certain Rev. Mr. Douglas, an obstreperous Covenanting minister, was a descendant of the captive Mary Stuart. However, Saint-Germain is said, like Kaspar Hauser, to have murmured of dim memories of his infancy, of diversions on magnificent terraces, and of palaces glowing beneath an azure sky. This is reported by Von Gleichen, who knew him very well, but thought him rather a quack. Possibly he meant to convey the idea that he was Moses, and that he had dwelt in the palaces of the Ramessids. The grave of the prophet was never known, and Saint-Germain may have insinuated that he began a new avatar in a cleft of Mount Pisgah; he was capable of it.

However, a less wild surmise avers that, in 1763 the secrets of his birth and the source of his opulence were known in Holland. The authority is the 'Memoirs' of Grosley (1813). Grosley was an archæologist of Troyes; he had travelled in Italy, and written an account of his travels; he also visited Holland and England,[46] and later, from a Dutchman, he picked up his information about Saint-Germain. Grosley was a Fellow of our Royal Society, and I greatly revere the authority of a F.R.S. His later years were occupied in the compilation of his Memoirs, including an account of what he did and heard in Holland, and he died in 1785. According to Grosley's account of what the Dutchman knew, Saint-Germain was the son of a princess who fled (obviously from Spain) to Bayonne, and of a Portuguese Jew dwelling in Bordeaux.

What fairy and fugitive princess can this be, whom not in vain the ardent Hebrew wooed? She was, she must have been, as Grosley saw, the heroine of Victor Hugo's *Ruy Blas*. The unhappy Charles II. of Spain, a kind of 'mammet' (as the English called the Richard II. who appeared up in Islay, having escaped from Pomfret Castle), had for his first wife a daughter of Henrietta, the favourite sister of our Charles II. This childless bride, after some ghostly years of matrimony, after being exorcised in disgusting circumstances, died in February 1689. In May 1690 a new bride, Marie de Neubourg, was brought to the grisly side of the crowned mammet of Spain. She, too, failed to prevent the wars of the Spanish Succession by giving an heir to the Crown of Spain. Scandalous chronicles aver that Marie was chosen as Queen of Spain for the levity of her character, and that the Crown was expected, as in the Pictish monarchy, to descend on the female side; the father of the prince might be anybody. What was needed was simply a son of the *Queen* of Spain. She had, while Queen, no son, as far as is ascertained, but she had a favourite, a Count Andanero, whom she made minister of finance. 'He was not a born Count, ' he was a financier, this favourite of the Queen of Spain. That lady did go to live in Bayonne in 1706, six years after the death of Charles II., her husband. The hypothesis is, then, that Saint-Germain was the son of this ex-Queen of Spain, and of the financial Count, Andanero, a man, 'not born in the sphere of Counts, 'and easily transformed by tradition into a Jewish banker of Bordeaux. The Duc de Choiseul, who disliked the intimacy of Louis XV. and of the Court with Saint-Germain, said that the Count was 'the son of a Portuguese Jew, *who deceives the Court*. It is strange that the King is so often allowed to be almost alone with this man, though, when he goes out, he is surrounded by guards, as if he feared assassins everywhere. ' This anecdote is from the 'Memoirs ' of Gleichen, who had seen a great deal of the world. He died in 1807.

It seems a fair inference that the Duc de Choiseul knew what the Dutch bankers knew, the story of the Count 's being a child of a princess retired to Bayonne—namely, the ex-Queen of Spain—and of a Portuguese-Hebrew financier. De Choiseul was ready to accept the Jewish father, but thought that, in the matter of the royal mother, Saint-Germain 'deceived the Court. '

A queen of Spain might have carried off any quantity of the diamonds of Brazil. The presents of diamonds from her almost idiotic lord must have been among the few comforts of her situation in a Court overridden by etiquette. The reader of Madame d 'Aulnoy 's contemporary account of the Court of Spain knows what a dreadful dungeon it was. Again, if born at Bayonne about 1706, the Count would naturally seem to be about fifty in 1760. The purity with which he spoke German, and his familiarity with German princely Courts—where I do not remember that Barry Lyndon ever met him—are easily accounted for if he had a royal German to his mother. But, alas! if he was the son of a Hebrew financier, Portuguese or Alsatian (as some said), he was likely, whoever his mother may have been, to know German, and to be fond of precious stones. That Oriental taste notoriously abides in the hearts of the Chosen People.

> Nay, never shague your gory locks at me,
> Dou canst not say I did it.

quotes Pinto, the hero of Thackeray's *Notch on the Axe*. 'He pronounced it, by the way, I *dit* it, by which I *know* that Pinto was a German,' says Thackeray. I make little doubt but that Saint-Germain, too, was a German, whether by the mother's side, and of princely blood, or quite the reverse.

Grosley mixes Saint-Germain up with a lady as mysterious as himself, who also lived in Holland, on wealth of an unknown source, and Grosley inclines to think that the Count found his way into a French prison, where he was treated with extraordinary respect.

Von Gleichen, on the other hand, shows the Count making love to a daughter of Madame Lambert, and lodging in the house of the mother. Here Von Gleichen met the man of mystery and became rather intimate with him. Von Gleichen deemed him very much older than he looked, but did not believe in his elixir.

In any case, he was not a cardsharper, a swindler, a professional medium, or a spy. He passed many evenings almost alone with Louis XV., who, where men were concerned, liked them to be of good family (about ladies he was much less exclusive). The Count had a grand manner; he treated some great personages in a cavalier way, as if he were at least their equal. On the whole, if not really the son of a princess, he probably persuaded Louis XV. that he did come of that blue blood, and the King would have every access to authentic information. Horace Walpole's reasons for thinking Saint-Germain 'not a gentleman' scarcely seem convincing.

The Duc de Choiseul did not like the fashionable Saint-Germain. He thought him a humbug, even when the doings of the deathless one were perfectly harmless. As far as is known, his recipe for health consisted in drinking a horrible mixture called 'senna tea'—which was administered to small boys when I was a small boy—and in not drinking anything at his meals. Many people still observe this regimen, in the interest, it is said, of their figures. Saint-Germain used to come to the house of de Choiseul, but one day, when Von Gleichen was present, the minister lost his temper with his wife. He observed that she took no wine at dinner, and told her she had learned that habit of abstinence from Saint-Germain; that *he* might do as he pleased, 'but you, madame, whose health is precious to me, I forbid to imitate the regimen of such a dubious character.' Gleichen, who tells the anecdote, says that he was present when de Choiseul thus lost his temper with his wife. The dislike of de Choiseul had a mournful effect on the career of Saint-Germain.

In discussing the strange story of the Chevalier d'Éon, we have seen that Louis XV. amused himself by carrying on a secret scheme of fantastic diplomacy through subordinate agents, behind the backs and without the knowledge of his responsible ministers. The Duc de Choiseul, as Minister of Foreign Affairs, was excluded, it seems, from all knowledge of these double intrigues, and the Maréchal de Belle-Isle, Minister of War, was obviously kept in the dark, as was Madame de Pompadour. Now it is stated by Von Gleichen that the Maréchal de Belle-Isle, from the War Office, started a *new* secret diplomacy behind the back of de Choiseul, at the Foreign Office. The King and Madame de Pompadour (who was not initiated into the general scheme of the King's secret) were both acquainted with what de Choiseul was not to know—namely, Belle-Isle's plan for secretly making peace through the mediation, or management, at all events, of Holland. All this must have been prior to the death of the Maréchal de Belle-Isle in 1761; and probably de Broglie, who managed the regular old secret policy of Louis XV., knew nothing about this new clandestine adventure; at all events, the late Duc de Broglie says nothing about it in his book *The King's Secret*.[47]

The story, as given by Von Gleichen, goes on to say that Saint-Germain offered to conduct the intrigue at the Hague. As Louis XV. certainly allowed that maidenly captain of dragoons, d'Éon, to manage his hidden policy in London, it is not at all improbable that he really entrusted this fresh cabal in Holland to Saint-Germain, whom he admitted to great intimacy. To the Hague went Saint-Germain, diamonds, rubies, senna tea, and all, and began to diplomatise with the Dutch. But the regular French minister at the

Hague, d 'Affry, found out what was going on behind his back—found it out either because he was sharper than other ambassadors, or because a personage so extraordinary as Saint-Germain was certain to be very closely watched, or because the Dutch did not take to the Undying One, and told d 'Affry what he was doing. D 'Affry wrote to de Choiseul. An immortal but dubious personage, he said, was treating, in the interests of France, for peace, which it was d 'Affry's business to do if the thing was to be done at all. Choiseul replied in a rage by the same courier. Saint-Germain, he said, must be extradited, bound hand and foot, and sent to the Bastille. Choiseul thought that he might practise his regimen and drink his senna tea, to the advantage of public affairs, within those venerable walls. Then the angry minister went to the King, told him what orders he had given, and said that, of course, in a case of this kind it was superfluous to inquire as to the royal pleasure. Louis XV. Was caught; so was the Maréchal de Belle-Isle. They blushed and were silent.

It must be remembered that this report of a private incident could only come to the narrator, Von Gleichen, from de Choiseul, with whom he professes to have been intimate. The King and the Maréchal de Belle-Isle would not tell the story of their own discomfiture. It is not very likely that de Choiseul himself would blab. However, the anecdote avers that the King and the Minister for War thought it best to say nothing, and the demand for Saint-Germain's extradition was presented at the Hague. But the Dutch were not fond of giving up political offenders. They let Saint-Germain have a hint; he slipped over to London, and a London paper published a kind of veiled interview with him in June 1760.

His name, we read, when announced after his death, will astonish the world more than all the marvels of his life. He has been in England already (1743-17—?); he is a great unknown. Nobody can accuse him of anything dishonest or dishonourable. When he was here before we were all mad about music, and so he enchanted us with his violin. But Italy knows him as an expert in the plastic arts, and Germany admires in him a master in chemical science. In France, where he was supposed to possess the secret of the transmutation of metals, the police for two years sought and failed to find any normal source of his opulence. A lady of forty-five once swallowed a whole bottle of his elixir. Nobody recognised her, for she had become a girl of sixteen without observing the transformation!

Saint-Germain is said to have remained in London but for a short period. Horace Walpole does not speak of him again, which is odd, but probably the Count did not again go into society. Our information, mainly from Von Gleichen, becomes very misty, a thing of surmises, really worthless. The Count is credited with a great part in the palace conspiracies of St. Petersburg; he lived at Berlin, and, under the name of Tzarogy, at the Court of the Margrave of Anspach. Thence he went, they say, to Italy, and then north to the Landgrave, Charles of Hesse, who dabbled in alchemy. Here he is said to have died about 1780-85, leaving his papers to the Landgrave; but all is very vague after he disappeared from Paris in 1760. When next I meet Saint-Germain he is again at Paris, again mysteriously rich, again he rather disappears than dies, he calls himself Major Fraser, and the date is in the last years of Louis Philippe. My authority may be cavilled at; it is that of the late ingenious Mr. Van Damme, who describes Major Fraser in a book on the characters of the Second Empire. He does not seem to have heard of Saint-Germain, whom he does not mention.

Major Fraser, 'in spite of his English (*sic*) name, was decidedly not English, though he spoke the language. ' He was (like Saint-Germain) 'one of the best dressed men of the period.... He lived alone, and never alluded to his parentage. He was always flush of money, though the sources of his income were a mystery to every one. ' The French police vainly sought to detect the origin of Saint-Germain 's supplies, opening his letters at the post-office. Major Fraser 's knowledge of every civilised country at every period was marvellous, though he had very few books. 'His memory was something prodigious.... Strange to say, he used often to hint that his was no mere book knowledge. '"Of course, it is perfectly ridiculous," ' he remarked, with a strange smile, '"but every now and then I feel as if this did not come to me from reading, but from personal experience. At times I become almost convinced that I lived with Nero, that I knew Dante personally, and so forth." '[48] At the major's death not a letter was found giving a clue to his antecedents, and no money was discovered. *Did* he die? As in the case of Saint-Germain, no date is given. The author had an idea that the major was 'an illegitimate son of some exalted person' of the period of Charles IV. and Ferdinand VII. of Spain.

The author does not mention Saint-Germain, and may never have heard of him. If his account of Major Fraser is not mere romance, in that warrior we have the undying friend of Louis XV. and Madame de Pompadour. He had drunk at Medmenham with Jack Wilkes; as Riccio he had sung duets with the fairest of unhappy queens; he had extracted from Blanche de Béchamel the secret of Goby de Mouchy. As Pinto, he told much of his secret history to Mr. Thackeray, who says: 'I am rather sorry to lose him after three little bits of *Roundabout Papers.*'

Did Saint-Germain really die in a palace of Prince Charles of Hesse about 1780-85? Did he, on the other hand, escape from the French prison where Grosley thought he saw him, during the French Revolution? Was he known to Lord Lytton about 1860? Was he then Major Fraser? Is he the mysterious Muscovite adviser of the Dalai Lama? Who knows? He is a will-o'-the-wisp of the memoir-writers of the eighteenth century. Whenever you think you have a chance of finding him in good authentic State papers, he gives you the slip; and if his existence were not vouched for by Horace Walpole, I should incline to deem of him as Betsy Prig thought of Mrs. Harris.

> NOTE.—Since the publication of these essays I have learned, through the courtesy of a Polish nobleman, that there was nothing mysterious in the origin and adventures of the Major Fraser mentioned in pp. 274-276. He was of the Saltoun family, and played a part in the civil wars of Spain during the second quarter of the nineteenth century. Major Fraser was known, in Paris, to the father of my Polish correspondent.

XIII

THE MYSTERY OF THE KIRKS

No historical problem has proved more perplexing to Englishmen than the nature of the differences between the various Kirks in Scotland. The Southron found that, whether he worshipped in a church of the Established Kirk ('The Auld Kirk '), of the Free Church, or of the United Presbyterian Church (the U.P. 's), it was all the same thing. The nature of the service was exactly similar, though sometimes the congregation stood at prayers, and sat when it sang; sometimes stood when it sang and knelt at prayer. Not one of the Kirks used a prescribed liturgy. I have been in a Free Kirk which had no pulpit; the pastor stood on a kind of raised platform, like a lecturer in a lecture-room, but that practice is unessential. The Kirks, if I mistake not, have different collections of hymns, which, till recent years, were contemned as 'things of human invention, ' and therefore 'idolatrous. ' But hymns are now in use, as also are organs, or harmoniums, or other musical instruments. Thus the faces of the Kirks are similar and sisterly:

> Facies non omnibus una
> Nec diversa tamen, qualem decet esse sororum.

What, then, the Southron used to ask, *is* the difference between the Free Church, the Established Church, and the United Presbyterian Church? If the Southron put the question to a Scottish friend, the odds were that the Scottish friend could not answer. He might be a member of the Scottish 'Episcopal ' community, and as ignorant as any Anglican. Or he might not have made these profound studies in Scottish history, which throw glimmerings of light on this obscure subject.

Indeed, the whole aspect of the mystery has shifted, of late, like the colours in a kaleidoscope. The more conspicuous hues are no longer 'Auld Kirk, ' 'Free Kirk, ' and 'U.P. 's, ' but 'Auld Kirk, ' 'Free

Kirk,' and 'United Free Kirk. ' The United Free Kirk was composed in 1900 of the old 'United Presbyterians ' (as old as 1847), with the overwhelming majority of the old Free Kirk, while the Free Kirk, of the present moment, consists of a tiny minority of the old Free Kirk, which declined to join the recent union. By a judgment (one may well call it a 'judgment ') of the House of Lords (August 1, 1904), the Free Kirk, commonly called 'The Wee Frees, ' now possesses the wealth that was the old Free Kirk 's before, in 1900, it united with the United Presbyterians, and became the United Free Church. It is to be hoped that common sense will discover some 'outgait, ' or issue, from this distressing imbroglio. In the words which Mr. R.L. Stevenson, then a sage of twenty-four, penned in 1874, we may say 'Those who are at all open to a feeling of national disgrace look forward eagerly to such a possibility; they have been witnesses already too long to the strife that has divided this small corner of Christendom. ' The eternal schisms of the Kirk, said R.L.S., exhibit 'something pitiful for the pitiful man, but bitterly humorous for others. '

The humour of the present situation is only too manifest. Two generations ago about half of the ministers of the Kirk of Scotland left their manses and pleasant glebes for the sake of certain ideas. Of these ideas they abandoned some, or left them in suspense, a few years since, and, as a result, they have lost, if only for the moment, their manses, stipends, colleges, and pleasant glebes.

Why should all these things be so? The answer can only be found in the history—and a history both sad and bitterly humorous it is—of the Reformation in Scotland. When John Knox died, on November 24, 1572, a decent burgess of Edinburgh wrote in his Diary, 'John Knox, minister, deceased, who had, as was alleged, the most part of the blame of all the sorrows of Scotland, since the slaughter of the late Cardinal, ' Beaton, murdered at St. Andrews in 1546. 'The sorrows of Scotland ' had endured when Knox died for but twenty-six years. Since his death, 332 years have gone by, and the present sorrows of the United Free Kirk are the direct, though distant, result of some of the ideas of John Knox.

The whole trouble springs from his peculiar notions, and the notions of his followers, about the relations between Church and State. In 1843, half the ministers of the Established Kirk in Scotland, or more, left the Kirk, and went into the wilderness for what they believed to be the ideal of Knox. In 1904 they have again a prospect of a similar exodus, because they are no longer rigid adherents of the very same ideal! A tiny minority of some twenty-seven ministers clings to what it considers to be the Knoxian ideal, and is rewarded by all the wealth bestowed on the Free Kirk by pious benefactors during sixty years.

The quarrel, for 344 years (1560-1904), has been, we know, about the relations of Church and State. The disruption of 1843, the departure of the Free Kirk out of the Established Kirk, arose thus, according to Lord Macnaghten, who gave one of the two opinions in favour of the United Free Kirk's claim to the possessions held by the Free Kirk before its union, in 1900, with the United Presbyterians. Before 1843, there were, says the sympathetic judge, two parties in the Established Church—the 'Moderates' and the 'Evangelicals' (also called 'The Wild Men', 'the Highland Host' or the 'High Flyers'). The Evangelicals became the majority and 'they carried matters with a high hand. They passed Acts in the Assembly ... altogether beyond the competence of a Church established by law.... The State refused to admit their claims. The strong arm of the law restrained their extravagances. Still they maintained that their proceedings were justified, and required by the doctrine of the Headship of Christ ... to which they attached peculiar and extraordinary significance.'

Now the State, in 1838-1843, could not and would not permit these 'extravagancies' in a State-paid Church. The Evangelical party therefore seceded, maintaining, as one of their leaders said, that 'we are still the Church of Scotland, the only Church that deserves the name, the only Church that can be known and recognised by the maintaining of those principles to which the Church of our fathers was true when she was on the mountain and on the field, when she was under persecution, when she was an outcast from the world.'

Thus the Free Kirk was *the* Kirk, and the Established Kirk was heretical, was what Knox would have called 'ane rottin Laodicean.'

Now the fact is that the Church of Scotland had been, since August 1560, a Kirk established by law (or by what was said to be a legal Parliament), yet had never, perhaps, for an hour attained its own full ideal relation to the State; had never been granted its entire claims, but only so much or so little of these as the political situation compelled the State to concede, or enabled it to withdraw. There had always been members of the Kirk who claimed all that the Free Kirk claimed in 1843; but they never got quite as much as they asked; they often got much less than they wanted; and the full sum of their desires could be granted by no State to a State-paid Church. Entire independence could be obtained only by cutting the Church adrift from the State. The Free Kirk, then, did cut themselves adrift, but they kept on maintaining that they were *the* Church of Scotland, and that the State *ought* in duty to establish and maintain *them*, while granting them absolute independence.

The position was stated thus, in 1851, by an Act and Declaration of the Free Kirk's Assembly: 'She holds still, *and through God's grace ever will hold*, that it is the duty of civil rulers to recognise the truth of God according to His word, and to promote and support the Kingdom of Christ without assuming any jurisdiction in it, or any power over it....'

The State, in fact, if we may speak carnally, ought to pay the piper, but must not presume to call the tune.

Now we touch the skirt of the mystery, what was the difference between the Free Kirk and the United Presbyterians, who, since 1900, have been blended with that body? The difference was that the Free Kirk held it to be the duty of the State to establish *her*, and leave her perfect independence; while the United Presbyterians maintained the absolutely opposite opinion—namely, that the State cannot, and must not, establish any Church, or pay any Church out of the national resources. When the two Kirks united, in 1900, then, the Free Kirk either abandoned the doctrine of which, in 1851, she said that 'she holds it still, and through God's grace ever will hold it,' or she regarded it as a mere pious opinion, which did not prevent her from coalescing with a Kirk of contradictory ideas. The tiny minority—the Wee Frees, the Free Kirk of to-day—would not accept this compromise, 'hence these tears, ' to leave differences in purely metaphysical theology out of view.

Now the root of all the trouble, all the schisms and sufferings of more than three centuries, lies, as we have said, in some of the ideas of John Knox, and one asks, of what Kirk would John Knox be, if he were alive in the present state of affairs? I venture to think that the venerable Reformer would be found in the ranks of the Established Kirk, 'the Auld Kirk. ' He would not have gone out into the wilderness in 1843, and he would most certainly have opposed the ideas of the United Presbyterians. This theory may surprise at a first glance, but it has been reached after many hours of earnest consideration.

Knox 's ideas, as far as he ever reasoned them out, reposed on this impregnable rock, namely that Calvinism, as held by himself, was an absolutely certain thing in every detail. If the State or 'the civil magistrate, ' as he put the case, entirely agreed with Knox, then Knox was delighted that the State should regulate religion. The magistrate was to put down Catholicism, and other aberrations from the truth as it was in John Knox, with every available engine of the law, corporal punishment, prison, exile, and death. If the State was ready and willing to do all this, then the State was to be implicitly obeyed in matters of religion, and the power in its hands was God-given—in fact, the State was the secular aspect of the Church. Looking at the State in this ideal aspect, Knox writes about the obedience due to the magistrate in matters religious, after the manner of what, in this country, would be called the fiercest 'Erastianism. ' The State 'rules the roast ' in all matters of religion and may do what Laud and Charles I. perished in attempting, may alter forms of worship— always provided that the State absolutely agrees with the Kirk.

Thus, under Edward VI., Knox would have desired the secular power in England, the civil magistrate, to forbid people to kneel at the celebration of the Sacrament. *That* was entirely within the competence of the State, simply and solely because Knox desired that people should *not* kneel. But when, long after Knox 's death, the civil magistrate insisted, in Scotland, that people should kneel, the upholders of Knox 's ideas denied that the magistrate (James VI.)

had any right to issue such an order, and they refused to obey while remaining within the Established Church. They did not 'disrupt,' like the Free Church; they simply acted as they pleased, and denounced their obedient brethren as no 'lawful ministers.' The end of it all was that they stirred up the Civil War, in which the first shot was fired by the legendary Jenny Geddes, throwing her stool at the reader in St. Giles's. Thus we see that the State was to be obeyed in matters of religion, when the State did the bidding of the Kirk, and not otherwise. When first employed as a 'licensed preacher,' and agent of the State in England, Knox accepted just as much of the State's liturgy as he pleased; the liturgy ordered the people to kneel, Knox and his Berwick congregation disobeyed. With equal freedom, he and the other royal chaplains, at Easter, preaching before the King, denounced his ministers, Northumberland and the rest. Knox spoke of them in his sermon as Judas, Shebna, and some other scriptural malignants. Later he said that he repented having put things so mildly; he ought to have called the ministers by their names, not veiled things in a hint. Now we cannot easily conceive a chaplain of her late Majesty, in a sermon preached before her, denouncing the Chancellor of the Exchequer, say Mr. Gladstone, as 'Judas.' Yet Knox, a licensed preacher of a State Church, indulged his 'spiritual independence' to that extent, and took shame to himself that he had not gone further.

Obviously, if this is 'Erastianism,' it is of an unusual kind. The idea of Knox is that in a Catholic State the ruler is not to be obeyed in religious matters by the true believers; sometimes Knox wrote that the Catholic ruler ought to be met by 'passive resistance;' sometimes that he ought to be shot at sight. He stated these diverse doctrines in the course of eighteen months. In a Protestant country, the Catholics must obey the Protestant ruler, or take their chances of prison, exile, fire and death. The Protestant ruler, in a Protestant State, is to be obeyed, in spiritual matters, by Protestants, just as far as the Kirk may happen to approve of his proceedings, or even further, in practice, if there is no chance of successful resistance.

We may take it that Knox, if he had been alive and retained his old ideas in 1843, would not have gone out of the Established Church with the Free Church, because, in his time, he actually did submit to many State regulations of which he did not approve. For example, he certainly did not approve of bishops, and had no bishops in the Kirk as established on his model in 1560. But, twelve years later, bishops were reintroduced by the State, in the person of the Regent Morton, a ruffian, and Knox did not retire to 'the mountain and the fields,' but made the most practical efforts to get the best terms possible for the Kirk. He was old and outworn, and he remained in the Established Kirk, and advised no man to leave it. It was his theory, again, as it was that of the Free Kirk, that there should be no 'patronage,' no presentation of ministers to cures by the patron. The congregations were to choose and 'call' any properly qualified person, at their own pleasure, as they do now in all the Kirks, including (since 1874) the Established Church. But the State, in Knox's lifetime, overrode this privilege of the Church. The most infamous villain of the period, Archibald Douglas, was presented to the Kirk of Glasgow, and, indeed, the nobles made many such presentations of unscrupulous and ignorant cadets to important livings. Morton gave a bishopric to one of the murderers of Riccio! Yet Knox did not advise a secession; he merely advised that non-residence, or a scandalous life, or erroneous doctrine, on the part of the person presented, should make his presentation 'null and of no force or effect, and this to have place also in the nomination of the bishops.' Thus Knox was, on occasion, something of an opportunist. If alive in 1843, he would probably have remained in the Establishment, and worked for that abolition of 'patronage' which was secured, from within, in 1874. If this conjecture is right the Free Kirk was more Knoxian than John Knox, and departed from his standard. He was capable of sacrificing a good deal of 'spiritual independence' rather than break with the State. Many times, long after he was dead, the National Church, under stress of circumstances, accepted compromises.

Knox knew the difference between the ideal and the practical. It was the ideal that all non-convertible Catholics 'should die the death.' But the ideal was never made real; the State was not prepared to oblige the Kirk in this matter. It was the ideal that any of 'the brethren,' conscious of a vocation, and seeing a good opportunity, should treat an impenitent Catholic ruler as Jehu treated Jezebel. But if any brother had consulted Knox as to the propriety of assassinating Queen Mary, in 1561-67, he would have found out his mistake, and probably have descended the Reformer's stairs much more rapidly than he mounted them.

Yet Knox, though he could submit to compromise, really had a remarkably mystical idea of what the Kirk was, and of the attributes of her clergy. The editor of *The Free Church Union Case*, Mr. Taylor Innes (himself author of a biography of the Reformer), writes, in his preface to *The Judgment of the House of Lords*: 'The Church of Scotland, as a Protestant Church, had its origin in the year 1560, for its first Confession dates from August, and its first Assembly from December in that year. ' In fact, the Confession was accepted and passed as law, by a very dubiously legal Convention of the Estates, in August 1560. But Knox certainly conceived that the Protestant Church *in*, if not *of*, Scotland existed a year before that date, and before that date it possessed 'the power of the Keys ' and even, it would perhaps seem, 'the power of the Sword. ' To his mind, as soon as a local set of men of his own opinions met, and chose a pastor and preacher, who also administered the Sacraments, the Protestant Church was 'a Church in being. ' The Catholic Church, then by law established, was, Knox held, no Church at all; her priests were not 'lawful ministers, ' her Pope was the man of Sin *ex officio*, and the Church was 'the Kirk of the malignants '— 'a lady of pleasure in Babylon bred. '

On the other hand, the real Church—it might be of but 200 men—was confronting the Kirk of the malignants, and alone was genuine. The State did not make and could not unmake 'the Trew Church, ' but was bound to establish, foster, *and obey it*.

It was this last proviso which caused 130 years of bloodshed and 'persecution ' and general unrest in Scotland, from 1559 to 1690. Why was the Kirk so often out 'in the heather, ' and hunted like a partridge on the field and the mountain? The answer is that when the wilder spirits of the Kirk were not being persecuted they were persecuting the State and bullying the individual subject. All this arose from Knox's idea of the Church. To constitute a Church no more was needed than a local set of Calvinistic Protestants and 'a lawful minister. ' To constitute a lawful minister, at first (later far more was required), no more was needed than a 'call ' to a preacher from a local set of Calvinistic Protestants. But, when once the 'call' was given and accepted, that 'lawful minister' was, by the theory, as superior to the laws of the State as the celebrated emperor was superior to grammar. A few 'lawful ministers' of this kind possessed 'the power of the Keys;' they could hand anybody over to Satan by excommunicating the man, and (apparently) they could present 'the power of the Sword' to any town council, which could then decree capital punishment against any Catholic priest who celebrated Mass, as, by the law of the State, he was in duty bound to do. Such were the moderate and reasonable claims of Knox's Kirk in May 1559, even before it was accepted by the Convention of Estates in August 1560. It was because, not the Church, but the wilder spirits among the ministers, persevered in these claims, that the State, when it got the chance, drove them into moors and mosses and hanged not a few of them.

I have never found these facts fully stated by any historian or by any biographer of Knox, except by the Reformer himself, partly in his *History*, partly in his letters to a lady of his acquaintance. The mystery of the Kirks turns on the Knoxian conception of the 'lawful minister,' and his claim to absolutism.

To give examples, Knox himself, about 1540-43, was 'a priest of the altar,' 'one of Baal's shaven sort.' On that score he later claimed nothing. After the murder of Cardinal Beaton, the murderers and their associates, forming a congregation in the Castle of St. Andrews, gave Knox a call to be their preacher. He was now 'a lawful minister.' In May 1559 he, with about four or five equally lawful ministers, two of them converted friars, one of them a baker, and one, Harlow, a tailor, were in company with their Protestant backers, who destroyed the monasteries in Perth, and the altars and ornaments of the church there. They at once claimed 'the power of the Keys,' and threatened to excommunicate such of their allies as did not join them in arms. They, 'the brethren,' also denounced capital punishment against any priest who celebrated Mass at Perth. Now the lawful ministers could not think of hanging the priests themselves. They must therefore have somehow bestowed 'the power of the Sword' on the baillies and town council of Perth, I presume, for the Regent, Mary of Guise, when she entered the town, dismissed these men from office, which was regarded as an unlawful and perfidious act on her part. Again, in the summer of 1560, the baillies of Edinburgh—while Catholicism was still by law established—denounced the death penalty against recalcitrant Catholics. The Kirk also allotted lawful ministers to several of the large towns, and thus established herself before she was established by the Estates in August 1560. Thus nothing could be more free, and more absolute, than the Kirk in her early bloom. On the other hand, as we saw, even in Knox's lifetime, the State, having the upper hand under the Regent Morton, a strong man, introduced prelacy of a modified kind and patronage; did not restore to the Kirk her 'patrimony,'—the lands of the old Church; and only hanged one priest, not improbably for a certain reason of a private character.

There was thus, from the first, a battle between the Protestant Church and State. At various times one preacher is said to have declared that he was the solitary 'lawful minister' in Scotland; and one of these men, Mr. Cargill, excommunicated Charles II.; while another, Mr. Renwick, denounced a war of assassination against the Government. Both gentlemen were hanged.

These were extreme assertions of 'spiritual independence,' and the Kirk, or at least the majority of the preachers, protested against such conduct, which might be the logical development of the doctrine of the 'lawful minister,' but was, in practice, highly inconvenient. The Kirk, as a whole, was loyal.

Sometimes the State, under a strong man like Morton, or James Stewart, Earl of Arran (a thoroughpaced ruffian), put down these pretensions of the Church. At other times, as when Andrew Melville led the Kirk, under James VI., she maintained that there was but one king in Scotland, Christ, and that the actual King, the lad, James VI., was but 'Christ's silly vassal.' He was supreme in temporal matters, but the judicature of the Church was supreme in spiritual matters.

This sounds perfectly fair, but who was to decide what matters were spiritual and what were temporal? The Kirk assumed the right to decide that question; consequently it could give a spiritual colour to any problem of statesmanship: for example, a royal marriage, trade with Catholic Spain, which the Kirk forbade, or the expulsion of the Catholic peers. 'There is a judgment above yours, ' said the Rev. Mr. Pont to James VI., 'and that is God 's; *put in the hand of the ministers,* for "we shall judge the angels," saith the apostle. ' Again, '"Ye shall sit upon twelve thrones and judge" ' (quoted Mr. Pont), 'which is chiefly referred to the apostles, and consequently to ministers. '

Things came to a head in 1596. The King asked the representatives of the Kirk whether he might call home certain earls, banished for being Catholics, if they 'satisfied the Kirk. ' The answer was that he might not. Knox had long before maintained that 'a prophet ' might preach treason (he is quite explicit), and that the prophet, and whoever carried his preaching into practical effect, would be blameless. A minister was accused, at this moment, of preaching libellously, and he declined to be judged except by men of his own cloth. If they acquitted him, as they were morally certain to do, what Court of Appeal could reverse the decision of men who claimed to 'judge angels '? A riot arose in Edinburgh, the King seized his opportunity, he grasped his nettle, the municipal authorities backed him, and, in effect, the claims of true ministers thenceforth gave little trouble till the folly of Charles I. led to the rise of the Covenant. The Sovereign had overshot his limits of power as wildly as ever the Kirk had tried to do, and the result was that the Kirk, having now the nobles and the people in arms on her side, was absolutely despotic for about twelve years. Her final triumph was to resist the Estates in Parliament, with success, and to lay Scotland open to the Cromwellian conquest. What Plantagenets and Tudors could never do Noll effected, he conquered Scotland, the Kirk having paralysed the State. The preachers found that Cromwell was a perfect 'Malignant, ' that he would not suffer prophets to preach treason, nor even allow the General Assembly to meet. Angels they might judge if they pleased, but not Ironsides; excommunication and 'Kirk discipline ' were discountenanced; even witches were less frequently burned. The preachers, Cromwell said, 'had done their do, ' had shot their bolt.

At this time they split into two parties: the Extremists, calling themselves 'the godly, ' and the men of milder mood.

Charles II., at the Restoration, ought probably to have sided with the milder party, some of whom were anxious to see their fierce brethren banished to Orkney, out of the way. But Charles's motto was 'Never again,' and by a pettifogging fraud he reintroduced bishops without the hated liturgy. After years of risings and suppressions the ministers were brought to submission, accepting an 'indulgence' from the State, while but a few upholders of the old pretensions of the clergy stood out in the wildernesses of South-western Scotland. There might be three or four such ministers, there might be only one, but they, or he, to the mind of 'the Remnant,' were the only 'lawful ministers.' At the Revolution of 1688-89 the Remnant did not accept the compromise under which the Presbyterian Kirk was re-established. They stood out, breaking into many sects; the spiritual descendants of most of these blended into one body as 'The United Presbyterian Kirk' in 1847. In the Established Kirk the Moderates were in the majority till about 1837, when the inheritors of those extreme views which Knox compromised about, and which the majority of ministers disclaimed before the Revolution of 1688, obtained the upper hand. They had planted the remotest parishes of the Highlands with their own kind of ministers, who swamped, in 1838, the votes of the Lowland Moderates, exactly as, under James VI., Highland 'Moderates' had swamped the votes of the Lowland Extremists. The majority of Extremists, or most of it, left the Kirk in 1843, and made the Free Kirk. In 1900, when the Free Kirk joined the United Presbyterians, it was Highland ministers, mainly, who formed the minority of twenty-seven, or so, who would not accept the new union, and now constitute the actual Free Kirk, or Wee Frees, and possess the endowments of the old Free Kirk of 1843. We can scarcely say *Beati possidentes*.

It has been shown, or I have tried, erroneously or not, to show that, wild and impossible as were the ideal claims of Knox, of Andrew Melville, of Mr. Pont, and others, the old Scottish Kirk of 1560, by law established, was capable of giving up or suppressing these claims, even under Knox, and even while the Covenant remained in being. The mass of the ministers, after the return of Charles II. before Worcester fight, before bloody Dunbar, were not irreconcilables. The Auld Kirk, the Kirk Established, has some right to call herself the Church of Scotland by historical continuity, while the opposite claimants, the men of 1843, may seem rather to descend from people like young Renwick, the last hero who died for their ideas, but not, in himself, the only 'lawful minister' between Tweed and Cape Wrath. 'Other times, other manners.' All the Kirks are perfectly loyal; now none persecutes; interference with private life, 'Kirk discipline,' is a vanishing minimum; and, but for this recent 'garboil' (as our old writers put it) we might have said that, under differences of nomenclature, all the Kirks are united at last, in the only union worth having, that of peace and goodwill. That union may be restored, let us hope, by good temper and common sense, qualities that have not hitherto been conspicuous in the ecclesiastical history of Scotland, or of England.

XIV

THE END OF JEANNE DE LA MOTTE

IN the latest and best book on Marie Antoinette and the Diamond Necklace, *L 'Affaire du Collier,* Monsieur Funck-Brentano does not tell the sequel of the story of Jeanne de la Motte, *née* de Saint-Remy, and calling herself de Valois. He leaves this wicked woman at the moment when (June 21, 1786) she has been publicly flogged and branded, struggling, scratching, and biting like a wild cat. Her husband, at about the same time, was in Edinburgh, and had just escaped from being kidnapped by the French police. In another work Monsieur Funck-Brentano criticises, with his remarkable learning, the conclusion of the history of Jeanne de la Motte. Carlyle, in his well-known essay, *The Diamond Necklace,* leaves Jeanne's later adventures obscure, and is in doubt as to the particulars of her death.

Perhaps absolute certainty (except as to the cause of Jeanne's death) is not to be obtained. How she managed to escape from her prison, the Salpétrière, later so famous for Charcot's hypnotic experiments on hysterical female patients, remains a mystery. It was certain that if she was once at liberty Jeanne would tell the lies against the Queen which she had told before, and tell some more equally false, popular, and damaging. Yet escape she did in 1787, the year following that of her imprisonment at the Salpétrière; she reached England, compiled the libels which she called her memoirs, and died strangely in 1791.

On June 21, 1786, to follow M. Funck-Brentano, Jeanne was taken, after her flogging, to her prison, reserved for dissolute women. The majority of the captives slept as they might, confusedly, in one room. To Jeanne was allotted one of thirty-six little cells of six feet square, given up to her by a prisoner who went to join the promiscuous horde. Probably the woman was paid for this generosity by some partisan of Jeanne. On September 4 the property of the swindler and of her husband, including their valuable furniture, jewels, books, and plate, was sold at Bar-sur-Aube, where they had a house.

So far we can go, guided by M. Funck-Brentano, who relies on authentic documents. For what followed we have only the story of Jeanne herself in her memoirs: I quote the English translation, which appears to vary from the French. How did such a dangerous prisoner make her escape? We cannot but wonder that she was not placed in a prison more secure. Her own version, of course, is not to be relied on. She would tell any tale that suited her purpose. A version which contradicts hers has reached me through the tradition of an English family, but it presents some difficulties. Jeanne says that about the end of November or early in December, 1786, she was allowed to have a maid named Angelica. This woman was a prisoner of long standing, condemned on suspicion of having killed her child. One evening a soldier on guard in the court of the Salpétrière passed his musket through a hole in the wall (or a broken window) and tried to touch Angelica. He told her that many people of rank were grateful to her for her kindness to Madame La Motte. He would procure writing materials for her that she might represent her case to them. He did bring gilt-edged paper, pens, and ink, and a letter for Angelica, who could not read.

The letter contained, in invisible ink, brought out by Jeanne, the phrase, 'It is understood. Be sure to be discreet. ' 'People are intent on changing your condition ' was another phrase which Jeanne applied to herself. She conceived the probable hypothesis that her victims, the Queen and the Cardinal de Rohan, had repented of their cruelty, had discovered her to be innocent and were plotting for her escape. Of course, nothing could be more remote from the interests of the Queen. Presently the soldier brought another note. Jeanne must procure a model of the key that locked her cell and other doors. By dint of staring at the key in the hands of the nuns who looked after the prisoners, Jeanne, though unable to draw, made two sketches of it, and sent them out, the useful soldier managing all communications. How Jeanne procured the necessary pencil she does not inform us. Practical locksmiths may decide whether it is likely that, from two amateur drawings, not to scale, any man could make a key which would fit the locks. The task appears impossible.

In any case, in a few days the soldier pushed the key through the hole in the wall; Jeanne tried it on the door of her cell and on two doors in the passages, found that it opened them, and knelt in gratitude before her crucifix. In place of running away Jeanne now wrote to ladies of her acquaintance, begging them to procure the release of Angelica. Her nights she spent in writing three statements for the woman, each occupying a hundred and eighty pages, presumably of gilt-edged paper. Soon she heard that the King had signed Angelica's pardon, and on May 1 the woman was released.

The next move of Jeanne was to ask her unknown friend outside to send her a complete male costume, a large blue coat, a flannel waistcoat, a pair of half boots, and a tall, round-shaped hat, with a switch. The soldier presently pushed these commodities through the hole in the wall. The chaplain next asked her to write out all her story, but Sister Martha, her custodian, would not give her writing materials, and it did not apparently occur to her to bid the soldier bring fresh supplies. Cut off from the joys of literary composition, Jeanne arranged with her unknown friend to escape on June 8. First the handy soldier, having ample leisure, was to walk for days about 'the King's garden,' disguised as a waggoner, and carrying a whip. The use of this manœuvre is not apparent, unless Jeanne, with her switch, was to be mistaken for the familiar presence of the carter.

Jeanne ended by devising a means of keeping one of the female porters away from her door. She dressed as a man, opened four doors in succession, walked through a group of the nuns, or 'Sisters,' wandered into many other courts, and at last joined herself to a crowd of sight-seeing Parisians and left the prison in their company. She crossed the Seine, and now walking, now hiring coaches, and using various disguises, she reached Luxembourg. Here a Mrs. MacMahon met her, bringing a note from M. de la Motte. This was on July 27. Mrs. MacMahon and Jeanne started next day for Ostend, and arrived at Dover after a passage of forty-two hours. Jeanne then repaired with Mr. MacMahon to that lady's house in the Haymarket.

This tale is neither coherent nor credible. On the other hand, the tradition of an English family avers that a Devonshire gentleman was asked by an important personage in France to succour an unnamed lady who was being smuggled over in a sailing boat to our south-west coast. Another gentleman, not unknown to history, actually entertained this French angel unawares, not even knowing her name, and Jeanne, when she departed for London, left a miniature of herself which is still in the possession of the English family. Which tale is true and who was the unknown friend that suborned the versatile soldier, and sent in not only gilt-edged paper and a suit of male attire, but money for Jeanne's journey? Only the Liberals in France had an interest in Jeanne's escape; she might exude more useful venom against the Queen in books or pamphlets, and she did, while giving the world to understand that the Queen had favoured her flight. The escape is the real mystery of the affair of the Necklace; the rest we now understand.

The death of Jeanne was strange. The sequel to her memoirs, in English, avers that in 1791 a bailiff came to arrest her for a debt of 30*l*. She gave him a bottle of wine, slipped from the room, and locked him in. But he managed to get out, and discovered the wretched woman in a chamber in 'the two-pair back.' She threw up the window, leaped out, struck against a tree, broke one knee, shattered one thigh, knocked one eye out, yet was recovering, when, on August 21, 1791, she partook too freely of mulberries (to which she was very partial), and died on Tuesday, August 23. This is confirmed by two newspaper paragraphs, which I cite in full.

First, the *London Chronicle* writes (from Saturday, August 27, to Tuesday, August 30, 1791):

'The unfortunate Countess de la Motte, who died on Tuesday last in consequence of a hurt from jumping out of a window, was the wife of Count de la Motte, who killed young Grey, the jeweller, in a duel a few days ago at Brussels.' (This duel is recorded in the *London Chronicle*, August 20-23.)

Next, the *Public Advertiser* remarks (Friday, August 26, 1791):

'The noted Countess de la Motte, of Necklace memory, and who lately jumped out of a two-pair of stairs window to avoid the bailiffs, died on Tuesday night last, at eleven o'clock, at her lodgings near Astley's Riding School.'

But why did La Motte fight the young jeweller? It was to Grey, of New Bond Street, that La Motte sold a number of the diamonds from the necklace; Grey gave evidence to that fact, and La Motte killed him. La Motte himself lived to a bad old age.

On studying M. Funck-Brentano's work, styled *Cagliostro & Company* in the English translation, one observes a curious discrepancy. According to the *Gazette d 'Utrecht*, cited by M. Funck-Brentano, the window in Jeanne's cell was 'at a height of ten feet above the floor.' Yet the useful soldier, outside, introduced the end of his musket 'through a broken pane of glass.' This does not seem plausible. Again, the *Gazette d 'Utrecht* (August 1, 1780) says that Jeanne made a hole in the wall of her room, but failed to get her body through that aperture. Was *that* the hole through which, in the English translation published after Jeanne's death, the soldier introduced the end of his musket? There are difficulties in both versions, and it is not likely that Jeanne gave a truthful account of her escape.

FOOTNOTES

[1] *Puzzles and Paradoxes*, pp. 317-336, Blackwoods, 1874.

[2] Paget, p. 332.

[3] My italics. Did Fielding abandon his belief in Elizabeth?

[4] See p. 38, *supra*.

[5] Paget, *Paradoxes and Puzzles*, p. 342. Blackwoods, 1874.

[6] See his *Paradoxes and Puzzles*, pp. 337-370, and, for good reading, see the book *passim*.

[7] Not only have I failed to trace the records of the Assize at which the Perrys were tried, but the newspapers of 1660 seem to contain no account of the trial (as they do in the case of the Drummer of Tedworth, 1663), and Miss E.M. Thompson, who kindly undertook the search, has not even found a ballad or broadside on 'The Campden Wonder' in the British Museum. The pamphlet of 1676 has frequently been republished, in whole or in part, as in *State Trials*, vol. xiv., in appendix to the case of Captain Green; which see, *infra*, p. 193, *et seq*.

[8] Really, the prosecution did not make this point: an oversight.

[9] They are in the possession of Mr. Walter Blaikie, who kindly lent them to me.

[10] Hachette, Paris, 1903. The author has made valuable additions and corrections.

[11] *The Story of Kaspar Hauser from Authentic Records*. Swan Sonnenschein & Co., London, 1892.

[12] *Proceedings of the Society for Psychical Research*, vol. vii. pp. 221-257.

[13] 'The True Discourse of the Late Treason,' *State Papers*, Scotland, Elizabeth, vol. lvi. No. 50.

[14] Burton, *History of Scotland*, v. 336.

[15] The story, with many new documents, is discussed at quite full length in the author's *King James and the Gowrie Mystery*, Longmans, 1902.

[16] I follow *Incidents in My Life*, Series i. ii., 1864, 1872. *The Gift of Daniel Home*, by Madame Douglas Home and other authorities.

[17] Home mentions this fact in a note, correcting an error of Sir David Brewster's, *Incidents*, ii. 48, Note 1. The Earl of Home about 1856 asked questions on the subject, and Home 'stated what my connection with the family was.' Dunglas is the second title in the family.

[18] The curious reader may consult my *Cock Lane and Common Sense*, and *The Making of Religion*, for examples of savage, mediæval, ancient Egyptian, and European cases.

[19] *Incidents*, ii. 105.

[20] *Journal S.P.R.*, May 1903, pp. 77, 78.

[21] *Human Personality*, ii. 546, 547. By 'Ectoplastic' Mr. Myers appears to have meant small 'materialisations' exterior to the 'medium.'

[22] *Journal S.P.R.*, July 1889, p. 101.

[23] *Contemporary Review*, January 1876.

[24] *Contemporary Review*, vol. xxvii. p. 286.

[25] Cf. *Making of Religion*, p. 362, 1898.

[26] *Quarterly Review*, 1871, pp. 342, 343.

[27] *Proceedings S.P.R.* vi. 98.

[28] Mr. Merrifield has reiterated his opinion that the conditions of light were adequate for his view of the object described on p. 184, *supra. Journal S.P.R.* October 1904.

[29] Gibbet.

[30] Fisher Unwin.

[31] The trial is in Howell's *State Trials*, vol. xiv. 1812. Roderick Mackenzie's account of his seizure of the 'Worcester' was discovered by the late Mr. Hill Burton, in an oak chest in the Advocates' Library, and is published in his *Scottish Criminal Trials*, vol. i., 1852.

[32] *Narrative of Frances Shaftoe*. Printed 1707.

[33] Boyer, *Reign of Queen Anne*.

[34] Article, 'Oglethorpe (Sir Theophilus).'

[35] Carte MSS.

[36] Macpherson, *Hanoverian Papers*.

[37] Carte MSS. In the Bodleian.

[38] Gualterio MSS. Add. MSS. British Museum.

[39] Wolff, *Odd Bits of History* (1844), pp. 1-58.

[40] The facts are taken from Ailesbury's, de Luynes', Dangeau's, and d'Argenson's *Memoirs*; from Boyer's *History*, and other printed books, and from the Newcastle, Hearne, Carte, and Gualterio MSS. in the Bodleian and the British Museum.

[41] The most recent work on d'Éon, *Le Chevalier d'Éon*, par Octave Homberg and Fernand Jousselin (Plon-Nourrit, Paris, 1904), is rather disappointing. The authors aver that at a recent sale they picked up many MSS. of d'Éon 'which had lain for more than a century in the back shop of an English bookseller.' No other reference as to authenticity is given, and some letters to d'Éon of supreme importance are casually cited, but are not printed. On the other hand, we have many new letters for the later period of the life of the

hero. The best modern accounts are that by the Duc de Broglie, who used the French State archives and his own family papers in *Le Secret du Roi* (Paris, 1888), and *The Strange Career of the Chevalier d 'Éon* (1885), by Captain J. Buchan Telfer, R.N. (Longmans, 1885), a book now out of print. The author was industrious, but not invariably happy in his translations of French originals. D 'Éon himself drew up various accounts of his adventures, some of which he published. They are oddly careless in the essential matter of dates, but contain many astounding genuine documents, which lend a sort of 'doubtsome trust ' to others, hardly more incredible, which cannot be verified, and are supposed by the Duc de Broglie to be 'interpolations. ' Captain Buchan Telfer is less sceptical. The doubtfulness, to put it mildly, of some papers, and the pretty obvious interpolations in others, deepen the obscurity.

[42] *Le Chevalier d 'Éon*, p. 18.

[43] Broglie, *Secret du Roi*, ii. 51, note.

[44] *Political Register*, Sept. 1767; Buchan Telfer, p. 181.

[45] One of these gives Madame de Vieux-Maison as the author of a *roman à clef*, *Secret Memoirs of the Court of Persia*, which contains an early reference to the Man in the Iron Mask (died 1703). The letter-writer avers that D 'Argenson, the famous minister of Louis XV., said that the Man in the Iron Mask was really a person *fort peu de chose*, 'of very little account, ' and that the Regent d 'Orléans was of the same opinion. This corroborates my theory, that the Mask was merely the valet of a Huguenot conspirator, Roux de Marsilly, captured in England, and imprisoned because he was supposed to know some terrible secret—which he knew nothing about. See *The Valet 's Tragedy*, Longmans, 1903.

[46] *Voyage en Angleterre*, 1770.

[47] The Duc de Broglie, I am privately informed, could find no clue to the mystery of Saint-Germain.

[48] *An Englishman in Paris*, vol. i. pp. 130-133. London 1892.

Printed in the United States
93844LV00005B/170/A